monsoonbooks

CHARLOT

Ian Masters is an award-w̶ ̶ ̶ ̶ ̶ ̶ ̶ ̶ ̶ :ked across Africa and Asia for over twenty years. As a freelance scriptwriter and creative consultant for BBC Media Action he has developed and written TV and radio dramas from Bangladesh to Indonesia, Cambodia to South Sudan. His first produced feature film script, *The Last Reel*, was Cambodia's submission to the Academy Awards in 2014. In 2018 he returned to the UK, where he continues to write and work as an international script consultant from Somerset. *Charlot* is his first novel.

Praise for *Charlot*

'A brilliant feat of imagination – reconstructing an episode from Charlie Chaplin's life and exploring its ramifications in a wholly fascinating and convincing way. An incredibly impressive debut.'
William Boyd, author

'Chaplin did not only want to make people laugh, he wanted to make them think and *Charlot* does the same. Richly atmospheric, it explores the struggle between the two sides of his character as it emerges on his journey through colonial Cambodia of the 1930s. Sensitive, articulate and impeccably researched, it restores fresh humanity to the man behind the mask of the Tramp.'
Nigel Barley, author

'What's inside *Charlot*? The charm of Charlie Chaplin, the pulse of a changing Cambodia, the call to speak up in the face of oppression – and a lot of strong G&Ts. Unique, powerful, and transporting – Masters knows Asia, and his way around words.'
Karin Tanabe, author of *A Hundred Suns*

Charlot

Ian Masters

monsoon

monsoonbooks

First published in 2023
by Monsoon Books Ltd
www.monsoonbooks.co.uk

No.1 The Lodge, Burrough Court, Burrough on the Hill,
Melton Mowbray LE14 2QS, UK.

ISBN (paperback): 9781915310125
ISBN (ebook): 9781915310132

Cover design by Estuary English.

Photograph on page 336: "Victor Goloubew, Paulette Goddard and
Charlie Chaplin, Angkor Wat, 1936" courtesy of Charlie Chaplin Image
Bank. Copyright©Roy Export Co. Ltd.

A Cataloguing-in-Publication data record is available from the British
Library.

Printed and bound in Great Britain by Clays Ltd, Elcograf S.p.A.
25 24 23   1 2 3

For Emie

'I suppose that's one of the ironies of life,
doing the wrong thing at the right moment.'

Charlie Chaplin (*Monsieur Verdoux*)

Preface

> **'CHAPLIN DEAD,'**
> **IS UNCONFIRMED**
> **RUMOR IN ASIA**
>
> *(Picture on Back Page.)*
> A Reuter's [British news agency]
> dispatch from London early this [Fri-
> day] morning says: "It is strongly
> rumored here that Charles Chaplin
> died in Indo-China. No information
> is presently obtainable."

The rumour of Charlie Chaplin's death in Indochina first appeared in the global press on the 22nd of April 1936, attributed to Reuters News Agency. There was no subsequent confirmation of the rumour, and history was to prove it wrong. The global star didn't die until 1977, and not in French Indochina but in Europe. What then was the truth behind this mysterious headline?

What we do know is that Charlie – Charlot to the French-speaking world – and his young co-star and lover, Paulette Goddard, visited Cambodia in 1936 along with Paulette's mother and Charlie's valet. Other than some photographs at Angkor Wat, and reports from a press conference held in Phnom Penh, not much else is known of this trip.

In this critical moment of his career, middle-aged, about to be eclipsed by technology and world events, Charlie Chaplin had vowed not to make another movie after *Modern Times*. By 1936, fascism was on the march in Europe and communism had emerged as a challenge to Western dominance. In Indochina, anti-colonial sentiment was rising. Cambodians were finding their voice against colonial exploitation in the rubber plantations. And somewhere between the release of *Modern Times* in 1936 and *The Great Dictator* in 1940, Charlie Chaplin also found his voice. He moved from silent movies to talkies, from social comedy to political satire. Could this profound change have been inspired by this trip? Could it explain the rumour of his death?

What follows then is a story about how an embittered Charlie Chaplin killed off his silent Tramp character and found his voice in the politically turbulent 1930s.

I

The river steamer from Saigon chugged through the murky brown of the Mekong Delta, silhouetted against the setting sun. Its metal chimney belched black smoke into the afternoon haze and the gentle wake rocked a passing sampan. The steamer engines droned through the thick air as if coming from somewhere beyond the shoreline. It was noisy, but not enough to drown the faint tinkle of laughter around piano keys from the shadier port side, as light and carefree as ice in a glass. Gerswhin on a gramophone, *It Ain't Necessarily So*.

It was far too hot to be on deck.

Even inside, the air seemed to hum from the heat. In a luxurious first-class cabin Charlie Chaplin sat at a desk, dressed in a stylish but now wilted tropical suit. It was so humid that when he'd sat down to write some letters, he'd been forced to place a towel under his elbow to absorb the sweat running freely down his forearm. This had done nothing to improve his already sour mood. He had long abandoned his correspondence and instead turned his attention to a stack of newspapers. They felt as thick and floppy as a flannel in his hands, and the headlines were equally flaccid.

'Governor Robin Hikes Taxes!' read one.

'Michelin Rubber Exports Exceed Quarterly Targets!' boasted another.

But beneath the fold of another, he found the headline he was looking for.

'Chaplin hangs up his derby after *Modern Times*.'

He stared at it for a moment without reading further. Then put it down with a cough and selected another. *The Straits Times* from Singapore contained an equally irksome headline.

'*Modern Times*: Modern Marvel or Social Manifesto?'

Beside him stood his smartly dressed Japanese majordomo, Frank Yonamori. The young man's hair was combed in the latest fashion, and he managed his facial expressions with the same dedication as he managed the affairs of his often-irascible boss. Whatever the circumstances, he was always just this side of cheerful; the half smile carefully designed to soothe rather than actually cheer. He'd learned quickly to walk the tightrope of service for the demanding global celebrity. He read aloud from another paper.

'*Modern Times* has been prohibited in Germany,' he read, in a voice that had not entirely lost its Japanese inflection. 'A Nazi spokesman indicated that the picture had a Communist tendency, and that—'

Charlie slapped away the newspaper in disgust and coughed again, an infection deep in his chest. He reached for some pills and a glass of iced water and then gestured to continue.

'And that …' Mr Yonamori faltered, 'and that Mr Shumyatsky himself, the head of the Soviet film industry, is reported to have counselled him on the ending.'

That was too much.

Charlie shoved back his chair in disgust and strode to the door. Pinned to it was a tourism poster for *Les Ruines D'Angkor*. After a disdainful glance, he turned to a derby hat and a cane on top of a cabinet. Frank had purchased them in Saigon as part of the publicity for the release of the film. But they seemed to mock him and mock his mood. Charlie snatched them angrily and stepped out to the deck, heading for the snub-nosed prow. There he put one polished shoe on the railing and glowered at the riverbank, where oxen were being washed in the shallows and rice paddies stretched endlessly between sugar palms.

He wished he was anywhere but there. He rolled the derby in his hands and tapped the railing absently with the cane. He wished that he was back behind the gates of 1085 Summit Drive, his mansion in Beverly Hills.

He had not been there long when the door to the steamer's lounge bar opened. Laughter and music spilled out into the shimmering heat, along with a young woman who clip-clopped across the deck in the latest strappy Rhythm Steps, and a dress more suitable for an evening reception than for travel. She held a gin and tonic, careful not to spill any.

Paulette Goddard approached the prow and Charlie coughed again, irritated by everything and everyone. Her concern caused her thin eyebrows to pull together and a wrinkle to appear on her elegantly pointed nose. It was an endearing expression that had made her a star – and a star's lover.

When she rubbed his shoulders, her engagement ring and wedding band caught the late afternoon sun.

'Darling, come inside before you wilt,' she whispered.

'We should have taken the car.' His voice was faint. It rasped over phlegm.

'But you love ships.' She nibbled his ear. 'That's where we first met.'

'Ships and yachts, yes. But not this rusty old—'

'We're not travelling steerage, darling.' Her normally easy laugh felt brittle, and she regretted it immediately. 'Buck up, would you? This was your idea.'

She sipped her gin and tonic, unsure whether to continue and looked out to the river shore as if for answers. A paddy farmer was scrubbing down his oxen. She smiled and waved to him, but he just stared stonily back beneath his conical straw hat.

'At least no one knows we're here,' she said eventually.

'The king does.'

When he turned to her, he had the kind of the face you'd forget in seconds. Under his curly hair, now with a streak of white, Charlie Chaplin looked weary and despondent, older and more ordinary than his onscreen alter-ego on whom he had built his fame. He held her gaze until she looked away. She didn't like him when he was like this. He wouldn't be cheered up and there was nothing she could do about it.

'Charlie, how do you refuse a king?' she said after a long pause.

The steamer puffed its way around a bend in the river and a town appeared ahead. A temple pushed through the abundant tree canopy on a low hill surrounded by the spires of traditional curved pagodas. There was little to show that this was the capital, Phnom Penh, or to prepare them for the impact this visit would have on their lives over the space of a few short days.

Paulette finished her drink and gestured for a refill, looking for an excuse to leave the heat and Charlie's moody introspection. When she kissed Charlie's cheek, he didn't even acknowledge her kindness. He did this often. As soon as she had gone, Charlie sighed deeply. He rolled the derby onto his head and leant heavily on the bamboo cane until it bent. Even without the topcoat and oversized shoes, against the setting sun the silhouette was unmistakeable. It was known and adored throughout the world.

Even here.

2

As Chaplin's chartered steamer rounded the bend in the Mekong, a theatre rehearsal was underway in Wat Botum, a pagoda inside the European Quarter of Phnom Penh. A bamboo stage was lashed together beneath the ornate curves and carvings of the main vihara, or temple, of the Buddhist wat complex. The late afternoon sun intensified the silk sheen of the costumes and the colourful make-up of a Lakhoun theatre troupe. A prince and a giant circled one another in a stylized battle-dance, part of the *Reamker*, a Cambodian interpretation of the *Ramayana*. The giant's face was painted as a grotesque black-and-white mask with a down-turned mouth. He brandished a long, straight staff, striped black and white. A princess cowered behind a bamboo thicket, looking on in fear for her life.

Watching in the shade were some devotees, and a group of Buddhist monks who re-wrapped their orange robes and paid the performance little attention. But the bare-chested children watched entranced as the prince was defeated and the princess was carried away by the giant. A group of musicians beat the rhythm on the *skor thom*, a big-barrelled drum, to signal the end of the act and a melodic interlude took over, led by the *kong vong toch*, ornate gongs arranged in a circle.

At the rear of the compound, Captain Le Favre assessed the threat through narrowed eyes, flanked by two uniformed officers of the feared colonial police, the Sûreté. He lit a cigarette and inhaled deeply. Why was he, the executive of the protectorate's security and a former legionnaire, tasked with watching a Khmer theatre rehearsal? Le Favre had been the main architect of the swift and brutal retributions which followed the suppression of a revolt in the French Colonial Army in Yen Bai six years earlier. The cold efficiency of his response had earned him a promotion and oversight of the rapid expansion of the Sûreté. He now had eyes and ears in every dark corner of the colony – but it came at a price. The vast network required constant management and he trusted no one. That's why, after one of his spies had informed him that a group of Khmer actors was poking fun at the French, he had personally come to the rehearsal. Better to snub out any hint of insurrection before it gained traction. But with a celebrity visit to manage, and a royal audience to police that evening, Le Favre longed to be anywhere but there.

All eyes were on the stage as two peasants ran on as if being chased. They wore baggy fishermen's pants, tied up with string. The smaller of the two turned to the audience as if suddenly aware of their presence. Beneath his dark eyes and face-paint was a toothbrush moustache daubed on in charcoal. Phirath was a muscular actor with a passionate intensity behind his comic performance. Offstage, booted footsteps approached. The two peasants scurried to hide behind the bamboo thicket in front of the forest backdrop. There was laughter now from the crowd as an actor entered stage right, dressed as the colonial governor with a red face and a cushion stuffed under his shirt. The overweight foreigner approached the front, peering out over the audience.

'Hoh-hi-hoh-hi-hoh!' he proclaimed in nonsensical French.

Phirath crept out and gave him a kick up the backside. The governor spun round. But Phirath had vanished behind the bamboo.

Le Favre scanned the crowd warily. The kids laughed, hiding their teeth behind their palms. Even the monks seemed to find it a mild distraction. But Le Favre was not amused. It was not anger in his eyes. It was a bored resignation that he had to intervene when there were other more important problems to attend to. Nevertheless, his spies had been right. This could not be allowed to continue. Nipping dissent in the bud was Le Favre's trademark. He nodded to his subordinate, who gave a shrill blast on a police whistle.

'Arrête!' the policeman shouted.

But there was no stopping Phirath now. With his back turned again, the governor received another kick from the left. More laughter. More nonsensical French, becoming increasing irate.

BANG!

A gunshot echoed off the pagoda walls. Le Favre held a smoking revolver, pointed at the sky, daring anyone to protest.

And just like that the rehearsal was over. The crowd scattered, avoiding the police and melting away into the pagoda complex. Even in the relative safety of the pagoda, they knew not to test the patience of the Sûreté.

A few minutes later and the stage too was emptied. The musicians packed up the instruments in silence as the monks prepared for nightfall and kids swept the compound. Phirath, still in costume, carried a heavy drum from the stage, helped by a round-faced boy. But as they brought it behind the stage, Phirath saw the giant, still in make-up, making a beeline for him. There was no hiding the anger in his eyes.

The frustration with Phirath's artistic and financial direction was not solely because of his provocation of the French authorities. The contemporary political commentary and satire broke a centuries-old tradition for the sake of slapstick laughs and political finger-pointing. The troupe followed his direction uneasily. Audiences, however, loved it, flocking to watch them perform in Phnom Penh, and in wats and pagodas across the country.

Lakhoun theatre was a strictly observed family tradition. Phirath had grown up in it; as a boy his first duty had been to ensure the offerings of incense sticks beneath the stage never burnt out during the performance. From that angle, he watched wide-eyed, and studied the performances of his father and extended family, until he was old enough to take a small role himself. But two years earlier his father had lost faith and had summarily disbanded the troupe. He was tired of the brutal circumstances they were forced to endure in the protectorate. The time for acting was over, he'd told the troupe. Now was the time for action. But within a few short weeks, the Sûreté had arrived at their compound in the Khmer Quarter and had taken him away. Phirath had not heard from him since, but knew that he'd been imprisoned with other political prisoners in Battambang.

Phirath had revived the troupe when he realised that his father would not be released. How else was he, and his wider family, to earn a living? There were other troupes who would perform, like them, on the banks of the Bassac River, but it was Phirath's idea to intersperse the well-known and well-loved traditional stories of Angkorian kings with comic entr'actes. His political awakening had been fuelled by his father's imprisonment but also, and to no less an extent, by his adoration for the Tramp, whose movies he'd devoured since he was a boy.

'Happy now?' the prince managed, as Phirath lowered the drum beside the others.

Before Phirath could reply, Le Favre strode over. The actor lifted his rice paddy hat in mock respect and addressed the captain in fluent French.

'Good afternoon, Captain. Did you enjoy our rehearsal?'

For an answer, the captain eyeballed the little man. Then, surprisingly fast, his hand darted out and smudged off the toothbrush moustache with his handkerchief. It smeared across Phirath's cheek. Without a word, Le Favre spun on his boots and strode away.

He had not gone more than a few paces when Phirath heard a foghorn sounding the arrival of a river steamer at the port. It took a moment to register, but then Phirath grinned.

'He's here!'

He grabbed a bicycle leaning against the pagoda steps and cycled off, making a show of wobbling as he passed Le Favre. He pedalled furiously, passing through the pagoda arch and into the boulevard beyond.

3

In 1936, Phnom Penh had the feel of a charming colonial backwater compared to Saigon, Singapore or Hong Kong. But as the impact of the Great Depression was increasingly felt across the Western world, French Indochina was hailed as a beacon of economic success. In fact, its rubber industry was the envy of the world, and largely it was administered from Phnom Penh. To maintain control, especially in the rubber plantations, the French protectorate used a combination of brutal taxation and fear, enforced by the Sûreté. But defiance of the colonial administration was growing.

Charlie neither knew nor really cared about that. The trip to Cambodia had been an afterthought while they were in Saigon. They had intended to sail on from there to Hong Kong, but Paulette and Charlie had stayed up until dawn on his birthday and thrilled themselves with the thought of an adventure to see the majestic jungle ruins of Angkor. Charlie's enthusiasm waned in the morning, but Paulette would not be dissuaded. And in the end, she had convinced Charlie that the ruins would be the perfect place from which to make their big announcement.

Frank Yonamori made all the arrangements. As Charlie's valet, this was his first big trip abroad since he had started working for the notoriously demanding filmmaker. On this occasion he'd taken Paulette's side, suggesting that the sudden switch of their well-advertised itinerary would thwart the press and give them some respite from their relentless attention. But word always gets out, and before he had even chartered the luxurious river steamer, they had received a telegram from Cambodia's Royal Palace requesting an audience. It wasn't this which had put Charlie in a dark mood, but he used the invitation and his stubbornly persistent cough, as an excuse to remain grumpy in the days that followed.

For all the praise and money *City Lights* gained, it was his critics who burrowed under Charlie's skin like jiggers and itched. He could take the criticism of his wealth and even his relationships, but it was their taunt that he had made a comedy in order to cash in on the crash which riled. How could he be branded 'an accomplice of capitalism' and a secret communist? And would either claim tarnish the legacy of his latest – probably last – film?

Charlie had been introduced to Paulette as a young starlet of twenty-one, on a party on his yacht *Panacea* sometime after he'd announced his retirement from motion pictures. He was revelling in the adoration for his pantomime masterpiece *City Lights* and invigorated by a long world tour. But motion picture companies and motion picture audiences were chewing through films at a breathtaking rate. Paulette had signed with producer Samuel Goldwyn in the same year as *City Lights* and had made six pictures by the time Charlie had returned from his tour in 1932. Paulette wasn't like his previous leading ladies with their round smouldering eyes and pouty little lips, perfectly suited to the hazy hedonism of the 1920s. She looked modern, a tougher face for the harsh realities of the 1930s. Her features were sharper, her nose more pointed and her cheekbones more pronounced. Her eyebrows puckered when she was angry and danced when she laughed. Unlike the hypnotically insipid screen vamps of the previous decade, she was spiky and adventurous, a knife between her teeth, and always in the thick of it.

Not long after, and with Paulette's encouragement, he began to work on an idea which would set his critics straight. It would be a film for the machine age, an indictment of the factory system. And he worked outwards from a central idea of workers ripping apart their factory in an outpouring of revolutionary justice. But as his relationship with Paulette deepened, and she moved into his home at Summit Drive, a parallel on-screen love story evolved for the Tramp and his Gamin. Paulette and he had laughed and discussed those first ideas, and slowly the righteous anger of the original vision had slipped further and further towards satire. More significantly, for the first time, Charlie Chaplin, the silent King of Comedy, had written a full script ... with dialogue. Paulette was delighted. She had a sharp tongue and liked to use it. Most importantly, she wanted to keep up with the times as a young woman at the start of her career in an industry that was changing at breakneck speed. As the details inevitably leaked out, there was nearly as much speculation about the woman who'd convinced the silent movie maestro to talk, as there was about how in fact the Tramp would speak. Would he have a cockney accent? Or the airs and graces of a fallen aristocrat with a voice to match? Charlie had stubbornly avoided the first scene with the talking Tramp for the first few days of production. He knew the first word the Tramp uttered would inevitably turn him into somebody else. Not even a week into shooting, he'd lost his nerve and changed his mind and to Paulette's considerable frustration, he fell back on his mastery of pantomime. *Modern Times* wasn't silent. But neither was it a talkie. Despite Paulette's misgivings, the critics and the public loved it.

But for how long could he continue his reign as the King of Comedy? And what next for Paulette, now signed with his company? New movies were released weekly, but he had made only two in eight years. Just five days after the release of *Modern Times*, at Grauman's Chinese Theatre in Hollywood, and with the reassurance of the reviews and the box office receipts, Charlie once more decided to escape from it all with Paulette and her mother. They sailed for a vacation in Honolulu on the 17th of February 1936 aboard the SS *Coolidge*. The decision to continue the tour into Asia was Charlie's. Paulette was far less enthusiastic. She'd not packed for such a long trip. But more than that, after four years in professional limbo, and with the glowing reviews of her performance as the Gamin, it was hardly the time for the ambitious young actress, not getting any younger, to leave the limelight.

Charlie knew this full well. In fact, there was a tinge of jealousy there which he did his best to hide. But having conquered the world with his silent movies, he was now at a professional, personal and creative crossroads. On the verge of being eclipsed by new technology and the demand for talkies, Charlie found himself the wrong side of middle-age and in danger of fading out and fading away. *Modern Times*, he protested to the press and fans, would be his swansong.

He had said the same about *City Lights* some five years earlier. Charlie stood at the prow fuming over the accusation of a communist conspiracy behind the production of *Modern Times*. The steamer chugged its way past the Royal Palace in the dying light. The spires of the palace shimmered gold and the large palms were silhouetted against an indigo sky. Further on, through the gathering gloom, he saw the little port of Phnom Penh.

It was perhaps fitting that Phnom Penh itself sat at a watery crossroads: the upper and lower reaches of the Mekong, and the Tonle Sap and Bassac rivers. The port gave little hint of the colonial charm of the European Quarter beyond, which earned the city its reputation as the Pearl of Asia. They docked as the last light faded. The river steamer was a shadowy bulk beside a regular ferry still puffing smoke. Lanterns and car lights picked out dockhands and port officials. The Saigon steamer's arrival was enough of an event to find the port crowded and noisy, but most were oblivious to the fame of the passengers who disembarked across a narrow gangplank to firm ground. Their high heels and loafers stepped through the muck and mud as around them lines of porters unloaded crates and sacks, paying them no heed.

Anonymity at last.

For a moment Charlie forgot his frustrations. Ahead of the disembarking passengers, Mr Yonamori opened a car door and beckoned them over. He had already organised the unloading of their suitcases from the steamer and they were carried over to the boot of another automobile. Charlie lifted his Keystone portable A-7 16mm camera to his eye, focussing the lens on the minutiae of the dockside tableaux. Lines of dockhands loaded rubber in sacks stamped with the name Michelin. Beyond the steamer, sampans had returned with their afternoon catch. A basket split open and fish flapped in the muck. A policeman dragged a stowaway to the Port Authority offices. Further along Charlie spotted a kid, no more than eight years old, saunter casually past an open crate of bananas. He broke off a hand furtively, then looked straight into Charlie's camera. But instead of running, the boy merely grinned, and saluted with the hand of bananas. Despite himself, Charlie saluted back, and the boy ducked between crates and disappeared. Charlie lowered the camera. In that twilight gloom which the French call *au crépuscule*, there was not enough light to film. But there was the flicker of a smile on his face as he held out his hand for Paulette's mother. She looked aghast, lifting her skirts to step along the wobbly planks that served as a pathway.

As Paulette and her mother clambered into the car, Charlie looked back one more time, his mind at work as he surveyed the scene, selecting moments, discarding, rearranging, examining, imagining until:

'Charlie?' There was a sharpness in Paulette's tone that checked Charlie.

Just before he climbed inside, he caught sight of Phirath barrelling through a line of porters on a bicycle. As they drove away, Phirath nudged his bicycle past a policeman.

'Charlot!' he called out. 'Monsieur Chaplin!'

He pedalled furiously after the receding brake lights. Inside the car, Paulette started to roll down the window when her mother stopped her.

'Please don't, sugar,' she begged with a hint of a Midwest drawl. 'I can endure the heat more than I can bear the odour.'

Charlie twisted round to look through the rear window. He saw Phirath peddling as fast his legs could pump, waving and calling out, but he lost control after a pothole, veered into a rickshaw and flew dramatically over the handlebars. He sat up, momentarily stunned. But not for long. He stood and dusted himself down, slicked back his dishevelled hair and rushed back to the bicycle. The frame was buckled, but that was not going to stop him. He pushed off, wobbling precariously across another junction before the car he was following turned into a boulevard.

Charlie laughed to himself.

'What's so funny?'

'Nothing darling,' he replied. 'No one.'

4

Not far from the port, as the crow flies, was the residence of the governor of the French colony. It existed in an altogether more tranquil world of wide boulevards flanked with tamarind trees, away from the bustle and business of the protectorate. The double-storeyed yellow stucco villas would not have looked out of place in Paris, or perhaps the headlands of the Côte d'Azur. Le Favre's boots clacked on the ochre and white veranda tiles. He marched towards two men dressed in tropical whites with their jungle helmets on the table in front of them.

'Governor Robin!' he called out.

Governor Robin was a middle-aged bureaucrat and an old Indochina hand, whose diplomatic rise in the East owed as much to the sickness of his superiors, as to his own competence. This was his third time as acting governor and he had already been two years in the post. He chose not to use the official residence, having his own villa, but attended official occasions and conducted much of his business from the cool shade of the veranda – mainly to get away from the tiresome snapping of his wife and children. The year had started off quietly and he was looking forward to Chaplin's visit as a welcome distraction from the ripples of discontent among the rubber plantation workers, and the tedious chore of overseeing tax collection across the provinces. He could afford to look casual, with a military force at his disposal known for its fierceness, but his carefree manner masked a cruel obsession with maintaining the status quo. He was taking an aperitif as he flicked through magazines. With him was Laurent Levalier, a young, ambitious plantation owner and fellow Frenchman. They exchanged glances as Le Favre marched up.

'Governor Robin! A royal audience? Governor—'

'Aperitif?' cut in the governor.

Le Favre stood to attention by the two civilians, his stiff poise and uniform awkward. Levalier half laughed, not looking up from his magazine.

'*C'est beaucoup de bruit pour rien*,' he exclaimed. A lot of noise about nothing.

'*Pour rien*?' blustered Le Favre, and snatched the copy of *Life* from Levalier's hands. The front cover showed French strikers in Paris.

It could almost be a frame from *Modern Times*.

'You want scenes like this in your rubber plantation?' He brandished it for effect. 'Or right here in the Khmer Quarter?'

Levalier refused to be goaded. Instead, he picked up a newspaper. Beneath the fold was the same headline of the celebrity couple's Far East tour.

'Chaplin hangs up his derby,' read Levalier out loud, adding, 'honestly, I thought he already had.'

'I'm glad you find this funny.'

'So, what would you have me do, Captain?' asked Robin, relishing his captain's flustered manner. 'I can hardly turn him away at the port. The king has extended a personal invitation to the palace.'

Le Favre took the cigarette which Robin offered as an olive branch. Calming himself between puffs, he addressed his seated superior.

'People around the world are convinced he speaks for them.'

'I thought the whole point was that he doesn't speak at all,' countered Levalier.

'Don't release his film,' implored Le Favre, ignoring the cocky businessman. 'At least until he's left the country.'

'You're over-reacting, Captain. *C'est beaucoup de bruit pour rien.*'

'Am I?'

At his tone, the thin line of the governor's smile faltered. Le Favre pressed home his advantage.

'The Communist Party in Saigon is growing bold. The Cao Dai sect believes him to be a prophet! Any comments, any support, any ... any defiance could spark something far worse than Yen Bai. You want to risk that for the sake of a movie? A comedy?'

He spat out the last word like a mouthful of soured milk.

The evening crickets filled the silence.

Governor Robin's good humour faded. Even Levalier seemed to sober at the thought of a Hollywood star's influence on the political tensions of the region. The governor nodded eventually.

'See to it. But the world will be watching, Captain. I know it won't come easy for you, but I beg you, be discrete.'

Le Favre snapped to attention and saluted. Then he clacked back down the tiled veranda and into the gathering gloom.

5

Charlie and his entourage drove from the port to the hotel in silence. The light had gone entirely, and there were only a few streetlights flickering as they crossed into the guarded European Quarter. They saw the armed police at the gates, but they didn't pay them any attention. Neither were they interested in the lines of rickshaw pullers huddled under lanterns playing chess and cards. The exotic East was no longer a mystery to them. They had been travelling for weeks on the capricious whim of those who pay no heed to expense. Each stop, in each city, in each country, had been part publicity for the film, and part holiday. As the convoy of two cars drove up the main thoroughfare, past the Royal Palace, Wat Botum and up to the Hotel Le Royal, Charlie was glad there were no crowds to welcome them. The tour had taken its toll. Charlie longed for a quiet period of anonymity, almost as much as he desperately feared being invisible. Or worse – ordinary.

The first weeks of their tour had energised Charlie to work on a new story. He'd set to work on it feverishly in the early mornings while Paulette and her mother were still in bed. The idea which he'd outlined to Paulette before they left the United States was the main reason she'd agreed to join him, despite it meaning her disappearance from the Hollywood scene at a critical juncture of her career. She saw it as some kind of reassurance that it wouldn't be a further five long years under exclusive contract before he produced his next motion picture. The working title was *The Countess of Shanghai*. It would be a vehicle for his muse and co-star, he assured her, about a down-on-her-luck Russian countess who stows away on an ocean liner and falls in love with an American millionaire. But the weeks of travel by ship hadn't proved the inspiration he'd hoped and had instead sunk the idea altogether. This was another reason why Charlie was in a stubbornly foul mood, and Paulette's patience had worn thin. If she was indeed his muse, then why was he not working?

Crowds and well-wishers and official audiences were a tiresome reminder of everything else that had gone wrong on the trip. Finally in Phnom Penh, a quiet backwater compared to Saigon, they hoped they might be free of the press and fans for a while.

But as soon as the car turned into the gravel driveway of the imposing Hotel Le Royal, it was immediately clear they were not travelling as incognito as they had hoped. Everyone in Phnom Penh it seemed was eager for a glimpse of the star and his companions. Flashbulbs exploded, blinding them as the press ran alongside the car. The police were there to help hotel staff keep the throng back as they pulled up at the lobby steps. Mr Yonamori opened the door and Charlie and Paulette clambered out, grateful that nightfall meant that at least the temperature had dropped to a tolerable level.

Paulette took Charlie's arm. She loved fame as much as Charlie did – even if he was making a show of hiding it at that moment. She flashed a dazzling smile at the journalists straining against the linked arms of the French police. More flashbulbs exploded. Behind them Mr Yonamori assisted Mrs Goddard as hotel porters unloaded, and Charlie led Paulette up the steps.

'Mr Chaplin!' It was impossible to make out the speaker in the din.

'Charlie, Charlot! Is it true that you'll be setting your next motion picture in the East?'

Charlie's sour mood returned twofold. He coughed and tried to pull Paulette inside past the bellboys holding open the grand doors. But Paulette loved the limelight. She turned back and waved and nudged Charlie to do the same. The two of them were blinded by the flashbulbs for the briefest of moments before they disappeared inside. Once gone, the press slipped back into the darkness. Someone imitated the Tramp's walk. There was a ripple of laughter and banter as they dispersed. And pushing through the high-spirited crowd was Phirath. He arrived at the steps just in time to see the celebrity couple disappear inside.

He slammed the broken bicycle to the ground in frustration. But as he retrieved it, he noticed the eyes of the French Sûreté on him. One whispered to the other and gestured in his direction. It was enough for Phirath to back the bicycle into the knot of press and fans, and slink back out of the gates.

He was too late. Again.

6

The Hotel Le Royal was the jewel in the crown of Phnom Penh's hospitality industry, a flamboyant combination of Art Deco and French colonial influence, designed in the 1920s by Ernest Hebrand. Frangipanis offered up their delicate scent to guests enjoying the pool, and there was a fusion of Khmer and European influence in the ballrooms, restaurants and breakfast cafés. The corridor leading from the lobby to the Elephant Bar was lined with framed photographs of its most famous guests. Only opened in 1929 it was still in its infancy of glamour but the corridor from the lobby to the Elephant Bar was already lined with framed photographs of its most famous guests. In time this would include writers and statesmen like Jackie Onassis, President de Gaulle and W. Somerset Maugham.

Chaplin's portrait didn't yet grace this famous corridor. Instead his reflection stared back at him from the bathroom mirror of the hotel's most luxurious suite. He lathered a shaving bowl, frothing the suds absently. He glared at the lines around his eyes, and that stubborn single streak of white in his tousled hair. His braces dangled over trousers, bare-chested. He was rather slight in frame.

'Coco Chanel or the Cartier?' called Paulette from the

bedroom. 'Something French would be appropriate, *non*?'

It snapped him out of his introspection, but he didn't answer. He took a little of the lather and placed it on his top lip as his iconic moustache, only now it was white. He daubed on some thick white eyebrows. He picked up the cut-throat razor, making a show of his hands shaking with age, performing for an audience of one. He steadied one hand with the other as he pressed the shaking cut-throat razor to his chin.

'Feeling your age, darling?' asked Paulette from the doorway of the bathroom. She was half dressed, eying the claw-foot tub as she sashayed over and put her arms around his slim waist.

'Mother used to tell me, "You're only as old as the woman you feel",' she whispered, her lips brushing his earlobes. She couldn't resist the playful dig at his reputation. 'Which makes you twenty-six and in your ... prime.'

She half expected an annoyed reply, but instead Chaplin wiggled his frothy eyebrows lasciviously. He walked the razor along the marble top like a woman's legs, swinging their hips as they reached Paulette's arm around his waist, and on up her forearm, continuing slowly upwards, until Paulette pulled away laughing.

'The Cartier then. And please hurry, Charlie. It won't do to keep the press waiting. Even here.'

Charlie didn't reply. The truth was he could barely speak. His voice, had he tried, would have rasped painfully through swollen tonsils. Paulette was grateful for his silence; in his current mood, he could be cruel with his tongue. She checked her own reflection in the mirror and tried a smile. Satisfied, she pulled off the engagement ring and wedding band and popped them into a clutch. Charlie watched her every move until she slipped back to the suite. When he returned to his shaving the fun had gone out of it. It was now simply mechanical, methodical, and necessary. His frown returned.

7

By the time the two stars had taken their seats for the informal press conference in the Elephant Bar, every word that came from Charlie's mouth required an effort. Normally garrulous and playful with the press, Charlie was trying his best for Paulette's sake, but it was clear he'd prefer to be alone in his suite – or better still back at Summit Drive in Hollywood.

The Elephant Bar could have been in Paris or London or New York. High ceilings with chandeliers, air thick with cigarette and cigar smoke that muffled the hubbub of conversation. Framed pictures of Angkor Wat adorned the walls, there was a large globe in a wooden holder, and Indochinese sculptures of apsaras and warriors were on every surface. A baby grand piano sat by the window. The style was Asian chic before the term was coined and imitated across the Western world. Waiters carried in Singapore Slings on silver trays, weaving through the knot of press to find Charlie holding court as best he could, defending his choice to make another silent movie, while the rest of the world had moved on to talkies.

'Dialogue may or may not have a place in comedy,' he answered hoarsely, trying not to let his frustration show. He had faced the same question a thousand times on this trip and had given the same answer. 'But it does not have a place in the sort of comedies that I make.'

He fidgeted in his chair, sipping iced water, willing the press conference over. The journalists nudged closer to hear his words.

'Have you *ever* considered speech in your films?' continued an American journalist from *Life* magazine.

'I've never considered jumping off Nelson's Column,' countered Charlie shortly. 'But I have the definite idea that it would be unhealthful.'

There was polite laughter. Paulette squeezed his hand and offered the photographers that same practised smile of a celebrity accustomed to their attention. Flashbulbs exploded; the more Charlie retreated, the more Paulette dazzled in his shadow.

But behind the press stood Le Favre, smoking his Gitanes and watching the celebrity couple through the smoke.

Charlie gestured to another journalist.

'If you'll permit me, there's one question to which many of my readers are desperate for an answer. Has Miss Goddard become Mrs Chaplin, or not?'

The question curled into the tendrils of cigar smoke. Even the waiters paused to listen. The hubbub died down and everyone inched closer, eager to hear his reply. Charlie studied his fingernails, as he considered his words. But none came. Paulette rubbed his shoulder. Was this a show of tender affection – or a deliberate gesture to make sure that her bare ring finger was on display? Eventually when the silence had stretched into an uncomfortable, almost embarrassing duration, it was Paulette who answered.

'I'm not denying I have the right to wear a diamond and platinum wedding ring on my left third finger,' she offered, 'but it's not our policy to discuss our private affairs.'

Charlie's look was full of gratitude. She had rescued him from an awkward question. It encouraged him and he retreated to familiar ground. He coughed for attention, stealing it back from Paulette.

'We are the only two live spirits in a world of automatons. We are children with no sense of responsibility,' he rasped, quoting his own picture.

'So you are, like the characters in your picture, "spiritually free"?' offered one, picking up the quotation from *Modern Times*.

'Whereas the rest of humanity is weighed down by duty.' A French journalist from *Le Figaro* continued the world-famous intertitles. 'But Monsieur, does "spiritually free" mean you are atheists?'

There was an audible intake of breath.

'Or anarchists?'

All eyes were on Charlie now. He got up from the armchair and paced the room, forcing the journalists to take a step back. He considered his words as he picked up and examined a bronze figurine on a cabinet, his back to the hungry press corps. Eventually he turned with a bow and offered, 'We are humanity crusading in the pursuit of happiness.'

'And will that "crusade" extend to Indochina?' rifled back the French journalist.

Le Favre stubbed out his cigarette, listening now with real interest. The tone of the interview had shifted. The journalist caught the captain's eye, and there was an almost imperceptible nod to press home the advantage.

Charlie spun the globe in its wooden holder.

'Have you even seen my picture?' he asked, anger rising.

'No, and I've never seen a Bengal tiger, yet I know of its danger. Sir, do you ever consider your political responsibility as a global star?'

'Sir, the Little Fellow is simply an entertainer! As for myself, that's my business, wouldn't you say?'

The gauntlet was thrown. The faintest curl of a smile appeared at the corner of Le Favre's lips. Once more Paulette rode to the rescue.

'Mesdames and messieurs,' she offered brightly. 'It has been a long journey from Saigon, and we have an important engagement at the palace. Would you please excuse us?'

A final wave beside Charlie, and she steered the flustered star out of the Elephant Bar and into the corridor. A coughing fit took over and he leant against the wall for support. How he hated not being able to speak. When it passed, all that remained was a rising anger that Paulette recognised immediately. He was spoiling for a fight and was about to round on her when a member of the hotel staff approached.

'Monsieur, a telephone call for you.'

Charlie looked puzzled.

'I have transferred it to a private office, monsieur. If you'll follow me.'

'Must be the studio,' explained Charlie to Paulette.

'I'll wait in the car with Mother,' she replied, with a fond but concerned expression. 'Don't be long, darling.'

Charlie followed the young man down the corridor. He opened a door marked private and Charlie entered a cluttered office. A phone was off its cradle. He walked over and picked it up, holding his hand over the receiver to clear his swollen throat.

'Yes?' he said eventually. 'Hello?'

There was no reply. He tapped the cradle, but there was no one there.

'Hello? Is that you, Alf?' he added, assuming it was his studio manager in Hollywood. But there was just more silence.

Confused, he replaced the receiver. Above the desk was a framed colour lithograph by Louis Delaporte. It showed the majestic ruins of Angkor Wat in the background as a French explorer hacked his way through the jungle to discover it. He checked the French inscription below it and read aloud.

'Angkor Wat. Built by a disappeared race; rediscovered by France.'

Behind him a match flared, and he whipped round to find Le Favre closing the door behind him. He stood in the shadows, assessing the little man with barely contained disdain.

'When I tell my children I have met Charlot himself, *mon Dieu*, they will not believe me. You smoke, don't you?' He offered a cigarette, but Charlie declined with a pantomime gesture to his sore throat.

'When you put the horse's shoe in your hands, *non*, your gloves! Changing the odds for the little – how do you say? The little ...?'

'The Little Fellow,' croaked Charlie, cornered.

'*Non, non*. Le Vagabond! The Tramp! Monsieur, you have many imitators, but no equals.'

'That's very kind of you to say,' he managed. 'But if you will excuse me, I must—'

'But this is not America.' The smile disappeared from Le

Favre's face. 'I will not say this again, Monsieur Chaplin. Le Vagabond's "defiance" is funny only if it is not taken too seriously, *non*? If it stays away from anything political.'

The two men eyeballed each other. Charlie fought back his rising anger, fuelled by the frustration of the press conference, the heat and his inflamed tonsils. He willed his vocal cords to work one final time.

'I think you have misunderstood, Captain. Maybe you haven't heard here what the rest of the world already knows. You see, I have retired from motion pictures. I am merely here to travel and experience the world—'

'Then thankfully we understand one another. And I hope that you will understand why, for the sake of security, the governor has decided not to allow *Modern Times* to be shown in his protectorate. Let me be perfectly clear, Charlot. Keep your Hollywood politics out of Indochina.' The thinly veiled threat hung in the air. He added as an afterthought – or a taunt. 'Enjoy your stay, Monsieur Chaplin. The ruins of Angkor; *c'est magnifique.*'

8

Outside the Hotel Le Royal, the crowd had barely diminished. It surged forwards when Charlie and his companions left the lobby and climbed into the waiting car. Tyres crunched over shattered flashbulbs, out of the gates and into the dark wide boulevards of the European Quarter. Frank Yonamori turned from the front seat and handed Charlie a derby hat and cane. The king had made an informal request on behalf of the young prince for Charlie to present himself with them. But what had seemed like a sound publicity move in Saigon now felt more like a taunt. And the exchange with Le Favre had left Charlie seething. He avoided Paulette's look of concern and instead stared into the darkness outside the window. It was Paulette's mother who broke the uncomfortable silence.

'You'd think the mercury would drop at night, but I swear to God it's actually gotten hotter,' she offered, fanning herself.

Her attempt to break the tension failed. Mr Yonamori tried again. 'I have overseen every last detail for the screening, sir. Everything is prepared. You'll be pleased to know that the king has spared no expense. He has acquired the very latest DeVry 35mm projector for the occasion.

Charlie ignored his manservant.

'Lighten up would you Charlie,' chided Paulette. 'It's a royal screening. Kings and queens.' Her patience was being tested by Charlie's persistent foul mood.

'Yes. A private screening!' he snarled back. His voice had almost totally gone now but the barbed comment was lost on them. He couldn't bring himself to explain. 'Tell them, Frank.'

'On the orders of the Governor of the Protectorate, *Modern Times* has been refused a general release in this territory.'

There was silence in the car for a moment.

Paulette was as incredulous as Charlie, but for different reasons. The income from the release in Cambodia would be negligible compared to European and American markets. They would be lucky if the numbers even registered on global sales.

'Charlie? Surely this can't be about money? I hardly think the income from—'

'Banned! Banned on the instruction of that jumped-up French captain! They think I'm a damned communist. You know he threatened me. He actually threatened ME!'

But the outburst was too much and he started coughing. Mrs Goddard reached into her purse and pulled out a packet of lozenges and offered them to Charlie.

'We swear by these in Utah. Soothes the adenoids.' But Charlie refused the peace offering and they drove on without a further word.

Not long after, they pulled up at the palace gates. A guard peered in. Charlie ran a finger under his collar and coughed. The formal attire only added to his frustration. The guard waved them through.

The Royal Palace was a lavish complex of throne halls, offices, residences and audience chambers nestled around the Temple of the Emerald Buddha – all in the distinctive Khmer style with *chedi*, or Buddhist stupas, *prang prasat*, or spires, and pillars, which were imitated in pagodas or wats around the kingdom. Between the buildings were broad traveller's palms, manicured lawns and topiary hedges. The display of wealth was breathtaking and fitting for a line of kings stretching back in time to the magnificent Angkorian era.

Maybe it was the heat, or the travel, or the viral infection in his throat, but the first part of the evening was a blur of protocol and formality. They were met by Governor Robin whom Charlie immediately dismissed as a small and tedious bureaucrat, who clearly viewed the celebrity couple with suspicion and annoyance. In a thick accent he offered them protocol advice before they were presented to King Sisowath Monivong in the Throne Room. The king wore a collarless white tunic, adorned with row upon row of medals and a wide sash over his royal silk *sampot*, or sarong, and stockings. It was his shoes that Charlie noticed. He liked to think he could tell a person's inner qualities by their footwear. The king wore immaculate polished Oxfords that looked like they might be a size or two too big and which seemed rather incongruous. Yes, he was the king, but he'd also been strong-armed into French 'protection' in return for remaining so. He was wearing a Frenchman's shoes in more ways than one. But compared to the frumpy governor's welcome, there was genuine pleasure and excitement in his broad smile. Despite having met kings and statesmen across the world in his travels, Charlie had never been comfortable around ceremony and protocol. He did the minimum not to appear rude. Paulette made up for his grumpiness, brightening the Throne Room with her smile and laughter after the formal introductions.

Before they started the royal screening, Charlie and his companions were treated to a dance from the classical Royal Ballet in the gardens. The graceful dancers, in their lavish costumes and ornate headdresses, and the hypnotic musical accompaniment, mesmerised the guests under the night sky. On any other occasion Charlie might also have been entranced by the spectacle, but he found his mind wandering. He tried to stifle a cough, not wanting to disturb the performance but also finding it soporific. He didn't want to fall asleep in front of the king. He fingered the derby in his lap. That was when he noticed another pair of eyes avoiding the performance. They belonged to the young Prince Sihanouk, who could barely contain his excitement at meeting the famous star. The prince had seen the royal ballet countless times, but he'd never been in the presence of Charlie Chaplin. But his wide smile faltered and his forehead puckered into a frown. Was this man sitting beside him really the Tramp? He almost seemed disappointed. Charlie got that a lot. It used to annoy him, but now he liked the growing distance between his middle-aged self and his iconic alter-ego. He softened for the prince. While all eyes were focussed on the ballet, Charlie made a few exaggerated eye gestures, a shoulder shake, a stifled yawn – all in the character of the Tramp. Prince Sihanouk hid a giggle. It was all he needed and now he knew that it really was Charlie Chaplin.

Charlie turned back to the performance in mock seriousness. The lead dancer, exquisitely beautiful and elegant, locked eyes with Chaplin and threw flower petals in his direction, her fingers pulled back at an almost impossible angle. There was polite applause as the ballet came to an end.

Afterwards the guests walked through the splendour of the palace gardens. Charlie barely listened to the governor's account of the French support for Cambodia. He spoke with hands behind his back like a tour guide.

'It was a request from King Norodom himself which prompted the French government to finance and build a palace befitting the king's god-like status among his people. That was when the royal capital was moved from Oudong to Phnom Penh.'

Even Paulette struggled to feign interest in the history lesson. From nowhere, Captain Le Favre fell in beside them and caught Charlie's bored eyes and nodded a greeting – without a smile.

'The Temple of the Emerald Pagoda, to your right, houses many national treasures and gifts presented to the royal family over centuries including many notable gold and jewelled Buddha statues. Perhaps most notable is actually one of the smaller items, a crystal Buddha made from Baccarat crystal in the 19th century and a life-size Maitreya Buddha encrusted with nearly ten thousand diamonds.'

Charlie scanned the gardens and noticed faces in the darkness peering at the procession. They were the dancers from the ballet, still in costume and their children, all trying to catch a glimpse of the celebrities.

The royal screening took place in the Moonlight Pavilion, an open-sided audience chamber used by the king to view parades on the boulevard beyond, and from which he addressed his subjects. Mr Yonamori fussed over the projector as a screen was rearranged on the stage. All the while, the teenage prince was transfixed by Charlie, making less and less effort to hide his stares. When all was set, Mr Yonamori nodded to the palace officials and Governor Robin ushered Charlie and Paulette to the front. Charlie held his derby and cane reluctantly. A nudge from Paulette and he put the hat on his head. Governor Robin beamed. Prince Sihanouk's eyes opened wider.

'Your Royal Highness, distinguished guests, may I present Mr Charles Chaplin, or as we call him here, Charlot. And his ... ah, companion and co-star Mademoiselle Goddard.'

Charlie noticed the deliberate pause. And so did Paulette's mother. There was applause and an excitable prince called out, 'Saklo, Saklo!' as Charlie stepped forward. He cleared his throat and tried to speak. But his voice was barely a croak. He tried again, but the rasp could barely be heard beyond the front row. He shot a pleading look to Paulette who came to his rescue. Again.

'Your Royal Highnesses, distinguished guests. Mr Chaplin is not feeling himself tonight. The days of travel have unfortunately taken their toll on his voice.' How she loved the spotlight, thought Charlie, jealous and grateful in equal measure.

Not wanting to be upstaged, he looked up at the colourful paintings of the *Reamker* that adorned the ceilings and pillars. His exaggerated movements caused a ripple of sniggers through the gathered dignitaries.

'Without wishing to speak for him, I'm sure he would, if he could, express his thanks to His Royal Highness for this opportunity to screen his latest and best motion picture.'

Charlie checked his fingernails with exaggerated nonchalance. His alter-ego edged out the frustrated filmmaker – and at the mention of the king he looked up bewildered and bowed so low the derby fell off his head and on to his waiting foot. He kicked it back up, a practised move that saw the derby land squarely back on his head. The laughter drowned out Paulette's introduction.

She looked to Charlie, beaming, and took his hand. He was back. The Charlie she fell in love with. The consummate entertainer.

'Your Royal Highness, *Modern Times*!'

The applause was genuine as the couple took their seats on the front row. Behind them the projector flickered to life and the music began. On the screen, under the moonlight, the film started – the hands of a clock and the opening title card, 'Charlie Chaplin in *Modern Times*', followed by another:

'*Modern Times*: a story of industry or individual enterprise. Humanity crusading in the pursuit of happiness.'

All eyes were on the screen in the darkness. All except Prince Sihanouk who grinned at the filmmaker. Charlie put a finger to his lips and winked. He left his derby hat and cane on the seat and sneaked his way along the line of dignitaries and ducked silently out of the screening. He couldn't face the heat, nor the idea of re-watching the film that he knew intimately, frame by individual frame. He longed for escape and to be by himself.

In the palace gardens, Charlie paced and smoked between the palm trees. He was close enough to hear the music from *Modern Times*. Palace staff, their children, and the dancers from the ballet, peered into the open sides of the pavilion, careful to stay out of sight. One of them was the same round-faced boy who'd helped at Phirath's rehearsal at Wat Botum earlier that afternoon. He saw Charlie pacing back and forth and walked over, imitating the infamous shuffle of the Tramp. It wasn't a bad attempt but Charlie wasn't in the mood. Not wanting to engage, he fished in his pocket for a piastre coin and offered it to the boy. Then he strode off to the gates to find the solitude he so desperately craved.

Back in the pavilion, Le Favre noticed Charlie's absence. All that remained of the star was the derby hat and cane resting on his empty chair. Amidst the laughter, Le Favre gestured over a Sûreté policeman and whispered in his ear. The policeman nodded and ducked out of the pavilion. His instructions were clear. He was not to let the celebrity out of his sight.

Charlie walked out of the palace gates and the guards snapped to attention. The night was bright beneath a half-moon, and the boulevard beyond was lit by a few streetlights and lanterns, which adorned the palace walls. There was a line of rickshaws and a few horse-drawn cabs. All the while he was watched by the same mysterious boy. He fingered the coin in his palm, and then followed Charlie to the gate.

Beside the line of rickshaws, Phirath waited with his buckled bicycle. He had changed out of his theatre costume and was now dressed uncomfortably in a Western suit not quite the right size. The toothbrush moustache has been wiped clean from his top lip and cheek. As soon as he saw Charlie leaving the gates he rushed over.

'Monsieur,' he blurted out. 'Pardon, monsieur?'

'*Oui*,' said Charlie, guarded, but with a faint smile.

'Is he there?' Phirath gestured inside the palace gates. 'Inside.'

'Who?'

'Monsieur Chaplin.'

'I'm Charlie Chaplin,' replied the star, momentarily confused. '*Moi. Je suis*—'

'*Non, non!*' Phirath continued in Khmer. 'Is Mr Chaplin still inside the palace?'

Charlie blinked, uncomprehending.

'Chaplin? Charlot?' added Phirath. And to make his point, he did an impression of the Tramp's walk. The shuffle-step was spot on. He grinned at Charlie, who returned his look coldly, the smile vanishing from his face.

'I believe he already left,' he said, and walked over to the nearest of the cabs and climbed in. The driver flicked the reins and the horses snorted.

'The Chinese Quarter please,' he instructed the driver. '*Quartier Chinois*.'

The cab pulled away before Phirath realised his mistake. He grabbed his buckled bike and pedalled furiously after them. The policeman arrived at the gates to find the boulevard deserted and still, except for the young boy watching from the shadows.

'Which way did he go?' barked the policeman in rough Khmer.

Without missing a beat, the kid gestured in the opposite direction and the policeman set off in pursuit.

9

Phnom Penh in the mid 1930s was a segregated city – and with good reason if you were French. Flooding the kingdom with Chinese opium had done much to dull resistance in the French colony, but resentment was building. The French kept mainly to the European quarter, but beyond their beloved 'Paris in the East' were the Chinese and the Khmer quarters, both of which were separated by wide canals and a network of guarded bridges. The cab crossed one such bridge, and Charlie sat back and felt the frustrations and anxiety of the past hours melt away. Since leaving New York, their vacation had turned into an endless run of receptions, screenings and parties. Back in Hollywood, he was able to seek solace in the quiet of Summit Drive. But more than anything, he loved to wander the streets of Los Angeles, often ending up at the downtown boxing rings. It was not that he was less well known in these areas. Everywhere he was a champion for the poor and possessed. But there he could talk to ordinary people who weren't obsessed with the pursuit of fame or the purchase of pleasure. He was excited to see the Chinese quarter and escape the stiff formality of the king's reception and screening, the sycophantic well-wishers just wanting a photograph or a piece of gossip to fuel the dullness of colonial life. He longed to melt into nothing for a few hours and watch people – without them watching him.

The Chinese Quarter, described at length in his Indochina *Baedeker*, did not disappoint. The cab turned off the main boulevard, across the bridge over the canal and under a pillared archway. He may as well have crossed into a different country. The road passed between a row of colonnaded Chinese shophouses, but the road was so narrow there was barely enough room for the cab. At the first opportunity he paid and stepped down, ignoring the driver's warnings.

'How will you find your way back?' asked the cabbie. 'Should I wait?'

'No need,' replied Charlie, already distracted by the nightlife unfolding before him.

His outsider's gaze pierced the smoke from a hundred cooking fires. From the light of dozens of lanterns he saw the Chinese Quarter bursting with animated exchanges, transactions and altercations. Families gathered around steaming bowls at food stalls. All manner of animals, from ducks to pigs to chickens, added to the cacophony which drowned out the memory of the tedious polite conversation and fake bonhomie of the European Quarter. While his alter ego would be recognised immediately, the real Charlie was as anonymous as any other European, and the shadows and flickering lanterns allowed him to melt into the melee.

At last he smiled.

He stopped for a moment at a stall selling lacquerware – exquisitely painted bowls and plates and lathed wooden pots. His wonder at the craftsmanship was interrupted by the sound of a drumbeat. At a crossroads, he caught sight of a procession of people in brightly coloured robes – some red, others yellow and blue. They beat time on a drum and then disappeared into a doorway of what looked like a temple. Charlie walked on taking it all in. His magpie mind surveyed every detail, every interaction, mining it for possibilities, storing away scenes.

He watched a moment play out at a shophouse opposite. An elderly Chinese shopkeeper stood teetering on a trestle table to replace a lantern. Beneath him were sacks of produce. Watching the shopkeeper was a boy, no more than seven or eight years old. Seizing his chance with the shopkeeper distracted, the boy dug his hand into the nearest sack and stuffed handfuls of rice into his sarong. But the shopkeeper spotted him. He shouted something in Chinese and stepped to the side of the tabletop. The table tipped under his weight. He very nearly lost his balance. Just in time, the boy pulled the table down from the other side to right it. The shopkeeper regained his balance, but it didn't stop him shaking his fist at the boy. So the kid responded by letting go. The table lifted once more, forcing the shopkeeper to readjust and rebalance himself. The kid grinned again – in control for once. Then he saw the strange European man watching him from across the street.

Charlie took out a notebook from his jacket pocket and began to scribble down notes, fuelling the boy's curiosity. In Charlie's imaginings the sounds faded out, and the colour leached away. The scene continued as a black and white tableau, like a silent two-reeler, accompanied by piano music ...

* * *

FADE IN: A shopkeeper's stall in the Chinese Quarter.

The shopkeeper falls to the ground with the lantern jammed hard on his head. He staggers to his feet, spinning one way and then the next, shaking his fist, before ripping the paper lantern clear. He launches himself after the kid, but the little boy is no longer a little Chinese boy. He is the Tramp, holding his derby hat, oversized trousers, undersized topcoat and cane. His hat is full of stolen rice and he ducks under the trestle table to evade the shopkeeper. He trips the shopkeeper with his cane and the big man flies into the sacks of rice in his own shophouse.

***

Charlie's imaginings were interrupted by a loud blast on a whistle. The scene returned to reality – the colours and sounds flooded back. And this reality was a harsh one. He saw a Sûreté policeman charging into the fray. The boy's eyes widened. This was serious. He legged it. The policeman gave chase and Charlie flattened himself against the doorway to let them run past. Charlie was about to follow when a hand grabbed him and pulled him back.

It was Phirath, sweating, beside his broken bicycle.

'Monsieur Chaplin!' he said in English. 'I'm sorry I didn't recognise you. My name is Sok Phirath. I've been waiting for you.'

Before the bewildered Charlie could respond, they saw the Sûreté return to the scene of the crime with the captured boy. From nowhere, the boy's father threw himself at the Sûreté's feet, begging, palms pressed together above his head, a *sampeah* – a sign of respect normally reserved for monks or Buddha himself. His desperate pleas were ignored and he received a beating from a baton for his trouble. He clung to his wayward son. Charlie started forward to intervene, the punishment way beyond the measure of the crime, but Phirath held him back.

'Against the law for Cambodian to be in Chinese Quarter after curfew,' he explained.

'But—'

'It is law. You cannot change it. Not like this.'

A siren wailed and a police van stopped at the wider intersection, scattering stalls and people. More police streamed out. Among them was the policeman from the palace. He spotted Charlie and Phirath in the doorway and left the fracas by the shophouse.

'Monsieur Chaplin!' he shouted.

Phirath grabbed Charlie's hand and pulled him away.

'Arrêtez!' he shouted. But Charlie and Phirath had gone. 'Merde!'

Charlie and Phirath ran through the dark alleys pursued by the whistles and boots of the police. Out of breath but exhilarated, Charlie eventually stopped. Ahead was a police checkpoint between the Chinese and Khmer quarters. The policeman on duty heard the shouts and whistles and drifted away from his post to check out the commotion. Seizing the chance, Phirath pulled Charlie in a crouch-run through the barrier.

They were free.

IO

Charlie and Phirath walked calmly through the Khmer Quarter as if nothing had happened, but Charlie's heart was racing. The king and governor and the odious Captain Le Favre were all forgotten in the exhilaration of their escape. He stole a glance at his new companion beside him. He felt no fear, despite being beyond the protection of the European Quarter, wandering a city he didn't know, with a man he barely knew. Phirath's hair was still slicked back, though the run had left it a little dishevelled. He was the same size and build as Charlie, and with the same athletic sinewy power that Charlie had possessed in his prime, some twenty years earlier. Charlie laughed to himself and checked his watch. He'd been gone from the palace barely twenty minutes.

The Khmer Quarter was laid out in a grid. There were few streetlights here and only the moon and occasional lanterns provided any light. Phirath knew his way in the dark and Charlie followed without thought to his own safety. He could just make out the traditional Khmer houses built on large stilts. Under the raised wooden rooms he caught sight of daybeds, livestock and large water jars – a communal space for all the household activities. Wooden steps led up to the houses proper, where the wealth and private possessions were kept, and where the occupants slept. It was into one of these compounds that Phirath led Charlie. Beside a broad tamarind tree, the house was a silhouette against the night sky. This wasn't just Phirath's home. It was also the base for the theatre troupe. A group of men and women of all ages huddled in heated discussion beneath the house. Around them were trunks of props, and costumes hanging from nails. Phirath strode forward but Charlie hung back, suddenly aware of his intrusion into a different world. Phirath's mother seemed both relieved and angry to see the actor return. He greeted her respectfully, palms together, but she brushed it off.

'We thought you'd been taken,' she said in Khmer. To Charlie's ears, her guttural intonations in Khmer sounded more like a bark than an expression of concern. Then she caught sight of Charlie, still in his formal clothes. Everyone stared. From the dark, their eyes were not friendly, viewing him with deep and understandable suspicion.

'You brought a *barang* here, a Frenchman?' she muttered.

'This is Charlie Chaplin. Charlot!' he said in Khmer. Then added, 'Saklo!'

The mood immediately shifted. There were whispers between shadows and eyes peered closer. One of the men, the actor who played the prince, looked him up and down, unconvinced. He barked something indifferently and shook his head.

'They don't believe me, Saklo,' offered Phirath to Charlie with a cheeky grin. 'They will. Sit down, please. Sit down.'

'I really should be heading back to the palace. I'm the guest—'

'One moment, please.'

Charlie did as he was told and sat on the daybed. Despite their suspicion, they cleared the area around him. Charlie scanned the faces in the gloom – a mixture of curiosity and doubt. Phirath poured himself a drink and downed it. It was rice wine and he grimaced, then grinned. The troupe hovered, unsure how to respond or react to Saklo in the flesh, out of costume and now sitting in their midst. Like most people, they only knew Charlie from his films. The man they saw before them was without make-up or his world-famous moustache. He was older, there were lines around his eyes, and streaks of white in his hair. He was a far cry from his exuberant, expressive on-screen persona.

'Saklo!' Phirath offered again to the gathering.

He put down the cup and bottle and retrieved a worn-out rice paddy hat, performing as if he was already drunk. When he sat down, he missed the edge of the daybed, staggered into an old man before stumbling to the floor. The kids were the first to laugh. They made space to allow Phirath to perform. Word soon spread throughout the neighbourhood. More faces peered into the gloom as Phirath did his very best Charlie Chaplin impression. And he had it down pat, using props and the setting to bring his impersonation to life. A shrug, a shuffle, a look – and soon everyone was laughing.

'You do a better me than me,' said Charlie mournfully, although his eyes sparkled under the lantern light.

'I've seen every one of your pictures, Saklo. Every single one.'

'Not *Modern Times*,' said Charlie back, and his smile faded.

'Not yet. I hear it's your best. A communist manifesto on film!'

Without waiting for a response, Phirath opened a trunk and took out some props. There was a sword and a staff. One of the musicians grabbed a drum and began to beat a rhythm.

Another joined in with a *troh*, the one-stringed instrument found throughout the region. A semi-circle formed, as Phirath and the prince faced off. The rehearsed steps were given an extra drunken dimension in an impromptu Lakhoun performance.

Charlie was utterly entranced.

The light, the whine of mosquitos, the laughter, the colour of headdresses and costumes, the exaggerated movements of each step, and the whole magical incongruity of the moment was intoxicating. Charlie felt his sickness seep away and his energy return. When the prince tripped and his stick fell at Charlie's feet, the prince beckoned Charlie to join them.

For a moment, Charlie hesitated. But when he picked up the stick and felt it in his hand, the energy of the moment surged through him. For the first time he grinned to his audience, finally enjoying himself without the trappings of fame and fortune. This was pure entertainment, like the turn-of-the-century Vaudeville acts which had made such an impression on Charlie's childhood.

As much as he tried afterwards, Charlie could never recall the exact performance, the double-act he improvised with Phirath in the theatre troupe's compound in the Khmer Quarter of Phnom Penh. This would be a private memory, never shared in his memoirs or writings, nor with friends back home, nor even with Paulette. This was a memory only for himself, a moment of pure expression that vanished as soon as it was completed. A perfect synchronisation between the unknown amateur Khmer actor and the most famous star in the whole world.

But finally Charlie stepped back panting. There was no doubt from any of the troupe now as to his bona fides. He gestured to the props and costumes.

'A theatre troupe?' he asked simply.

'We call it Lakhoun Bassac,' Phirath replied. 'Traditional Khmer theatre based on ancient stories from centuries ago – what we call the *Reamker*. But unlike the ballet, we have a bit more ... fun with it, for the popular, rather than the royal audiences. We have adapted it, with comic' – he searched for the word – 'in French they call them entr'actes. Moments in which we stop showing the past and speak to the audience about the present. In that, my friend, we are inspired by you, Saklo.'

Charlie was humbled. He has been mobbed by fans in London, Berlin, New York and Singapore, but it was here and on this day that he caught a real glimpse of what his life's work had really meant to people – ordinary people – in the furthest corners of the world.

'I don't know what to say,' he offered eventually. 'Where do you perform?'

'Mainly in pagodas, sometimes on the riverfront. That's why people call it Lakhoun Bassac. After the river. Our troupe has become popular although we dared to modernise the performance. We perform wherever we are allowed. But the French worry we are becoming too popular, and too critical. They try to stop us, but our people won't let them. This is entertainment – but politics is never far behind. Wouldn't you agree?'

Charlie stammered his agreement.

'It's enchanting. But I really must get back to the palace. I'm screening *Modern Times* for the king. It wouldn't do to be absent from the palace when the film ends.'

A few moments later, and after some heartfelt goodbyes, Charlie found himself sharing a rickshaw with his number one fan heading back to the European Quarter. As they approached the checkpoint, Phirath gestured for the rickshaw driver to stop and took leave of his hero.

'The newspapers report that you intend to set your next motion picture in the East. Perhaps here.'

'You shouldn't believe what you read in the papers. Others will tell you I've retired entirely from motion pictures—'

'You mustn't, Saklo! I mean, you must not retire but you must make your motion picture here. I will help you.'

He stepped out of the rickshaw before Charlie could reply.

'We rehearse every day at Wat Botum. We are preparing for the touring theatre season. We will be there from five o'clock tomorrow. Come, Saklo. We can discuss it more.'

The rickshaw rode on. Charlie turned round to see Phirath standing in the shadows at the edge of the Khmer Quarter. His spirits soared.

II

When Charlie arrived back at the Royal Palace, he spotted the policeman rushing back, puffing and belligerent. Charlie doffed his hat in mock respect – only making things worse. He strode across the gardens to the Moonlight Pavilion in time to hear the final scene of *Modern Times*. On screen in the pavilion, the Tramp put on his oversized shoes, sat beside the Gamin in scrubland. But the Gamin looked defeated. She buried her face in her arms and collapsed onto a boulder causing the Tramp to look on in concern.

'What's the use of trying?' read the intertitle, her despair clear in her eyes.

'Buck-up, never say die. We'll get along,' was the Tramp's reply.

He helped her up, encouraged and ready to face the world, and they walked off down a winding road towards a distant horizon of misty hills.

Charlie returned to his seat just as the Tramp and his Gamin were heading off to an uncertain future. Prince Sihanouk noticed his return and smiled. Charlie puts his finger to his lips and shrugged. But his disappearance had not gone unnoticed by Paulette. She wasn't smiling. Not one bit.

'The End' read the final intertitle.

The gathered audience rose to their feet in applause and cheers. Paulette and Charlie stood and bowed politely. As the hubbub died down, Le Favre ambled over.

'Enjoy your walk, Charlot?' he whispered in Charlie's ear, making a show of shaking his hand and congratulating him on the film.

'I needed some air,' replied Charlie brightly.

'In the Chinese Quarter?' It was not a question. He wanted Charlie to know he was going to be watched throughout his stay.

'Are you spying on me, Captain?' countered Charlie.

Before the captain could reply, the celebrity couple were surrounded by well-wishers. They were guided out of the screening room to a reception being held in their honour. It was an extravagant affair. A band played European jazz for the guests, and waiters passed between them with trays of canapés and champagne. No expense had been spared. Under normal circumstances, such an event would have irked Charlie, but the experiences in the Chinese Quarter had invigorated him, almost as much as his disappearance has infuriated Paulette. His magpie mind was buzzing with vignettes and possibilities for the Tramp in Indochina. These vignettes hadn't settled into any kind of order, but he found himself smiling inwardly as they played out on the screen in his mind.

Sometime later, Charlie found himself alone with the king but he was barely listening to the monarch. He couldn't take his eyes off Paulette, who was surrounded by a gaggle of Frenchmen, some in dress uniform, others in reception attire. She wanted Charlie to see her, beside the flamboyant Laurent Levalier, laughing and flirting, and in her element. Charlie stood stiff and formal as the king's clipped voice continued.

'... and it has always surprised me that you have chosen not to embrace the future with "talkies" as you Americans call them.'

Charlie thought better of challenging his assumption that he was American.

'The technology is there, *n'est ce pas*?' pushed the king.

'It's my belief, Your Majesty,' said Charlie before his silence appeared rude, 'that motion pictures need sound as much as Beethoven's symphonies need lyrics. But it appears that I am in a minority. A relic of a bygone age. Out of step with ... modernity.'

The king brushed this off with a laugh and guided him to a quieter corner of the hall beside some Angkorian-era sculptures. He made a show of discussing them but lowered his voice to whisper.

'Should I speak to the governor? Ask him to lift the ban on *Modern Times* and approve its release in the Kingdom? I can do this.'

'Your Highness doesn't share his fear of the picture?' asked Charlie cautiously.

'Perhaps, Mr Chaplin. But the real question is, what do *you* think?'

Although the politics of the protectorate were a mystery to Charlie and he was reluctant to be drawn into them on his holiday, he couldn't let the governor's political ban go.

'It's a motion picture. Only entertainment. The Little Fellow is defiant of any form of injustice. My critics wouldn't agree, but I hold firm in my belief that the film displays an underlying concern with humanism, not communism.'

The king considered this reply, but before he could answer, the star-struck teenager Prince Sihanouk rushed over with the royal photographer. The king and his son presented themselves with Charlie to be photographed. A flashbulb exploded, blinding Charlie momentarily, the practised grin fixed on his face.

'You've made quite an impression on the prince, Mr Chaplin.'

'Is that so, Your Highness? Are you interested in motion pictures?'

The little prince nodded, speechless, but pleased as punch. Charlie bowed and, as arranged, offered his derby hat to the prince. He took it wide-eyed with wonder, and grinning. The king gestured for Paulette to join them. She sashayed over, turning heads throughout the room. Still smiling, she leaned close to Charlie's ear and whispered fiercely, 'Where the hell did you go?'

But there was no time for chit-chat or recriminations. Governor Robin approached them, accompanied by an eccentrically dressed white Russian émigré who sported an impressive white moustache and military medals pinned to an ill-fitting and outdated suit.

'Mr Chaplin, Miss Goddard. May I present Victor Goloubew, a Russian aristocrat in exile in our humble corner of the globe, and perhaps the only true expert on the lost civilization of Angkor.'

Victor took Paulette's hand, bowed low and kissed it gallantly.

'*Ochen pryantna*, Mademoiselle. A very great pleasure indeed. Victor Victorovich Goloubew at your service.'

He bowed low to Charlie too. 'I am at loss for words.' And he added in Russian, 'In my country we have Stakhanov, but in America, workers revolution has very different hero!' He guffawed at his own joke, pumping Charlie's hand up and down so vigorously his jowls shook. The governor came to the bewildered guests' rescue.

'Victor speaks more than twelve languages. Mostly at the same time.'

There was laughter at the familiar joke and Victor shrugged, beaming.

'And you, Mr Chaplin. How many do you speak?'

'I try not to speak at all.'

Victor found this the funniest riposte he'd ever heard. He clapped Charlie on the back so hard he spilt his champagne.

'You are comedian in real life too!'

'Did you enjoy my picture, Mr Goloubew?' asked Charlie, changing tack.

'Count Goloubew. But Bolsheviks have little time for titles. And what of titles here? Count this, Baron that.' Seeing the king he hastily added, 'Present company excepted, of course. But here we have no need for European titles. We are in the presence of Angkor. A civilization more *grandiozny* than pyramids of Egypt. More technologically advanced than ...'

He trailed off, looking hard at Charlie and Paulette.

'My dears, if I can be of any assistance during your visit. *Nyet!* I insist!'

Charlie and Paulette exchanged a glance as he answered his own unfinished question with an equally opaque answer.

'Accompany me as my guests! I leave for my home in Battambang in two days and would be delighted to give you a personal tour of the temple complexes.'

But while Paulette politely declined, Charlie enthusiastically accepted. The count took Charlie's side.

'That's settled then! *C'est magnifique!*' He beamed.

As they posed for another photograph with the king and the curious count, Paulette wasted no time in showing Charlie her displeasure.

'We're supposed to be leaving for Angkor Wat in the morning, Charlie. What the hell are you up to?'

12

Phirath squatted on his haunches along with the other members of the troupe, huddled around a flickering oil lamp. They leant close to listen as Phirath read from a newspaper.

'Workers, peasants, soldiers, youth, school students,' he read quietly in Khmer. 'Oppressed and exploited fellow countrymen! So, Ho Chi Minh calls on all in the Indo-Chinese Communist Party to rise up!'

But some of the troupe were not so swept up in his revolutionary fervour. The actor who played the prince glared at the younger performer, still dressed in stage-make-up and costume.

'With these?' he asked, brandishing the pole from the theatre performance.

'With our voices!'

'We're actors, not revolutionaries.'

'And who says we can't be both?'

He held up the newspaper for emphasis. The paper was the first in Indochina written in the curly Khmer script, a concession by the French that many in the colonial administration now regretted. It was a paper which spoke to them as proud Khmer people rather than as somehow deficient, indolent Frenchmen.

'Listen to the man who calls himself Original Khmer,"

continued Phirath, his voice dropping lower. It was still too dangerous to use real names, and the Sûreté had spies and informants everywhere. 'While the French insist that the race who built the Angkor Empire has disappeared, we <u>are</u> that race. We must wake up. We were once proud. We must be again.'

'And how do you propose to do that? From prison like your father?' countered the prince, doubtfully.

'Our party friends from Saigon will bring us what we need.' There was no dampening Phirath's spirit. He stood defiant in his costume as a Khmer peasant. 'Our champion has arrived. The world will listen now that Saklo is with us.'

'And is he?'

'He will be.'

Not too far away there was another kind of fervour overtaking Charlie – the fervour of creation. Under normal circumstances it was something that Paulette might have indulged. She loved it when Charlie got the bit between his teeth for a new idea. She could listen to his thoughts come tumbling out of his head for hours. And, if she was honest with herself, it was this very passion, not his celebrity status or wealth, which Paulette had fallen in love with. When Charlie got an idea in his mind, the world bent to it, and he couldn't be silenced. But here and now and after his mysterious disappearance she was still fuming and feeling somehow excluded from his process. She removed her jewellery at the dressing mirror in their suite while Charlie raced on, his voice much improved – and his spirits infinitely so.

'Colonial Subjects!' he announced triumphantly. 'That's what I'll call it. Set right here in Indochina. The Tramp's Eastern debut. Look around you. Think about the possibilities!'

He came up behind Paulette, his braces dangling below his trouser pockets, bare-chested and on fire. Paulette made a face.

'Leaving motion pictures behind,' he said.' Paulette pouted and brushed away his hand on her shoulder.

'Who am I, if I'm not the Little Fellow?'

For a moment the two of them stared at their reflections in the dressing mirror, side by side, but seemingly a gulf apart. The enthusiasm of Charlie's outburst caused a small coughing fit. He hacked as he selected a fresh shirt.

'Mother gave me some of her lozenges before she went to bed.' Paulette checked him out in the mirror as he paced with his new idea, thrilling himself with its possibilities. 'And what about the *Countess of Shanghai*?'

It was a barbed aside, designed to annoy him. She knew he moved on from one idea to the next and didn't like to be reminded of his previous passions. And not just the creative ones.

'You were cooped up for weeks in your cabin on our way out here. Working every hour on it, and leaving me and Mother to entertain ourselves.' Charlie didn't respond. She dug the knife in. 'It was during our holiday, Charlie. It was why we joined you on this trip. I was your inspiration, you said.'

But Charlie wasn't listening. He was wrapped up in his own head. On the table in the centre of the suite was a basket of exotic fruit and a packet of lozenges. Charlie took one of the lozenges out of the packet and considered it, his eyes sparkling.

'Strange word, "lozenge",' he muttered to himself. He rolled the word around his mouth relishing its sound. 'It sounds like it should mean something else. That's the strange thing about words. Deceptive little buggers. Lozenge. Lozenge.'

Paulette carried on dressing for the evening. It was only now, past ten o'clock in the evening, that it felt fresh enough to enjoy the night.

'Lausaaange,' Charlie offered in a French accent, rolling out the vowels.

'Lotzengah!' he barked in a caricature of a German accent.

When Paulette eventually looked up, there was a forgiving smile as she watched him perform for her. He rolled the lozenge between his fingers. She couldn't stay mad with him for long.

'I think I preferred you when you'd lost your voice,' she quipped with a smile.

'Lotzengah!' Charlie slammed his hand down on the table in mock anger. '*Lotzengah für alle, Lotzengah für Deutschland, die Menschen, das Land. Lotzengah für alle. Alle!*'

The impression of Hitler was uncannily and uncomfortably accurate. He raised his hand in a Nazi salute, not outstretched and domineering, but effetely bent at the elbow with his delicate hands and long manicured nails pointed.

'*Lotzengah für alle. Aber nicht für die dummkopfen meddle-machen Franzosen!*'

Paulette laughed. He popped the lozenge into his mouth and joined her at the dressing mirror where he stared at her reflection with a fierce intensity that she knew all too well.

'The Little Fellow stows away in San Francisco to find better work in Europe. But he boards the wrong ship – and, and – ends up in Indochina by mistake!'

One arm snaked around Paulette's waist. He leant closer to her ear and whispered.

'Where he falls hopelessly – and helplessly! – in love with the beautiful daughter of the governor-general. A spiteful, cruel man ...'

His eyebrows danced suggestively. Paulette removed his hands and stood up, letting her dress fall to the floor. She selected another, less formal but equally daring, lifting the straps over her shoulders to present herself to Charlie. Momentarily distracted by her pale porcelain back, he zipped up the dress, starting just above her coccyx, one hand running up her spine, relishing the touch of her skin.

'And then?' she asked.

'And then ... and then ... Who knows! But the characters! Count Victor whatisname. The Opium King! The peasants in their rice paddy hats. You know what they call me here? "Saklo". Their way of saying Charlot. Ha! That'll give the captain something to swagger about.'

He trailed off when he realised Paulette had stopped dressing and was staring at him, a dawning realisation on her face. This was nothing to do with a new idea for a movie. Or at least not entirely.

'It's about the ban, isn't it? It's about being told "no" for once in your life!'

Charlie didn't answer. He didn't want to.

'Charlie? Where did you go during the screening? What happened?'

'I'll be on the side of the Khmer subjects,' Charlie said, rather than answering her question. 'Restoring balance, fighting injustice and oppression. A comic revolutionary!'

Paulette scoffed at that. She didn't buy it one bit.

'My God, Charlie. It's not even the money, is it? It's because they dared to ban your film. This little French backwater, and some jumped up official dared to defy the great King of Comedy himself. Charlie, you're incorrigible!'

'And you wonder why I don't let you talk!' Charlie fired back. And instantly regretted his spiteful tone. But Paulette was perfectly capable of giving as good as she got. They'd sparred many times before. She was neither a puppy-eyed sycophant nor a teenage plaything. She was in fact perhaps the only person Charlie had ever known intimately who wasn't a conquest or purchase but an equal.

'Thank God we didn't tour Germany on holiday! What would you have done there!'

Charlie considered that. Before he could respond, Paulette offered him the end of a necklace to clasp behind her neck. As he did so, she added as casually as she dared, 'Will he talk?'

Charlie's hands froze. For a moment they stared at each other in the mirror.

'Will I?' Paulette pressed on. As soon as her necklace was secured, she turned to face him. 'Charlie, you promised. Give your fans what they want. Give me what I want,' she implored him.

Charlie's excitement faded as quickly as breath on a windowpane.

'If he speaks, the magic is gone.'

He spat the lozenge into the bin and walked out. Paulette bit her lip. She'd gone too far too soon, and she knew it. She would pay for it later, but for once that only strengthened her defiant mood.

That defiance was no less diminished when the celebrity couple entertained guests at the Elephant Bar in the Hotel Le

Royal. The alcohol had fuelled Paulette's rebelliousness, and she was draped over the piano, cocktail in hand, with Victor Goloubew and some French residents of the European Quarter. Charlie sat apart, cigarette in his hand and a tolerant smile on his face, as a song came to an end. Across the bar, Levalier and Le Favre were deep in conversation, but Charlie clocked the darting eyes of the French businessman checking out his wife in the gown that she'd chosen for just that purpose.

A French pianist started a new song. Somehow his doleful expression never matched the upbeat choice of the show-tunes he played. When Paulette clapped her hands in delight and started to sing along, Levalier left the captain and joined her at the piano. Whether by design or by circumstance, the song the pianist had selected was 'I'll be Hard to Handle'. For Paulette it was a double-handed dig to Charlie, not just because of the lyrics, but because it was from *Roberta*, a much-loved contemporary talkie starring Fred Astaire and Ginger Rogers. And Ginger's character of the Countess Scharwenka twisted the knife further – a reference to his now-abandoned *Countess of Shanghai*. Paulette knew Charlie well enough to know the references would land. So, while she flirted innocently with Levalier and the other expatriate hosts, who had crowded round her at the piano, she was really only performing for Charlie. She put on an accent for the song.

'I'll be hard to handle,' she sang in a clear strong voice, with a casual glance in his direction.

I'll be hard to handle
When we've said, 'I do.'
See there's no hope,

I just got a dope,
When I took you!

There was laughter from the guests, but it was too pointed for Charlie, and he slipped out of the Elephant Bar unnoticed. He could still hear her voice carrying down the corridor.

I'll be living my life in bed
But they'll always be twin beds
And I warn you, you'll be living like a monk
Our affair is now a past one.
So don't think you've pulled a fast one.
Just remember, I think you're a punk.

Back in their suite, Charlie opened the double French doors onto a balcony. The streets beyond the hotel were empty and dark, except for one car parked in a pool of light from the hotel gates. A policeman leant against the car, and his gaze travelled up the façade of the hotel to where Charlie stood. For a moment the two men exchanged glances. Then Charlie tossed his cigarette, waved and disappeared inside.

13

The next morning Charlie dressed in light casual slacks and an open shirt. He loaded new film into his 16mm camera with practised ease, and there was a sparkle in his eyes that Paulette knew well. Gone was the sour mood, and with it the infection in his chest and sore throat. Paulette lay back on the pillows, with slices of cucumber over her eyes. She was over-hung and feeling a little sorry for herself. She groaned when he threw back the heavy curtains and the morning sunlight streamed into the room.

'Try one of your mother's lozenges, darling. She swears by them.'

'I thought you despised sarcasm?' fired back Paulette.

There was a knock at the door and Mr Yonamori entered with a tray of breakfast. As he poured some coffee for Paulette, he asked, 'Will you be needing me this morning?'

'Not unless you can pour yourself into a glass and change your name to Gin Sling,' Paulette's sharp tongue had not been dulled by the alcohol of the night before or the throbbing behind her eyes in the morning.

Frank took an invitation from the tray and handed it to Charlie who glanced at it with little interest.

'A garden party at Governor Robin's at four,' he read. 'Sounds like a hoot.'

He popped it back on the tray and tucked a pen into his notebook, nearly ready.

'I might take a walk this morning before it gets too hot,' Charlie announced casually to no one in particular.

'With your notebook and camera?' asked Paulette sharply. She propped herself up on the pillows and removed the slices of cucumber from her eyes. 'My God, you're serious, aren't you? You're working on a new idea already. You've only been here a day!'

But Paulette's quips and barbs glanced harmlessly off his newfound good humour. He kissed her forehead with a genuine fond smile.

'Nothing bed and rest won't fix,' he offered. Adding a 'darling' as an afterthought.

Paulette threw a pillow at him as he ducked out of their suite and into the corridor. But as Charlie and Mr Yonamori reached the top of the grand stairs, they spotted Le Favre waiting at the bottom, with a handful of his officers. It was too late to hide so Charlie stepped down the stairs with a broad grin on his face.

'Are you planning to "get some air" this morning, Monsieur Chaplin?' Le Favre asked.

'I thought I might, yes,' replied Charlie, playing along.

'Then please allow us to escort you.' It was not an offer.

Charlie considered the captain's offer with mock indignation.

'But, Captain, I'm just here on holiday. I thought I might take a walk, that's all.'

'Then you won't mind us accompanying you. The streets are not always safe for someone as well-known as yourself.' Le

Favre's granite complexion was as unlikely to change as his mind, and Charlie thought better of trying.

'Very kind, Captain. Then why don't I meet you in the lobby in five minutes. Frank?'

And he retraced his steps up the staircase. Le Favre watched him go. What was he up to?

Nearly half an hour later, Le Favre was still waiting in the hotel lobby at a window where he could maintain a commanding view of the main entrance and gardens. He was smoking and pretending to read a newspaper. The lobby was full of press, hoping to catch a glimpse of the star and snag a comment for the weekend editions. Le Favre checked his watch. Something wasn't right.

And then he spotted Charlie in his derby hat and cane hurry out of a hotel side door, making a beeline for the gates. Le Favre whistled through his teeth. His officers jumped to attention and the press grabbed their cameras and stampeded out of the main entrance, calling Charlie's name.

'*Merde!*' hissed Le Favre, flicking away his cigarette. 'That little tramp!'

He snapped his fingers to his officers and gestured for them to follow. They ran down the main steps in time to see Charlie change direction on the lawns beside the frangipani trees, and head towards a side gate. But he almost seemed to be slowing down, as if waiting for the press and Sûreté to catch him. Le Favre was halfway across the front lawn of the hotel when he realised his mistake. When the man turned, they realised immediately that it was Frank, disguised in Charlie's derby hat and coat. Le Favre whipped back to the main entrance but there was no sign of Charlie.

Meanwhile, Charlie stepped through the hotel's staff entrance, carrying a bag, onto a back street and into a waiting cab, with a nod of gratitude to the hotel chef.

'The docks, please,' Charlie instructed the driver, and they pulled away.

14

Charlie sauntered through the dockside bustle towards a grubby-looking café beside the customs offices. There were a few tables outside and from there Charlie could view the port and all its activity. He took a table in the shade of a gnarly mango tree and shooed away a street dog. A waiter approached.

'*Un café au lait,*' said Charlie with a smile, fanning himself with his hat. Flies hovered and sweat started to trickle down his neck. He opened his notebook, pen poised, and scanned the docks. Rubber was being loaded into a barge by the sack load, carried by "coolies" from two idling trucks with the Michelin logo emblazoned on their sides. A dog yelped as it was kicked away from a pool of rice-water discarded from the customs office kitchens.

The details of the daily chaos of the working poor mesmerised and inspired him. Perhaps it was the comfortable distance of his wealth that made him find solace in watching their back-breaking work. Or perhaps it was the faded memory of his own childhood poverty and his time in the workhouses. Was it sympathy for their lives, or empathy – or both? The waiter interrupted this line of thought when he set down the café au lait and momentarily broke Charlie's line of sight. When Charlie looked down at his notebook once more, his sweat had smudged the lines and date already, and the paper was thick and soggy. So instead, he retrieved his 8mm camera and lifted the eyepiece. Through the lens the dock no longer appeared as the scene in front of Charlie. It was a version of it, as if filmed in a studio, and in the flickering black and white of a two-reeler motion picture.

***

WIDE SHOT: *Phnom Penh port and the docks.*

The camera tracks alongside dozens of crates being unloaded from a steamer, all under the watching, bulging eyes of a burly Sûreté policeman. A whistle hangs from his lips – alert to any infraction. The smallest crates are carried manually across the dock to a waiting truck. We follow one crate stamped 'PARIS, FRANCE'. It's carried on the back of a Cambodian dockhand. He's bent double and stumbles along a line of planks over the mud and crosses a line of other 'coolies' carrying sacks of rubber on their shoulders.

Back at the steamer the largest crate, six feet square, is offloaded by crane. A coolie, played by Phirath in a conical rice paddy hat, supervises, guiding it to the ground in view of the policeman. It's the last of the cargo and Phirath leans against it, sweating in the morning heat.

But a noise from inside startles him.

THUMP! The sound of boots on wood. The lid of the crate is kicked open from within by one oversized boot.

Phirath and his colleague lean closer, intrigued and a little fearful. They move the crate lid to the side and peer in to see the Tramp. He sits surrounded by an elegant bone china tea set, tucking into a meal of foie gras, cheese and wine. He dabs his mouth with a handkerchief relishing every morsel. Finished, he catches Phirath's eyes and shrugs as if this is the most normal thing in the world. He grins and climbs out of the crate. Phirath is about to protest when the Tramp hands him a new bottle of wine, a jar of foie gras and a round of cheese, oblivious to his bewildered expression. A nonchalant shrug and his lips move:

INTERTITLE: Ah! Paris. The city of love!

The Tramp scans the dock. His smile fades into a look of confusion, cutting to a tableau of the Phnom Penh port, the Mekong flanked by sugar palms, bananas being unloaded, Cambodian coolies in fishermen's pants and rice paddy hats. A young boy grabs a hand of bananas from a crate and salutes with them in the Tramp's direction. His eyes widen.

He doffs his derby to the bemused coolies and climbs back into the crate and tries to replace the lid.

Phirath hauls him back out by the scruff of the neck and dumps him in the muck of the dockside on his backside. The Tramp staggers up, brushes himself down and shakes his fist at Phirath before attempting once again to climb back into the crate.

Phirath swings at him with the wine bottle, but the Tramp ducks and instead it smashes over the head of the other labourer. Momentarily stunned, he staggers, overbalances and then topples into the crate. Quick as a flash the Tramp slides the crate top closed over the coolie and sits on it … as the policeman saunters over. A nonchalant smile to the policeman as if nothing has happened. But the policeman is having none of it. He shoves the Tramp aside and slides off the crate lid. His eyes bulge even more, *and he shouts at the groggy coolie.*

INTERTITLE: A stowaway!

The policeman hauls the coolie out by his shirt but before his punishment can be meted out, the steamer foghorn blares so loudly behind him that he starts in surprise. The Tramp turns to see the French governor in his grand formal attire, stepping off the steamer deck and navigating the narrow gangplank onto the dockside. The French governor is also played by Charlie Chaplin, but unlike the Tramp, he's the picture of wealth and privilege. Behind him follows his daughter, played by Paulette, who looks bewildered and scared, and clutches a small poodle to her chest. But it's her beauty that catches the Tramp's eye. He doffs his hat, instantly smitten, but she doesn't see him, stepping closely behind her father, past them and on towards a waiting car.

Back to his task, the policeman carries away the mistaken stowaway. But as the governor and his daughter pass beside the Tramp and Phirath and the opened crate, he stops. He glares at the open-mouthed Phirath, still clutching cheese in one hand and the broken neck of the wine bottle in the other, and then snatches the foie gras from his hand.

Eager to distance himself from the unfolding drama by the crate, the Tramp saunters off in the opposite direction. He twirls his cane and shuffles through the hustle and bustle of the dock as if it was the most normal thing in the world.

It's an image we've seen countless times before in his films.

The walk that made him famous, and very, very rich.

15

At the Hotel Le Royal, Paulette's hangover had finally evaporated under the mid-morning heat, but it had left her dehydrated and not in the best of spirits. She couldn't decide whether her mouth had shrunk or her tongue had grown, but either way there didn't seem to be enough room to swallow – no matter how much water she drank. So she opted for a gin and tonic instead. She lay in an electric blue swimsuit on a lounger by the pool, fanning herself with a magazine. Beads of sweat formed on her neck and ran down her back. The heat made everything appear to move in slow motion: the waiters and guests, the lapping water, even the frangipani petals, which broke free and spun hypnotically down into the water. There was nothing to do, and it was too hot even to try.

Compared to Paulette, Alta Goddard was more conservatively dressed – and made it perfectly clear what she thought of her daughter's daring swimsuit. She wasn't a prude, but she did belong to a generation that had frowned on Hollywood's twenties excess, and was extremely glad that Paulette had finally persuaded the millionaire filmmaker to put a ring on her finger after so many years of speculation. This was no small feat considering his reputation and the number of Hollywood hopefuls who were used and discarded like the latest fashionable hat. She huffed in her head at the very thought of it. She had one thought on her mind: to get her daughter's wedding announcement into the press, so that it was finally real. Although she longed to believe in Charlie's love for her daughter, she was brought up to err on the side of caution. Once the announcement was in the press it would be harder for Charlie to wriggle out of it, and she could finally breathe.

That was the first thought. The second was how much longer did they need to stay travelling in this interminable heat and on this interminable vacation? It was all very exotic and fascinating, and sometimes even rather thrilling, but mainly it was just damned hot and exhausting. And this was not helped by her stubborn refusal to adapt her dress in any way to the tropical climate.

In fact, Alta continued, she had three thoughts, but the problem was that when she tried to add to the second, she struggled to remember the first. It must have been the heat. It was only then that she realised she was talking out loud.

'The truth, my dear, is I'm still not sure I understand a damn why we have to travel back in time to a ruined civilisation, simply in order to announce your future? And now you're telling me, he's decided to stay here for another day. Because of an idea that popped into his head?'

Paulette was barely listening. She loved her mother. Of course she did. But there were times when her voice and her attitude were as irritating as the flies that buzzed around her hair-of-the-dog highball. She lay back and closed her eyes with a sigh.

'You know Charlie. He says he'll quit after every picture, but he can't. It's not the money – heaven knows *Modern Times* has made him plenty. But once he gets an idea in his head—'

'And how is that more important than your announcement?' interrupted her mother, nearly overbalancing from her lounger in an attempt to swat a fly with a menu card. She steadied herself before continuing. '"Companion", they called you. Companion!' And she hurrumphed as if it were a personal affront to her.

'I'm under contract, Mother,' countered Paulette, tired by the familiar conversation.

'*Two* contracts! And don't you forget it even if, at the moment, there's only one the public knows anything about. I don't know why we couldn't just announce the marriage in Singapore without all this hullabaloo to tell the world from Anchor Wat.'

'It's pronounced "Ang-kor". It's romantic. Different. And besides, that's what we wanted to do, so that's what we will do. We'll just be delayed by a few days. It's not as if there's any rush.'

'Of course there's a rush, dear. Believe me, young lady, men like Mr Chaplin need chaining down before their eyes start to wander – and I'm not talking about chasing idle ideas for his pictures.' Seeing her daughter's exasperated glare, she added, 'You know what I mean. You won't be young much longer, dear. And if he only manages to make one film every five years, well, where will that leave you? Hmmm? Am I right?'

Alta knew she'd hit a nerve. It was the issue that had consumed Paulette since they started their trip. If Charlie was finished in motion pictures, as he so often proclaimed, then where did that leave her? Professionally … and personally? And so, while she was as annoyed as her mother about Charlie's disappearance that morning, more than anything she was secretly pleased that he was working again, chipping away at his first thoughts and scene ideas. She knew that he was a perfectionist, but perhaps he might find the inspiration he needed right here in Indochina. That was certainly preferable to the other hovering thought. The thought that perhaps he was just chasing ghosts, another idea like the *Countess of Shanghai*, an obsession for a while, all too soon discarded. Or that he was using this as an excuse for some time apart. What if the constant presence on the trip had made him tire of her, rather than bringing them closer? She knew he needed time alone and was more than happy to oblige. When he'd moved her in to Summit Drive, he'd begged her not to be upset if he disappeared every now and again – to wander downtown on his own perhaps, or to sit up with Alf his studio manager watching old two-reelers, or to obsessively research an economic theory or practice a piece of music on his violin. He reassured her that she should never interpret this as him tiring of her. It was just his way. And for all his faults and foibles, Paulette never doubted it. But here on their travels, perhaps he did feel a little trapped. She tapped her glass on her teeth at the thought of it.

'Don't do that darling,' said her mother, even more riled.

Paulette continued, pretending not to hear, until a waiter walked over with a refill. She flashed him a grateful smile, but he hovered above her like the damned flies. She shaded her eyes from the midday sun and looked up.

'Mademoiselle, there is a call for you. Would you follow me?'

Paulette and her mother exchanged a glance. Who on earth knew they were there?

Paulette gathered a silk robe around her and followed the waiter inside. Her first thought was that something must have happened to Charlie, or perhaps someone back home. Their itinerary had not been well publicised although the press managed to get wind of their arrival in Phnom Penh and the press conference might have made the early editions.

'Paulette Goddard,' she said into the receiver, fearing the worst.

'Good evening, Miss Goddard.' It was a male voice and one that Paulette knew well, although it belonged to a world so far removed from their adventures in the East that it took her by surprise.

'How did you get this number,' she said cautiously.

'Do you really expect a couple of your status to travel incognito?' The man paused before adding, 'We sent several telegrams, but—'

'Then I believe you've wasted your time, David. I'm not breaking my contract,' snapped Paulette, cutting him off. Her frustration was building at the thought of how David Selznick, a Hollywood producer, had managed to track her down on what was supposed to be a personal and private escape. She immediately suspected Mr Yonamori. Despite Charlie's utter devotion and reliance on the man, he had not yet earned her trust. But why would someone so eager to please in his new role, and so anxious to ingratiate himself on Paulette after his predecessor's demise, take such a risk and to what end? She whisked the thought away and was about to politely end the conversation when David cleared his throat.

'I think you'll like my offer, Miss Goddard. It's for my next project, a new picture.' He paused for impact, and then added the cherry on top, 'It's a talkie.'

A few hours later, the telephone call was still uppermost in her mind, but Charlie had not returned from his explorations. Paulette was dressing for the afternoon reception. She pumped some perfume from the atomiser and checked herself in the mirror. She knew she'd turn heads in her daring evening gown and would normally relish the thought. After all, she was a leading actress, the star of one of the world's biggest movies that year – even if she wasn't making as many films as her competitors on the studio circuit.

'Are you ready, Miss Goddard,' came the familiar voice of Frank Yonamori.

But she was lost in thought, mulling Selznick's offer and weighing up Charlie's inevitable response when he heard of it. She adopted a pose, her face at an angle, and tried a pout for the mirror – and for Frank. She looked every inch like a movie star – the face which stared back at her was like a promotional portrait for a movie poster or photograph.

'Miss Goddard?' pressed Mr Yonamori.

It snapped her out of it. She smiled and caught his eye with a nod.

'Did you mention our itinerary to any one back home?' she asked as casually as she could.

'Back home, Miss Goddard?'

'The studios. Hollywood.'

'Of course not. I was under the strictest of instructions not to …'

'Yes, I know, but somehow our presence, even where we are staying, seems to have reached across the damned Pacific Ocean before we could make it to our first dinner.'

'That, Miss Goddard, is the price of fame. The palace I believe were so excited by your imminent arrival that they leaked your itinerary to the press. And the press conference last night, well of course there was no hiding that from the morning editions.'

Paulette stared hard at him. There was no doubt that his loyalty was to Charlie, not to her, but now she doubted whether he would have informed Selznick's office. He was probably right. It must have been the palace. The king had been so enthralled to host them, and the prince did look as cute as a button in a derby hat trying to imitate the Tramp's walk for the press. So what if David Selznick had found her? It showed that she still had currency in Hollywood even while she was away. But what would Charlie think about it?

'Too much for a garden party?' she asked standing up and presenting her evening gown with a twirl.

'I would imagine a little glamour is exactly what the governor expects, Miss Goddard.'

'Ever the diplomat, Frank. Is mother ready?'

'She's resting. She complained that the mosquitos whined worse than a Hampton's debutante, even from beyond the net – and so she asked for some Veronal.'

'That sounds like mother. And Charlie?'

'He, ahem, hasn't returned.'

'Alone again,' sighed Paulette, adopting the exaggerated, doleful expression of a silent movie vamp. 'Come on then, Frank. Looks like it's you and me.'

16

Charlie's observational research and two-reeler imaginings at the docks had left him invigorated and excited, but in no mood to return to the hotel to face the inevitable barbed comments from Paulette and her mother. He took a leisurely lunch in the European Quarter in a courtyard bistro in the shade of a banyan tree. His sour mood, brought on by creative ennui, sickness and the veiled threats of the police captain had vanished, along with the morning breeze. His mind wandered back to the stolen, unplanned meeting with Phirath and the theatre troupe the night before – and Phirath's invitation to attend their rehearsal. Having asked the bistro owner for directions to Wat Botum, he realised he had some time to pass, and the idle people watching from his outside table at the bistro gave him a little more context and detail for his research. He made notes on the rickshaws, the dress of the Europeans, and snippets of conflicts and interactions – particularly between the Europeans and the Cambodians who worked for them and who were allowed in the more salubrious European Quarter.

Later in the afternoon, he arranged with the bistro owner for a rickshaw and headed south past the Royal Palace to Wat Botum to find Phirath. He scanned the streets and people – not with the anodyne interest of a tourist, but with a voracious appetite for moments, images and exchanges to be stored and catalogued for the motion picture forming in his mind's eye. It would be called *Colonial Subjects* and would be the first outing of the Tramp in the East.

Perhaps the press had been prescient in their questions after all, he thought with a rueful smile.

The rickshaw pulled up at the arched entrance of the Wat Botum pagoda and Charlie stepped out and paid the driver. He spotted the same boy he'd seen in the palace now keeping guard by the arch, but when he walked past, the boy greeted him respectfully in the Khmer custom, palms pressed together at his chest with a little bow. The *sampeah* was earnest and genuine and Charlie offered a stiff bow in return, without breaking his stride.

From within the pagoda complex, the sound of traditional music echoed off the stone walls. The theatre troupe was rehearsing once more on the bamboo stage beneath the main vihara. Musicians performed from the sides of the stage. Charlie approached the seated devotees and monks, but he paused and waited at the back. From his bag he retrieved his camera and lifted it to his eye after adjusting the exposure settings. Once again, the giant and the prince performed their precisely choreographed fight dance, ending when the giant bettered the prince and stole away the princess. When they left the stage, Phirath and his comic counterpart entered stage left, dressed as peasants. Phirath sported the distinctive moustache daubed onto his lip. Charlie raised a hand in greeting, but Phirath didn't notice, absorbed in his performance. After he had chased away the French governor, he approached the front of the stage and the tone shifted from comic performance to an altogether more serious – even political – speech.

'They are few and we are many,' he projected in Khmer. 'They think we are nothing more than rice farmers, but the same blood flows through our bodies as filled the veins of the great Angkorian kings who came before us and built an empire that stretched for a thousand miles in every direction.'

He spoke in Khmer but Charlie heard the passion in his voice and was in no doubt about the political slant to the words even though the exact meaning was lost on him. Monks stopped their chores to listen. Those seated in front of the makeshift stage leant forward to catch every word. Their smiles had gone, replaced by grim attention. Phirath commanded the space and demanded their ears and hearts, entreating them to wake up and take the initiative against the French.

'They try to rob us of our history,' he shouted, gesticulating like a politician. 'They sever the line between our ancestors and us, convince the world that we belong to a different, indolent, inconsequential race more suited to opium and brawling than discourse and intellectual argument. But they cannot stop us—'

'Police!' The alarm came from the look-out boy.

Phirath broke off mid-sentence and whistled through his teeth. The performers snapped out of the spell he'd so effectively cast and prepared for the arrival of the police. It was only then that Phirath caught sight of Charlie at the back. He grinned and beckoned his new friend to follow. Charlie needed no encouragement. There was a dynamism and purpose about the troupe's defiance which was infectious and lit a fire under his own dulled passion for change. For years he'd poured his own passion into his motion pictures but it had inevitably faded with the business of production and promotion, and with the ennui of wealth he had accumulated. Charlie ducked behind the stage with Phirath just in time to avoid being seen by the police, who marched into the pagoda compound with Le Favre at their head. The music started up again, and the prince and the princess appeared together on stage performing the countenanced traditional drama. Le Favre scanned the gathering, his eyes settling on the look-out boy at the gate, who insolently grinned back at the Frenchman.

Behind the stage, Phirath pulled Charlie towards the main vihara, grabbing his regular clothes from a pile. They made an odd couple. Charlie in his Western tropical flannels, Phirath in his baggy fisherman's pants, the moustache still on display. He changed out of his theatre costume and wiped off the stage make-up, forgetting for a moment the moustache.

'Nice moustache,' offered Charlie, but Phirath didn't understand. Charlie pointed to his lip and Phirath grinned in realisation and wiped it clear. Behind them the boy crept over to listen to their conversation.

'I knew you would come,' said Phirath.

'Do the police always visit your rehearsal?' asked Charlie.

'I, we – how do you say, poke? – yes, poke fun at the French. It is not only theatre.'

'What do you say which so upsets them?'

'The truth. That this is not their country. That we are not under their "protection" but under their domination to exploit as they see fit. Why we pay taxes for the king's new palace while our people go hungry? Hunger makes us slaves.' And he smiled then at Charlie. 'You showed us that.'

The boy was even closer now, and Charlie caught sight of him watching their discussion.

'Who is that? I saw him at the palace last night.'

'The boy? His cousin is a royal dancer in the ballet, and – everyone believes – one of the king's concubines. He stays at the pagoda for his education with the monks, but he also helps with our show and keeps an eye out for the police. His name is Saloth Sar. This way, please. Follow me.'

Phirath pulled on the jacket of his suit and slicked back his black hair. He pulled Charlie away and out of sight. As soon as they had gone, Saloth Sar spotted Le Favre approaching.

'Where is he?' barked the captain.

Saloth Sar's eyes widened in mock fear but, once again, he pointed the policeman in the opposite direction.

17

As the sun dipped towards the horizon and Charlie was deep in political discussions with his new friend, an altogether different occasion was underway on the other side of the European Quarter. The great and the good of Phnom Penh's expatriate community (and many who merely aspired to be) had gathered on the governor's manicured lawn beneath the grand old trees. Governor Robin had arranged the lavish garden party in his official residence in honour of his celebrity guests, and the event was not a disappointment. A jazz band played an upbeat tune in the shade, and as happened throughout the colonial world, guests were drawn into tight rowdy knots around the free bar. There was nothing like the whiff of celebrity to bring the bugs out of the woodwork; the tantalising possibility of a glimpse of something as truly glamourous as a Hollywood movie star was an occasion which rarely graced this part of the world.

Paulette was not alone in dressing up for the occasion, with a gown more fitting for an evening reception than an afternoon garden party. But it wasn't long before the polite chit-chat and star-struck stares had begun to irritate her. Having made up for Charlie's absence with her effortless good humour and grace, she'd finally managed to excuse herself from the gawping and stood alone for the first time since she'd arrived. She cradled a flute of champagne, staring up at the scudding high clouds with a whimsical smile. How had she, a girl from Utah, ended up as the guest of honour of the Governor of French Indochina? Light-headed from the champagne and the heat, she imagined the world has stopped turning for a moment. In the absence of its gravitational pull, she saw herself floating up into the sky, looking down at those irritating guests still gathered around the silk-draped occasional tables, or dancing on the lawn. But she was free. She gave in to the reversed gravity and drifted upwards, carefree, alone, with a darkening blue above her and the first glimpse of the stars beyond, turning away from the angry red glare of the setting sun …

'You'll damage your eyes.' It was Laurent Levalier, and his own eyes plunged into her cleavage with little attempt to hide it. Levalier had that effortless confidence of a man used to money.

'And you'll go blind,' she retorted sharply, plummeting back to earth. She adjusted her dress, but it was only a nod to modesty.

'A fate worse than death, in your company, Mademoiselle.'

Paulette had to consciously stop herself from rolling her eyes. He probably pours himself into his shoes in the morning, she thought with a smile. He's as slippery and oleaginous as only a Frenchman in lust can be. But for once she kept her thoughts in her head.

'But where is your … companion?'

Paulette finished the remaining champagne in her flute and sighed, melodramatically.

'He abandoned me! Left me to my fate in a foreign land, full of savages and beasts.'

'Oh, you poor, poor thing. More champagne?'

Paulette laughed despite herself. She was tipsy and felt no need to hide it. Levalier grabbed a bottle from a passing waiter and filled her glass until it bubbled over her hands. It wasn't an accident, and he was there immediately with a handkerchief for just such an unforeseen occurrence. He held onto her hand a little too long.

'Are you trying to get me drunk?' slurred Paulette, whipping her hand away, but only after allowing him to hold onto it for longer than strictly necessary.

'You can never have too much of a good thing.'

'It wouldn't be a good thing if it was commonplace. Bottoms up then.'

She chinked her flute against his, trying to ignore his irksome clichés. And when the band launched into a playful foxtrot, she allowed herself to be taken by the arm and fell into step, both loving and resenting the attention in equal measure. Soon others joined them. Heels sank into the earth, but this was Phnom Penh and when there was an excuse for a dance, no matter the impracticality, there was a host of expatriates bored enough to give it a go. She didn't notice Mr Yonamori watching them discretely. She was caught up in the movement of the moment, her head thrown back and her alabaster neck on display for any potential vampires.

'He's done the world a great disservice, you know,' whispered Levalier.

'Who has?' answered Paulette, a little out of breath.

'Charlot. Monsieur Chaplin of course.'

'How so?' Paulette pulled out of the foxtrot and the two of

them walked away from the other dancers.

'By not letting you speak – or sing – in his pictures. I never knew you had such a wonderful voice until I heard you sing last night at the hotel. The world should know.'

'Perhaps they will.' She leaned her head on his shoulder and whispered in his ear, 'Selznick wants me for his new picture. *Blowin' in the Wind* or some such thing. He requests, no he demands, my immediate return to Hollywood!'

'Then why don't you?'

'Because I haven't yet seen *Les Ruines d'Angkor*. I didn't cross the deep blue sea to leave such a sight unseen. I hear they are truly "*magnifique*".'

'They've been there a thousand years, a week or two won't make any difference.'

He grabbed two more flutes from a waiter and offered her one, his eyes suddenly serious. 'But since you are already in our corner of the world, my home is en route to the temples. If that is truly your intention, I would be honoured if you would stay a night with me at my plantation residence. In fact, I insist.'

'You and the Russian count. Is everyone in Indochina so … insistent?' And she flashed her most alluring smile, a smile which was neither a *non* nor a *oui*.

'Excuse me.' She sashayed away, knowing full well that Levalier's eyes would be lingering on her figure as he tried to work out which way her mind would turn.

18

On the other side of the European Quarter, Charlie was blissfully oblivious to Levalier's interest in his wife, and Paulette's half-hearted attempt to deflect it. His mind was consumed with his new friend and his stories of colonial excess and exploitation. He listened intently in the rickshaw as Phirath pointed out this building and that canal, each new landmark given a political slant or a cultural resonance. It was nearly dark by the time they pulled up in front of the light-yellow Art Deco façade of the Central Railway Station. The two towers on either side of the entrance cast shadows over the square in which rickshaw drivers huddled around a cluster of market stalls. Dusk was fast approaching and some of the traders were lighting lamps. Phirath and Charlie headed to the station entrance, passing a line of rickshaws. Two drivers played a game of Khmer chess in the half-light but many of the others were asleep.

'Look at us,' snapped Phirath in disgust. 'Asleep. Hungry. Spending what we earn on the poppy. In IndoChine it is opium which is the religion of the masses. We must wake our people up!'

'It will take more than comedians for the French to give up their pearl,' said Charlie. His introduction to the politics of the protectorate -- and in particularly the cruel reality of the rubber plantations in the French colony – had been a wake-up call. He found the clandestine discussions with his unlikely companion intoxicating and inspiring in equal measure.

'How can they stop us? All around the country the signs are clear. Change is coming.'

'Isn't it always?' replied Charlie, quickly regretting his easy Western cynicism.

'We have Khmer newspaper. First time. Khmer graduates from the lycée. The Communist Party of Indochina. The time for acting is over. Now is the time for action.'

They crossed the grand threshold and into the cool dark interior. It was busy with porters and hawkers.

'If we're lucky our people compete to earn a few piastres as labourers or porters. But this is just scraps the French throw to us, a cruel competition which turns us against each other.'

He peered through the railings to the rear of the station, following the platforms until they extended beyond the main structure and into the open air. A handful of steam locomotives idled. Porters rushed with suitcases, trunks and cargo. Charlie joined him as the Battambang train arrived at the platform. The din and the smell of coal were an elixir. Steam hissed, whistles blew and there was a screech of brakes.

The two men exchanged glances. There was something in Charlie's expression that made Phirath smile. He saw that familiar moment of inspiration, that first fizz of an artist's creative neurons reacting to stimulus. 'Tell me what you see.'

'A railway scene, a set piece. After his arrival in the docks as a stowaway from America, this will be the moment that launches the story of *Colonial Subjects*.'

'Explain.'

'The Little Fellow's unexpected departure on the train to Battambang in pursuit of the governor's daughter.'

'Go on. Maybe I can help?'

For an answer, Charlie lifted his camera to his eye and looked through the lens. The station was no longer the scene in front of Charlie. It was the studio backlot version of it, in black and white – an embryonic first vision of a Chaplin silent comedy.

***

ESTABLISHING SHOT: the main station's grand art deco façade.

Tilting down a pillar on one side of the entrance to a sign which reads 'Porters Required'.

There's a queue in front of the sign – a line of labourers all wearing identical rice paddy hats. As we pan down the line, the pattern is broken by one lone derby hat – belonging to the indomitable Tramp. He's beside Phirath in the line but Phirath shakes his head dismissively at the Tramp's inappropriate choice of headwear. The Tramp looks first to Phirath, then to the porters to his left, clearly worried.

Before the Tramp can react, a French station master in uniform emerges and the line surges. In the hubbub the Tramp swaps his hat for his neighbour's. A whistle blows and the labourers flatten against the station wall for inspection as the station master walks down the line. Until he reaches the derby on the unsuspecting Khmer labourer's head. He's yanked from the line and sent to the back. This starts a pantomime of hat swapping down the line as everyone tries to pass on the offensive derby. Distracted by this, the labourers don't notice as Phirath pulls the Tramp down to a crouch and they crawl through the station master's legs to reach the front of the line. The Tramp taps the burly official on the shoulder and gestures inside with a sheepish grin. The station master's bulging eyes narrow. He checks the line, then the odd couple at the front of it, perplexed. Undeterred, the Tramp pulls out a handkerchief and dusts down the station master's lapels with a shrug and a grin, desperate to find favour. The station master bats him away irritably, but nods for them to go inside.

WIDE SHOT: a steam train idles inside the station. Smoke and steam billow.

CUT TO: The Tramp and Phirath wait on the platform. They are now dressed in the uniforms of official station porters complete with baggage trolleys. The Tramp picks up a discarded cigarette butt and puts it in his pocket for later as a train rumbles into the station billowing more smoke and steam. All the porters wait, eyeing the doors (and each other) – primed for customers. The first door opens and the Tramp is off, rushing over to the nearest door with his trolley, but another porter beats him to it and shoves his trolley aside. Further down the train another door opens. The Tramp runs over, but with the same outcome. He's being outmanoeuvred by the more experienced porters.

At the second carriage, a porter has positioned himself to help an ELDERLY DOWAGER preparing to disembark. The Tramp taps him on the shoulder and gestures back to an irate-looking station master glaring in their direction. The porter gulps, worried – but while his back is turned, the Tramp kicks the porter's trolley away and replaces it with his own. He doffs his derby for an elderly grand dame dowager and offers his hand to help her off *the train. She hangs her hatbox on it, ignoring his gallantry.*

But when he turns to put it on his trolley, the disgruntled porter has pushed the Tramp's trolley down the platform and replaced it with his own. And gives the Tramp an angry glare. The Tramp is livid. They push and shove each other's trolleys, ramming each other out of the way and shaking their fists, until they realise that Phirath has snuck through and is now helping the grand dame dowager with her baggage. The trunks and cases are piled precariously on his trolley.

That's when a poodle runs through their legs. The argument is forgotten as the Tramp sees again the governor's daughter beside the governor, approaching from the end of the platform. She looks horrified, hand up to her mouth and shouting:

INTERTITLE: Descartes! My darling Descartes!

Descartes, the poodle, has climbed to the top of the pile of the grand dame dowager's luggage on Phirath's trolley. The furious porter, feeling cheated by both the Tramp and Phirath, pulls the bottom case of the pile out to put on his trolley. The pile jolts lower, with Descartes on top. Each case is swiped out; each time a bewildered Descartes plunges lower and lower until finally it leaps into the Tramp's arms.

The governor's daughter is there in an instant and the Tramp hands over Descartes with a shy smile. A hand taps him on the shoulder. It's the governor. He glares at the Tramp and shouts:

INTERTITLE: Put our luggage on the Battambang Train. First Class.

He hands the Tramp a piastre coin. The Tramp grins.

CUT TO: the interior of the baggage compartment on the Battambang train. The Tramp whistles to himself, pleased as punch, as he stacks the last of the governor's trunks on the train. Job done, he walks down the carriage, nodding to the French passengers, and doffing his derby to the ladies. He passes the governor's daughter in her seat by an open window, her folded parasol and dog beside her. The heat is unbearable, and she fans herself. The Tramp doffs his derby, but she's completely oblivious to him and stares instead at the bustle on the platform. But Descartes sees the Tramp. He barks once and then leaps out of the open window. The governor's daughter shrieks. A handkerchief dabs her eyes, she looks to the Tramp, pleading. He nods gallantly, about to set off when the whistle hoots and the train begins to pull away ...

As the train moves slowly out of the station, the Tramp sees Phirath holding Descartes. He grabs the parasol from beside the governor's daughter and runs down the carriage, leaping over the connections to the next carriage, and the next, until he's at the back of the train.

Phirath is running towards him, hands outstretched holding Descartes.

Closer and closer Phirath runs, but the train is building up speed. The Tramp holds out the parasol from the tip and hooks Descartes collar and pulls him into the train as Phirath leaps aboard. They clap each other on the back as the tracks rush away beneath them.

INTERTITLE: Tickets please!

Shock on their faces. They turn to see the ticket collector passing through the last carriage checking and punching tickets. He sees them at the back of the train holding a poodle and a parasol. His eyes narrow. The Tramp and Phirath look back, but the tracks are rushing away too fast now to jump.

The Tramp retrieves the piastre coin from the governor but Phirath shakes his head.

'It's OK for you,' he says. 'But the punishment for Khmer to ride train with no ticket is ten years. Ten years hard labour.'

The Tramp stares at him open-mouthed.

'What?' asks Phirath, confused.

'What are you doing?' the Tramp shouts, ignoring the ticket collector barrelling towards them.

'I don't understand.'

'You're … you're talking!'

'So are you,' quips Phirath.

***

Charlie's sketch came to an abrupt halt with Phirath's verbal intrusions. The filmmaker lowered his camera, annoyed. The younger actor looked at his idol with a sadness in his eyes.

'What must be said cannot be limited to intertitles, to a few cards,' he said, his voice firm but friendly.

'Then I need to rework the scene. The Little Fellow doesn't speak.'

'Think of the power if he did.'

Charlie glared at him, but the hour started to chime on the big station clock.

'I'm late.' And he put his camera back into his bag and rushed through the station and into the twilight. He was already at the line of rickshaws when Phirath caught up with him.

'Forgive me, Saklo,' Phirath said, worried that his comment had jeopardised their budding friendship and creative collaboration. There was a lot riding on it, although Charlie didn't know that yet. Before Charlie could respond they saw the headlights of a police car enter the square and circle round in front of the station entrance, coming to a stop close to the line of rickshaws. The driver immediately stepped down and opened the rear passenger door. It was Le Favre.

'*Merde*,' muttered Phirath.

'Do you think he wants my autograph?' said Charlie. The captain's persistence was beginning to rattle the filmmaker.

Phirath leant into Charlie so they wouldn't be overheard and whispered, 'It's he who stopped Yen Bai in Vietnam. Forty men sentenced to death. Over nothing. And don't be fooled by the governor either. He and the rubber plantation owners are in this exploitation together. They take what they like, do what they like. We will talk more, but now you must go.'

He told the rickshaw driver where to take his guest and Charlie climbed into the back. Before they pulled away, Phirath grabbed Charlie's arm.

'Saklo, in two days we perform in Battambang. It would be an honour if you would grace the performance with your presence. I must be honest with you. It is not just an honour. If you believe that we have the right to challenge the excesses of the French protectorate, your presence would … it would give us greater … visibility. The press follows you everywhere. Think about it, I beg you.'

Charlie barely had time to acknowledge this heartfelt request when the captain barrelled over. Phirath turned his face away.

'Was I not clear, Monsieur Chaplin?' said the captain.

For a moment Charlie was caught between Phirath's request and Le Favre's irritating threats. But it was the manner of the Frenchman's intrusion which made up his mind.

'I'll be there,' he whispered to Phirath. 'I promise.'

The young actor walked off into the darkness. Charlie turned his attention to Le Favre and offered his wrists to the policeman. 'I wasn't aware that taking a walk was a criminal offence, Sergeant Le Favre.'

'It's Captain Le Favre. As you well know.'

Le Favre trailed off when he caught sight of Phirath melting into the darkness beyond the night-time street stalls. His eyes narrowed.

'What do you want to achieve in Indochina, Mr Chaplin? Perhaps it would be best if you would just speak your mind.'

Charlie thought about that for a moment, choosing his words carefully. It was an opportunity, and he knew it.

'Very well,' he replied eventually. 'I am struggling to understand why *Modern Times* has been approved for screening in every country of the Far East and beyond, every single one, except for French Indochina? I believe that this was on your insistence. I am no threat, and neither are my motion pictures.'

Le Favre glared at the filmmaker. 'Perhaps in America they are seen only as light entertainment. But it is the opinion of the governor that you and your films are dangerous to the status quo of this colony. In America you may be a celebrity, Monsieur Chaplin, but here you are a guest of French-administered Cambodia, and I would remind you once again to keep your Hollywood politics out of Indochina. Do I make myself clear?'

'Is that a threat, Captain? Are you going to arrest me for

walking? Now that would be front page news.'

He dropped his wrists and eyeballed the captain. It was the Frenchman who looked away first.

'Very well then. If you'll excuse me, I'm late for the governor's garden party.'

19

It was past seven in the evening by the time Charlie arrived at the governor's garden party. The event was reaching its inevitable drunken climax. A string of firecrackers exploded, and guests clapped and cheered. The whole spectacle was illuminated by Chinese lanterns. Charlie walked through the gathering looking for Paulette but found Mr Yonamori first. His manservant looked concerned.

'I'm glad you're here, sir,' he said quietly. 'It's ... it's Miss Goddard.' And he guided Charlie towards a group of guests seated on the residence veranda.

Unseen by Charlie, Le Favre arrived and made a beeline for the governor, interrupting an anecdote and deflating the governor's punchline.

'Can this wait, Captain?'

'I don't think so. It's Monsieur Chaplin.' Le Favre steered him away from his guests. 'We lost him for a while.'

'You lost the most famous face in the world? What are we paying you for?'

'Sir, he made it clear that his intention, his defiance to our requests, is for one reason only. He wants the ban on *Modern*

Times lifted.' And before the governor could protest, he added, 'Sir, we saw him with Sok Phirath.'

The name meant something to the governor. His jovial manner hardened instantly.

'We can't afford another incident,' he said, the tone of the preceding anecdote replaced by an icy calm. His look was an order, and one that Le Favre was only too eager to carry out.

On the other side of the residence, Paulette was holding court, surrounded by men. She was clearly the other side of tipsy, her eyes were half closed, and her champagne flute was almost horizontal. Levalier was beside her, his jacket draped over her shoulders.

'Miss Goddard, just a hint. An approximate figure,' asked one of the guests.

'Don't you know, a real lady never tells.' Paulette slurred with a laugh.

Levalier saw Charlie approaching. 'Ah! Monsieur Chaplin! At last.'

Charlie eyed the company and digested the situation in an instant. His apology was clipped but courteous.

'My apologies. Unfortunately, some business at my studios in America required my urgent attention,' he lied.

'No matter.' Levalier's smile was almost feline. 'Fortunately, your companion Miss Goddard has been entertaining us with tales of Hollywood excess.'

Charlie smiled politely as he helped Paulette to her feet. He pulled her close and murmured in her ear. Levalier caught his jacket before it fell to the ground.

'We were speculating on the figure for her next motion

picture. With David ... what was his name?'

'Snezlick,' struggled Paulette, and then corrected herself. 'Selznick.'

The name was like a slap in the face to Charlie.

'To telephone Miss Goddard all this way in French Indochina – and while you are vacationing – well, he must be serious, mustn't he? And this inevitably turned to an expatriate's favourite pastime – financial speculation. That degree of interest must suggest a substantial fee, wouldn't you say?' Levalier twisted the knife with the same humourless smile.

'Selznick called you?' Charlie asked Paulette quietly.

'I've always believed that wealth is wasted on the poor,' needled Levalier, enjoying the star's evident discomfort. 'But your own rise from rags to riches seems to disprove my theory.'

'Wealth is wasted by everyone,' said Charlie sharply.

'Spoken like a true champagne-drinking communist!'

'Did someone mention champagne?' slurred Paulette, hoping to diffuse the rising tension.

But Levalier pressed home his point. He adopted a sudden serious tone. 'And if we were to suddenly burden these lazy rice farmers, plantation workers and ... coolies' – he spat out the word with evident disgust – 'if we were to burden them with all the wealth of our Colony, what then?'

The question was a challenge, and one to which Charlie had no intention of responding.

'Darling,' he said to Paulette instead. 'Let's get you back to the hotel.'

'But you've only just arrived.' And she pulled Charlie into a dance step on the veranda. Charlie was not in the mood. He grabbed her hard by the arm and steered her away from the group of Frenchmen.

'If you'll excuse us, I fear that the heat and champagne, has taken its toll. Please pass on our gratitude to the governor. My apologies once again.'

Even angry he could perform the part of a celebrity. But inside, in his anger, he saw them all, tongues out like dogs around a bitch in heat. As they were walking away, with the sound of the coarse jibes in French in their ears, Levalier called after them.

'Miss Goddard, will you consider my offer? It would be a great honour.' The question registered on Charlie's face and he turned back. Levalier grinned. 'My plantation is en route to Angkor. I merely offered to accompany Paulette and her mother tomorrow. I understand you are otherwise engaged.'

Charlie imagined himself striding back to Levalier and punching him in his arrogant nose. But he did nothing. Merely smiled politely and fumed internally.

As soon as they arrived back at their suite at the Hotel Le Royal, Charlie slammed open the door and Paulette kicked off her shoes. One flew through the air and hit a lamp, which fizzed, flickered and died. Seeing Charlie's expression, she giggled drunkenly.

'Oh darling, lighten up.'

But Charlie was not laughing. Not even on the inside. Her smile faded and she poured herself a drink, but she missed the glass, splashing bourbon over the cabinet. She collapsed onto the bed with a sigh.

'You left me alone,' she signed. 'The whole day. What's a girl like me supposed to do?'

Charlie didn't answer.

'Levalier was my knight for the ... night.' She giggled again at her own bad joke. 'You know he's the richest man in Indochina. And a duke back in France.'

'How much gold can one woman dig!' spat Charlie.

Paulette's face crumpled. Her drunken teasing was instantly deflated with real hurt, and she turned her back. Charlie regretted the words as soon as they'd left his mouth. He started to undress unsure how to come back from such an unnecessarily cruel comment.

'You left me, Charlie,' Paulette said again, in a quiet faraway voice. 'Alone in a foreign land.'

But it wasn't Levalier's flirtation that had infuriated Charlie. That was hardly a new thing. In fact, Charlie enjoyed watching her flirt with other men at parties in Summit Drive, or at events and film premieres in America. He admired how she controlled them with a phrase, a look or a laugh – as consummately as a conductor and his orchestra. Ever since they got together, there was never any doubt where her heart lay, nor which bed she would return to after the fun and games were over. No, it wasn't the flirting or the Frenchman's invitation or how drunk she was.

'When were you going to tell me? Answer me!' A note of savage anger crept into his voice. But Paulette didn't answer immediately.

'You're under contract, if case you're unaware!' His voice had risen to a shout.

'Which contract are we talking about? You know I get so confused.'

By then she had taken her wedding and engagement rings

from the clutch and held them in her palm. Her mascara had run, her tears were silent. Seeing her distress, Charlie softened immediately. He couldn't stay angry with Paulette for long. He joined her on the bed and took her hand.

'Don't work for Selznick,' he said, softly, simply.

'Why not, Charlie? Should I wait another five years for a silent role in your next picture?'

'I can't write without you. In every scene all I see is you with me. The Little Fellow needs his Gamin.'

'The governor's daughter, you mean,' said Paulette sleepily. She felt suddenly and utterly exhausted and lay back on the bed. 'Please, Charlie, let me go.'

'To Sleazenik? How can you ask me that?'

'Not to David. To Kampong … damn the names. Kampong something. With Monsieur Levalier and Mother. You can continue your work here, and we can meet at his plantation en route to Battam-bambalang.'

'Battambang,' corrected Charlie.

'That's the one. That's all I ask. And from there we can continue to Angkor Wat and from there … and from there we can tell the whole damned world.'

Charlie stared at her. Her eyes were closing. She curled up on the bed.

'Like you promised me, Charlie. Tell the world about the only contract that really matters.'

And with that Paulette was asleep.

20

Phirath was in a jubilant mood, buoyed by Charlie's presence at his troupe's rehearsal and their subsequent political and creative discussions as they wandered around Phnom Penh. And most of all he was thrilled that his idol had accepted his invitation to attend their performance in Battambang. That had happened much sooner than he had anticipated. He smiled when he realised that that it was the captain's interruption which had ironically forced Charlie's hand.

But there was more on his mind than their forthcoming performance as a truck reversed into his family compound. It parked next to their own battered truck with the name of the troupe painted on the side. Before it had even stopped, Phirath leapt athletically into the back and hung a storm lantern to the side. The truck was crammed with sacks of rice. Someone tossed him a rice sickle with a serrated inner curve and a wooden handle ending in a carved snake. He prodded the sacks with the handle until it hit something solid. He beckoned over Saloth Sar, and he and another actor dragged the sack off the back of the truck. Phirath took the sickle and sliced it open. Rice spilled out revealing a wooden crate. They lifted the crate out as Phirath returned to the truck to find other contraband. Before long there were four crates on the dirt, lit by the headlights of the truck.

Phirath jumped down. He grabbed a crowbar and jimmied open the first crate. Inside, lying in straw, were two pistols and a handful of sticks of dynamite. The other crates were similarly loaded with weapons and explosives. They lined them up on the daybed beneath the wooden house. For a moment they stared at the goods. The danger of their whispered plans was now one step closer to realisation.

'Quickly!' Phirath barked.

He handed out the weapons to the troupe and they hid them with their theatre equipment. Some were hidden in drums, others beneath costumes in a metal trunk. A large cooking pot was filled with a bundle of dynamite and then packed with straw. The enormity of the delivery was evident on the faces of the gathered actors. They were stepping beyond the political statements of the comic entr'actes to something far more serious and the penalties for such actions were all too clear. From this moment on, they were committed, and if they were caught, the punishment for them, and their families and anyone who knew them would be severe, and most probably fatal.

Phirath slapped the side of the truck and it farted into life. He walked to the cab and *sampeahed* the driver. 'Thank our communist friends in Saigon,' he whispered in Vietnamese.

The truck bucked into gear and drove out of the compound which returned to a fragile calm. Beyond Phirath's home, a few night stalls served customers soup and fish *amok* by kerosene lamplight. Water buffalo rested in the shadows and oxen chewed straw in the sheds beyond the homes. Khmer chess. But this uneasy calm was disturbed by the growling of diesel engines followed by shouts from down the street. Mothers grabbed their kids, and men scurried from their daybeds up ladders and inside houses, as a police car and a van rumbled into view.

The shouts were heard in Phirath's compound too. The actors pushed Phirath away and took up their rehearsed roles – acting for real now as they swept the compound and loaded their own truck with costumes and trunks of stage props. Phirath bolted through the fence and out the back of the compound. He ran between houses and crossed a street, then burst out onto the main road, just as a police convoy drove into view. He froze for a second, caught in the headlights of the leading vehicle. Then he was off again, down a narrow path, heading towards a more built-up area of two-storey shophouses. The police car skidded to a halt in the dirt, the dust clouding in the headlights of the truck behind. Policemen poured out from the cars and vans and sprinted after Phirath, whistles blowing.

A gunshot rang out in the night air.

Remaining in the passenger seat of the leading police car was Le Favre. He leaned back in the seat and lit a cigarette.

Phirath sprinted down alleyways, vaulting cooking pots, leapfrogging buffalo and skidding beneath stairwells, until he turned into a dead end between a series of two-storey buildings covered in rickety bamboo scaffolding. The police shouted behind him, closer and closer. Phirath didn't break his run, and instead leapt into the scaffolding, clambering up as the torch beams of the police found him. Just in time he swung over the top rung of the scaffold as—

BANG!

A tile shattered by his head. He ducked and ran as fast as he could across the rooftops. The nearest policeman was just twenty feet behind. Ahead, the crowded rooftops opened between a wide boulevard. It was surely too wide to vault. Phirath looked behind. His calm composure was now replaced by real fear. The police were close. Too close. More shots were fired.

Phirath changed direction abruptly, dislodging a roof tile which fell to the alleyway below, shattering beside a drunk Khmer man staggering home from a local drinking spot. He looked up and saw Phirath leap across the night sky above him – legs pumping, arms flailing.

Phirath tumbled into a roll and looked back for the briefest of seconds. The distance between the roofs must have been more than five metres. He muttered a prayer of thanks. The police would never attempt such a jump. And it would take would them minutes to retrace their steps. By then Phirath would be well hidden. He ran off once more, across the roof and down a coconut palm to the safety of the dark, labyrinthine alleyways of the Khmer Quarter. He stopped in a doorway, chest heaving, and considered his options. If they were looking for him, and if they set up their checkpoints on all the roads out of Phnom Penh, how would he get to Battambang?

21

The argument of the night before was not forgotten by the next morning, but it was packed away like the suitcases and hatboxes in Laurent Levalier's car outside the hotel. Charlie had learned to let their disagreements settle before taking any direct action. Twenty years ago he would not have been so calm, but the intense public scrutiny of his private affairs, the paternity suits and ugly and expensive divorce settlements had taught him to keep his anger in check, to let the emotion subside and to try to see things from Paulette's point of view, rather than speculate and imagine the worst. The truth was, he couldn't bear to argue with Paulette, mainly because she frequently won, but really because he had come to realise that without her, he was more than likely to lose his way. In fact, yesterday's outburst, as well as Charlie's adventures with Phirath, had become the subject of good humour over breakfast. And having spent the past months together every single day, they agreed that a day or two apart for Charlie to continue his research would not threaten their relationship or their plan to announce their marriage to the world at Angkor Wat. As for Selznick's call and his offer, they were of the same mind about it – they didn't need to decide right away. It could wait until their other more personal contract was finally and formally announced.

The press hovered on the steps waiting. Paulette wore sunglasses, modern and cool in culottes and a hat, compared to the frumpy frock of her mother still a little groggy from Mr Yonamori's over-generous nightcap. Charlie escorted them out of the lobby, safe in the knowledge that his manservant was more than capable of looking after the ladies for a night or two. Levalier was there to greet them; the cat that got the cream, gallantly holding back the press to shepherd them to his Rolls Royce Phantom.

'Don't look so worried, Charlot,' he purred. 'They'll be in good hands.'

'I have no doubt, Monsieur Chevalier,' replied Charlie.

'Levalier. Monsieur Levalier.'

'That's what I said.' And he turned his back on the Frenchman to say his farewells.

After a rather chaste kiss on the cheek, Paulette whispered in his ear. 'Stay out of trouble, dear.' It wasn't a threat or a warning. She said it fondly and kissed him back. Then she waved to the gathered press and joined her mother inside the car. Charlie waved them off then noticed the hotel's concierge waiting for him. He had a note from Victor Goloubew inviting him to meet at the National Museum. It was less of an invitation than a demand. But having not made any plans to meet Phirath that morning, and being intrigued by the count's eccentric manner, he was pleased by the possibility and made arrangements immediately. Over coffee in the Elephant Bar he studied his *Baedeker* and read that the National Museum was the first purpose-built museum in the French colonies. He skimmed the details. It was a grand example of Khmer architecture built with French money under the instruction of the Angkorian expert George Groslier. Located a stone's throw from the Royal Palace, the famous gardens were full of royal palms, hibiscus and large bushes of spiky bougainvillea. But Charlie found the description prosaic and dull. That was the problem with words. He wanted to see it for himself. Perhaps it might inspire a scene. Whether it did or didn't, it would be better than reading about it in his guidebook.

Not long after, Charlie climbed out of the rickshaw and walked through the museum gates into the gardens. They didn't disappoint. The red terracotta walls and roofs were set off by the deep green and purple of the bougainvillea. But it was the activity that drew his attention. Khmer workers unloaded wooden crates from a truck and pushed them on trolleys up a ramp positioned over the grand main steps and into to the dark interior.

Inside, Victor Goloubew barked orders (and insults) in his usual mishmash of languages. But it was clear that he was well regarded by the workers and his insults were as little understood as they were intended. That is until one worker dropped an end of the crate and it smashed into the tiled floor of the main hall. Victor slapped the offending worker around the head.

'*Bohze moy! Imbecilnik!* This is not sack of rice!'

But his anger vanished when he saw Charlie approaching.

'Comrade Chaplin!' he called out, laughing at his own joke. He pumped Charlie's hand and they followed the line of crates further into the museum.

'Angkorian bas-reliefs,' the count explained. 'And yet these imbeciles treat treasures without care! If not for French, they lost to jungle. Do you know much of the Angkorian period?'

127

Charlie shook his head. 'I read of the exhibition at the Bois de Vincennes in Paris in thirty-one. I think half the world did. But I never had the opportunity to visit. The photographs of the reconstruction were magnificent. In fact they played a big part in inspiring Paulette and me to come here to see for ourselves.'

'Propaganda!' exploded Victor. 'A crude attempt to pretend to world that French are not here to exploit riches of colonies. A "mutual exchange of culture!" Pah! In this the German accusations were correct. I hear they even projected the Tricolore – TRICOLORE! – onto temple replicas!'

His outburst caught Charlie by surprise. He assumed from their previous encounter that the count was apolitical. But after his earnest discussions with Phirath the day before, he had no desire to talk politics now. Fortunately, Victor was called away by a labourer and barked and guffawed in a mixture of languages. He could have been discussing Angkorian temples, debating Hitler's expansionist policies or arguing his preference for rich tea biscuits, thought Charlie with a smile. What a character! But who could play him? Who had that presence in the moment, that idiosyncratic, eccentric energy without even a hint of self-awareness? Hollywood and its movie stars were a long way away and felt rather irrelevant and inconsequential. He put them out of his mind and checked out the exhibits. Stone apsaras, carved female dancers from the temples, were presented on plinths, feet and hands bent in the same impossible angles as Charlie had witnessed in the flesh at the Royal Ballet. The lineage was clear. Other bas-reliefs had been mounted along a gallery wall. The detail and craftsmanship were breathtaking. Charlie brought his camera out of its case to film an exquisite statue which dominated the gallery to the left of the main entrance hall. He tracked and panned around the detail, hands as steady as if they were on tracks. It was a while before he realised that Victor had returned and was now watching him. He sighed with an almost reverential wonder and pointed out a detail with his forefinger.

'See here. Queen trampled to death by elephant.' Then he added as explanation, 'For infidelity.'

His reverie was cut short when he caught sight of more porters mishandling his precious artefacts. He bellowed again. '*Ostorozhny! Bohyze Moy!*'

He turned to Charlie. 'Hard to believe rice farmers and fishermen created wonders.'

'I was under the impression they were not the same race. That Angkor was built by a lost civilisation, a lost race of warrior-artisans?'

'French like to think that way. They look at Khmer now and look at grandeur then, and say, no way! For me, who cares who built. Only that they are protected, uncovered from jungle, studied and examined. For that, I give my life. Every day.'

Despite being several degrees cooler in the museum, it was still unbearably hot and humid. Charlie fanned himself with a hat and the sweat ran freely into the waistband on his trousers. Seeing his discomfort, Victor added, 'Charlot, there's only one thing to do at this time to take mind off heat. If you have time?'

Twenty minutes later, Charlie found himself sitting beside Victor in a Peugeot 601. Squashed into the driver's seat, the count's knees seemed to be up around his ears. He chain-smoked Russian black tobacco as they made slow progress through the narrow backstreets and mayhem of the Chinese Quarter. Chaplin filmed through the window only half listening to Victor's archaeological diatribe.

'But why, Comrade Chaplin, did empire collapse? Everyone, every damn scholar and stupid academic say same thing. Invading army! Pestilence! Disease! But I – only I – know truth. Water! Water is only reason for collapse!' And he pounded the steering wheel for emphasis.

But Charlie was no longer listening at all. He was distracted by a strange sight ahead. It was the same procession he'd seen on his first unplanned excursion to the Chinese Quarter. It was not a political procession, of that he was sure. Or at least not in the way that politics was arranged in the US. This was more like a religious sect. Their colourful robes dominated the street, and there was a crowd of faithful following them. Their drums beat and the car slowed to a crawl. Charlie looked to his guide for explanation. For a moment, the Count's obsession with water was forgotten.

'Cao Dai,' Victor spat, clearly not a devotee. He lowered his voice. 'Crazy spiritualists. Seances. Incense. The French scared of them. They know no boundaries, no borders, and don't care for the French laws and control. But careful, Charlie. To them, you are prophet.'

'I've been called many things ...'

'No joke, Charlie. Prophet in their church. Saint perhaps.' And he laughed so loudly some of the devotees at the back of the procession turned to stare. He immediately reduced his voice to a whisper. 'I'm serious. With Joan of Arc. Victor Hugo. Many artists and thinkers. East, West, North, South. Everywhere, the whole world.'

'So at least I'm in good company.'

'Perhaps. But my advice; keep well clear of them. Or they may not let you go!'

They watched in silence as the procession marched on towards their temple.

Charlie considered this new information. He'd been called many things: comic genius, millionaire tramp, champion of the downtrodden, a communist – but never a prophet and never a saint. He rather liked that, but respected Victor's words of warning. The count quickly grew impatient, gave a few loud blasts on the horn and spun the car down a narrow alleyway. It bumped over ruts and squashed through mulch, with Charlie hanging on to the door and his camera. They passed the same lacquerware store in the intersection where Charlie had met Phirath. And then on, down another quieter road. With no sign that they'd reached any specific destination, Victor slammed on the brakes and jolted to a halt. Charlie looked up and down the street, then to Victor beside him who was patting down his jacket to retrieve his black tobacco. Behind them an ox cart came to a halt. The car blocked the way entirely. Victor climbed out, ignoring the ox-cart driver and opened the door for Charlie.

'This way,' he said.

Charlie grabbed his camera bag and followed. After weeks of travel and the endless promotion of his last film, it was only since he'd stepped out of the royal screening and met Phirath by chance, that he'd made the decision to open himself up to other opportunities for chance and adventure, and Victor was as good a guide as any. He followed the count through a nondescript door and into what looked like a Chinese shophouse.

The afternoon heat penetrated the dark interiors where it wrapped around Charlie, dulling sounds and senses until it felt like he was gliding rather than walking. He followed Victor through narrow wooden corridors, up steps, past carved wooden panels, lanterns and paintings. The boards beneath their feet creaked as they walked further in. This was not a regular shophouse selling sacks of rice or farm implements or pottery. The double sliding doors at the end opened into a lounge room. Daybeds under open drapes were set against all the walls. Women in scarlet cheongsams embroidered with dragons cast their eyes at the two foreigners entering but paid them little attention. There were other opportunities already in the opium house. Frenchmen, many in uniform, were also taking a break from the afternoon heat. Victor caught the eye of the mamasan and gestured up. She nodded and dispatched a girl to accompany them. The girl led them through the lounge and out onto a landing. Charlie followed, keeping his head down, but looking at everyone and everything. He was grateful now that with his advancing age the resemblance to his famous alter-ego had diminished and there was little chance of being recognised. They continued down another corridor with doors leading to the left and right. The girl stopped at one and opened the door. As he was going inside, Victor gave Charlie a broad grin.

'Don't look so worried, Charlie.'

Once inside, the girl lit a spirit lamp and prepared the pea-sized ball of opium paste for a stained bamboo pipe decorated with a bone dragon. For a moment Charlie watched fascinated. He'd taken Victor's lead and thrown his jacket over an upright wooden chair and unbuttoned his shirt. Victor was already half dressed on a daybed. His barrel chest was covered in thick black hair and criss-crossed with scars. The girl looked up and caught Charlie's eye. He turned away surprisingly embarrassed by his own fascination with the process.

They could hear the drums of the Cao Dai procession even here, but they seemed to throb rather than beat through the thick smoke-filled air. Charlie crossed to the louvred windows and peered down to the street below. The Cao Dai marched right below the window. He could see some of their placards, held up like Orthodox icons, but with paintings of their prophets and saints. Just as Victor had said, there among others like Victor Hugo and Joan of Arc, Charlie saw an image of the Tramp. There were hundreds of thousands of pictures of the Tramp throughout the world, but Charlie recognised it immediately as taken from the poster of his first feature length motion picture, *The Kid*. He filmed for a moment on his 16mm camera – the high angle looking down on their heads covered in pointed silk hats made the devotees look like counters in a game of Chinese chequers. Charlie laughed to himself at the idea, his mind already racing with possibilities.

After the procession had passed out of sight, he turned back from the window in time to see Victor take a long, deep hit from the pipe in his reclining position. The girl took the pipe from him and he leant back on the triangular Khmer cushions and his eyes closed. Then the girl offered the pipe to Charlie. He nodded with a smile. The girl smiled back, covering her teeth with her palm. He packed up his camera and put it on the daybed, then lay down beside it, propped up on the cushions. Although he was comfortable and not really afraid, he was still a little hesitant when the girl handed him the pipe and gestured how to hold it over the spirit lamp. He took a small hit – the taste was strange, pungent but not unpleasant – and handed it back, but the girl shook her head and gestured for him to go again. He turned the bowl over the flame from the spirit lamp once more, and inhaled again, this time long and deep and sweet. The hit was instantaneous. He slumped back against the pillows, his hand dropping to the floor. The girl caught the pipe just in time, pulled his arm back onto the bed by his side and tiptoed out.

***

INTERIOR. *A Cao Dai Temple.*

We fade in on curling tendrils of smoke and hear chanting from far away. The faithful are seated in a large hall with ornate pillars decorated with dragons and Chinese symbols. They are all dressed in white. At the head of the hall are the groups of religious elders in coloured robes and long wispy beards. They are seated around an altar, beyond which there is a vast painted mural on the back wall. At the centre of the elaborate mural is an eye in the sky in a triangle emitting shafts of light.

TRACKING CLOSER: we pass through the congregants to the elders only then realising what they are doing. They are conducting a séance. Between them are the placards and icons of their saints and prophets. Jesus at the head, Mary beside him and an array of disciples and followers. And below them, Victor Hugo and Charlie Chaplin.

Smoke fills the frame and we:

CUT TO: a street in the Chinese quarter of Phnom Penh.

The Tramp hitches up his torn trousers and holds his stomach with hunger. He loiters at a Chinese noodle stall and takes a deep sniff of the soup broth, eyes closing in ecstasy. An old Chinese man with a long droopy moustache glares at him. The Tramp smiles back with a nonchalant suggestive nod to the noodles. The Chinaman shakes his head. Another smile, a shrug ... and another wink towards the noodles. This time the Chinaman raises his ladle threateningly. The Tramp saunters on, hitching up his trousers. But beside the noodle stall he spots a Khmer spirit house. It has a central column of carved teak on top of which is a platform for the spirit house itself – like a miniature carved pagoda. In front of it is a lacquerware bowl shaped as lotus leaves which contains the burnt-out sticks of incense. But what The Tramp has particularly noticed are the offerings – dragon fruit, bananas and lychees. The Tramp settles beside it, waiting for his chance, but the stall owner glares at him, suspicious. As soon as he looks away, the Tramp's hand reaches out for the banana. The stall owner snaps back round, and the Tramp snatches his hand away just in time. He gives the owner a grin and a shrug. The stall owner looks away again – trying to catch the Tramp out. And once more the Tramp just manages not to be caught in the act. The moment is interrupted by a loud blast on a whistle. A policeman has spotted him. He raises his baton in the Tramp's direction and swaggers over.

The Tramp runs off down the alleyway and around a corner where some rickshaw drivers are playing cards. He jumps into the nearest rickshaw as the policeman runs up, still blowing his whistle. A rickshaw puller leaves his game of cards to take his passenger, but he walks far too slowly. The Tramp jumps back out and starts pulling the rickshaw himself. Seeing that, the puller runs after him, furious, and jumps into the empty seat. In full motion they swap places. The Tramp settles into the seat, and the puller scrambles over him to pull his rickshaw. But he's still too slow and the policeman is gaining on them. Desperate, the Tramp leaps down to help pull the rickshaw himself. The two men start arguing, pushing and shoving each other as the policeman bears down on them, ever closer ...

Just as the policeman is about to grab the Tramp by the collar, he cuts his losses, runs away from the angry rickshaw puller and sprints with his trademark one-legged skid around a corner into the narrowest of alleyways. Up ahead a rickshaw faces back at him, almost entirely blocking the alleyway. Its two poles are on the ground, seat in the air and the driver nowhere to be seen. The Tramp looks behind him; two policemen are just metres behind. He sprints towards the rickshaw and jumps up onto the seat, and up and over – the poles of the rickshaw lift up behind him, catching the two policemen between the legs. They yelp and collapse to the floor as the rickshaw poles comes back down with a thump.

The Tramp escapes, for now, diving through a doorway and into:

CUT TO: The interior of the Cao Dai temple. At the altar the Cao Dai high priest invokes the spirit of Charlie Chaplin. There's incense, smoke and chanting from the devotees until their religious serenity is shattered when the door beneath the eye-in-the-sky emblem bursts open and the Tramp himself appears.

Pandemonium in the temple. The priests are startled and jump back as the Tramp looks around him to see the men in robes, chanting, and an icon of himself from the kid on a placard. But there's no time to investigate. He's spooked out, and runs through the temple, carving a line through the seated devotees. The congregation get to their feet and follow. You would too if you'd been praying for years for Charlie Chaplin as a saint, and he appeared through the door of your temple during a séance. Their solemnity is forgotten as they hoist up their robes and run as fast as they can after the fleeing Tramp.

Outside once more, the Tramp emerges from the Cao Dai temple in a cloud of smoke. He looks one way – policemen are gathered around a van, unaware of the Tramp's presence! So he turns the other way, head down, nonchalantly doffing his derby to a stall owner with a shrug and a grin and his iconic walk.

He doesn't look back, but behind him the Cao Dai faithful spill out of the temple and follow him from a respectful distance. Drums beat over the piano music. The Cao Dai hold up their icons for Charlie Chaplin and soon they're joined by others – Khmer and Chinese, workers and shopkeepers – until the Tramp is unknowingly leading a whole procession. It recalls his unwitting leading of a union protest in Modern Times. But he's not waving a flag, just minding his own business as the streets fill behind him.

Finally sensing the procession behind him, he spins around. When he sees the crowd, he speeds up. But they speed up too. He turns again to address them, hand up to say something, then changes his mind and walks away even faster until he's running, ducking into a side street in the Chinese Quarter. Phirath is there. He drags him out of sight behind a truck but there's nowhere to hide. They climb into the back of the truck and finally out of sight, the crowd runs past still shouting his name.

The Tramp grins his thanks to his saviour. Just then the truck begins to move and they topple onto one another and onto the cargo of sacks. The truck picks up speed. As it drives away, we see the name stamped on the side of the truck: Michelin Rubber Company.

22

Le Favre waited impatiently outside Charlie's hotel suite as a chambermaid opened the door. He pushed past her and stepped inside, checking the room with the professional economy of a lifelong policeman. There was nothing of interest in the cupboards, drawers or table. The cases were empty. It was over at the writing desk that he found what he was looking for. A completed notebook. It was full of scrawled notes in Charlie's spidery handwriting, some sketches and scene blocking diagrams. Le Favre flicked through it backwards until the first page, where his eyes rested on the printed words: 'Colonial Subjects'.

It was all the evidence he needed. Charlot's presence in Indochina was not a mere distraction or nuisance. A film with the Tramp in the East had the potential to disrupt the colony's fragile equilibrium, potentially fuelling more resistance to French control – quite possibly with violent repercussions.

While Le Favre was gathering evidence of Charlie's film project in Indochina, Charlie himself was coming round in the opium house. Shafts of light from the late afternoon sun pierced the louvre slats and illuminated the smoke from the incense sticks. His mouth felt as dry as cinders and he was annoyed to have woken from his imaginings so abruptly. Without dressing or taking the green tea left for him, he scrawled away in his notebook, chasing a rapidly fading memory of his opium-fuelled wanderings. Finally satisfied, he dressed in a hurry and only then registered that Victor was no longer there. The girl entered the room and presented Charlie with a note from the count explaining his departure and hoping to see him again that evening at Hotel Le Royal. They would travel to Battambang the following morning.

Moments later, Charlie emerged from the opium house into the late afternoon activity of the Chinese Quarter. He ignored the rickshaws touting for business and wandered away on foot. While he looked through trinkets in the artisan alleyways, he felt someone was following him. He spun around once but saw nothing out of the ordinary and continued. But his senses were heightened, and his nerves on edge from the come down of chasing his Cao Dai dragon. Was Le Favre's constant presence making him paranoid? He stopped again, lifting his camera to film a stall. But he just pretended to look through the eyepiece. Instead, he checked out the reflective surface of a polished silver bowl in a stall. That was how he spotted his tail. He walked on, less scared than grateful that it wasn't his delusional paranoia.

Charlie idled and sauntered until he was absolutely sure. Then he ducked into a doorway beside two tall Chinese pillars – and waited. Footsteps rushed up, a shadow followed by its owner's feet. They were a boy's feet. Charlie's arm shot out. He grabbed him around the scruff of the neck and yanked him backwards. It was Saloth Sar.

'What do you want?' hissed Charlie.

The boy didn't answer and only gestured for him to follow. Charlie relaxed his grip, his curiosity getting the better of his irritation. Saloth Sar pulled free of Charlie and walked away. Charlie was still debating whether to follow him or not, when the boy turned around and beckoned him over. There was something about his intense expression that made up Charlie's mind. He followed the boy into a broader street, then on towards the bridge where Saloth Sar greeted the guards and presented his documents. They waved him through with only a casual glance at his papers. But when Charlie followed, they looked at him curiously. He was white, but that wasn't unusual. Many Europeans spent their afternoons in the Chinese Quarter. Yet there was something about his face, a flicker of recognition that they couldn't quite place. Once again, Charlie was happy that his screen persona was better known than his real one.

Charlie followed Saloth Sar for a long while, becoming more and more annoyed and impatient with this game. They walked past the construction of the vast central market building. A lattice of bamboo scaffolding covered the dome and labourers scurried up and down it like ants. Charlie paused to watch and forgot his frustration momentarily. His mind raced with the visual possibilities of a scene for Colonial Subjects. The bamboo scaffolding offered great physical comedy opportunities, and the perfect context for the Tramp at work. But his imaginings were cut short by a fierce hiss. The boy was pulling at his sleeve.

'Where are we going!' insisted Charlie, but again he got no answer. The boy led him on, staying a few paces ahead, and never looking back. They passed the post office, but still the boy didn't stop. Charlie sped up to call it off, but the boy sped up too, until they reached the road which circled the hill of Wat Phnom – the hill which gave the capital its name. The boy crossed into the shade of the boddhi and banyan trees, heading towards the entrance to the pagoda. An ornate seven-headed naga balustrade ran up either side of a set of steps towards the wat at the top of the hill. The daylight was fading, and a few other Frenchmen enjoyed the shade beneath the banyan trees with wives or mistresses. When Charlie saw the boy climbing the steps it was the last straw. He waited at the bottom. Saloth Sar stopped his climbing and beckoned him up again. Charlie shook his head. The boy retraced his steps, took him by the hand and pulled him forward. Charlie stood his ground.

'Where are you taking me?' Charlie hissed, voice low so as not to attract attention.

'Not here,' said Saloth Sar in Khmer. 'Up there.' He gestured up the steps.

The steps were steep and intricately carved. They reached beyond the top of the tree canopy.

'Wat Phnom,' he said to himself as if to make up his mind. Charlie decided that if the boy didn't tell him what they were doing by the time he reached the top of the steps, he would come straight back down. But at least the view from the top would be worth the climb. By the time he reached the top he was out of breath, but the view didn't disappoint. He looked out across the city beneath him. It was quiet and still, far above the noise of the end of the day. He span around to challenge Saloth Sar but instead found himself face to face with an elderly sparrow seller holding a cage of birds. When he tried to pass, the sparrow seller blocked his path. Charlie sighed, then reached into his pocket for a coin. The man grinned and his one gold tooth glinted in the sunset. He grabbed two birds from the cage and pressed them into Charlie's hands.

What was he supposed to do? The sparrow seller nodded and smiled as if in encouragement, but Charlie couldn't understand what he was saying. That's when he noticed Saloth Sar miming throwing the birds up into the air.

'Good karma!' he said simply.

Once again, Charlie did as he was told. He held up his hand and opened his palms. For a moment the birds were unaware of their newfound freedom. Then they suddenly flew away, into the tree canopy below.

When he looked around again, Saloth Sar was taking off his shoes to enter the pagoda itself. Charlie followed, kicked off his loafers and entered the gloom. A vast carved Buddha dominated the far end of the temple, surrounded by hundreds of candles, figurines, and offerings. Monks in orange robes, prayed quietly or chanted. The faithful sat, feet tucked behind them, palms pressed together, praying for wealth, health and good fortune for themselves and their ancestors. Saloth Sar gestured for Charlie to follow him further in.

The tiles beneath Charlie's feet were cool and he was grateful for the respite from the heat. He dabbed his forehead with a handkerchief and stopped to view the intricate paintings on the temple walls. There was a section of Buddhist hell depicted in graphic detail. Birds pecked the insides of a screaming man. Black demons prodded terrified humans with spears, pushing them on towards the leaping flames. When Charlie turned away from the murals, he found himself looking not at Saloth Sar but at Phirath. The young man watched him with a gentle smile. He held a finger to his lips and motioned for Charlie to follow. In front of Lord

Buddha he counted out an odd number of incense sticks and lit them, gesturing for Charlie to do the same. Charlie followed suit, but when he was about to blow out the little lip of flame, Phirath shook his head.

'Breath is contaminated. We don't blow out the flame. Like this.'

He shook the bunch of incense sticks until the flame went out and they started smoking, and then placed them before Lord Buddha. He knelt and pressed his forehead to the floor three times. When he'd finished his devotions, he stepped back and whispered to Charlie.

'The Sûreté are looking for me. They will send me to prison if they catch me.'

It was not much of an explanation. Phirath guided him to the back, to a dark corner where they could whisper more freely. 'I must get to Battambang for our performance, but they will be checking every roadblock and guard post. Charlot, I need your help. Will you help me?'

The desperation in his voice and in his eyes was real.

'What can I do? Should I speak to the Governor?' Charlie offered.

'Talking won't help. Not now.'

'Then what can I do? Won't they just arrest you anyway at Battambang?'

'Perhaps.'

Phirath and Charlie walked out of the wat and around the pagoda compound deep in conversation. Charlie listened intently, face serious, occasionally breaking into a smile, then back to more nodding. Every now and again he would double-check a detail and by the time they had walked around the top of the hill and were back at the steps, Charlie knew what he must do. And why. Phirath took Charlie's hand in both of his and shook it warmly.

'Thank you, Charlie,' he said.

Charlie watched him go and considered the impact of the role he had agreed to play – for a man he barely knew. He never could nail down the reason why he'd said yes. In fact, since the visit to the opium house, nothing had felt real. And yet, compared to the receptions and garden parties and press conferences and screenings, he'd never felt more alive in his life.

23

For Paulette and her mother, the drive to Levalier's plantation estate was far less eventful. The convoy of cars drove through the beautiful Cambodian countryside for six hours. They sat in the back in silence because there was only one topic of conversation and neither wanted to pursue it. Her mother was not pleased with the arrangement with Levalier and had made her feelings clear. Any distance between Charlie and Paulette was unwelcome; Charlie's reputation had left her concerned for the relationship and the marriage, and Paulette's casual dismissal of her concerns had done nothing to allay her fears. So instead, they both stubbornly stared out of the windows at the sugar palms, the water buffalo and the rice paddies, passing the occasional archway and tree-lined approach to the pagodas that formed the hub of every village. Alta dozed and snored a little. Paulette was glad she wasn't in Levalier's car. She didn't want to make small talk and didn't have the energy to deflect his obvious interest.

As soon as they left Phnom Penh, it felt to Paulette that they had gone even further back in time. It could have been the 9th century. The sun was dipping towards the horizon by the time they turned off the main road and drove under an archway which displayed the name of the Levalier estate in French and Khmer.

From there they passed through endless rows of rubber trees. The trunks were scarred by rubber tappers and the workers themselves were silent and shadowy between the trees. They stopped their work and looked down to the ground as the convoy passed. When Paulette looked back, the workers were lost in the fine dust kicked up by the car. It reminded her of *Red Dust*, a movie she'd watched before she'd even met Charlie. It was a talkie, directed by Victor Fleming, and starred Jean Harlow, Clark Gable and Mary Astor, set in French Indochina and the colonial French rubber business. She recalled that there was a love triangle between Gable, the plantation owner, a prostitute on the run, played by Harlow, and the wife of an engineer. She smiled to herself as she remembered her favourite scenes. Would she find the real experience anything like the film?

Eventually the car drove out of the shade of the rubber plantation itself and crossed a wide lawn towards the imposing façade of a colonial villa. After Levalier had shown the ladies and Mr Yonamori to the east wing of his estate he excused himself to attend to some business. The east wing interior was dark and cool with high ceilings, but the fans did little to churn the muggy air. A heavy humidity dampened every surface and made every breath an effort. Their suite was lavishly decorated and there were framed lithographs hung on the walls depicting Angkor Wat and Wat Phnom, and tableaux of the countryside and rivers. A bookshelf was full of mildewed histories and cultural treatise on Indochina, more like a museum than a guest room. Paulette's mother picked up an opium pipe from its holder on a desk beside the louvred windows. The mouthpiece fell off and she looked around embarrassed and tried to replace it. But there was no doubting the wealth on display throughout Levalier's home.

'He's got more money than Charlie,' she whispered, her mood brightening.

Paulette rolled her eyes as she studied the framed poster of the Colonial Exposition of 1931 in Paris. A full-scale replica of Angkor Wat had been constructed for the exposition, bringing the wonders of the Khmer Empire to the Western world. It was this exposition, reported throughout the world in the press, that had drawn Charlie and Paulette's attention to this jungle-clad wonder and inspired their trip. Paulette particularly thought it would be a wonderful place from which to make their marital announcement to the world.

'The Exposition Coloniale of 1931.' Levalier's voice made Paulette spin around. 'I saw it in Paris and knew at once that I must come to Indo-Chine.' Levalier was in the doorway, oozing a now familiar charm. 'If you are settled in, perhaps you'd permit me to show you around my humble estate?'

And that's why moments later, as the sun set beyond the distant low hills, Levalier guided Paulette across the lawns towards the endless lines of rubber trees. Alta had politely declined the invitation, opting to lie down with a book after the long drive. So it was only Levalier and Paulette who strolled leisurely through the shade of the rubber trees. He was an entertaining host and did most of the talking. Paulette was happy to listen, taking it all in, and grateful for the opportunity of the walk after being cramped in the car since morning. She sipped on an iced gin and tonic as Levalier continued his explanation.

'I took over from the previous owner after a scandal involving the mamasan of a nearby establishment ... and an obstinate buffalo. It was not pretty.'

Despite herself, or perhaps because of the long monotonous drive and the gin in her bloodstream, she laughed at his intentionally vague account, imagining the possibilities.

'The dreary Parisian spring fuelled my thirst for the exotic. The orient beckoned. The *mission civilisatrice*. You see, we are encouraged to believe that beneath their stubborn, lazy exteriors, all our workers have the potential to become civilised Frenchmen.'

'And did you find what you were looking for here?' asked Paulette.

Levalier stopped at a tree and his fingers tested the latex sap collected in a small bowl.

'What I found was sixty thousand metric tonnes of rubber exported from Indo-Chine this year. And back home? A dreary château, the grind of parties and debutante balls, while outside my aristocratic bubble, nothing but strikes and depression. Herr Hitler and his stupid moustache. No offense to your … friend.'

Paulette was about to put him straight on the nature of their relationship but thought better of it, enjoying the Frenchman's attention.

'You don't worry about Germany?'

'Bof!' exclaimed Levalier dismissively, a perfect caricature of a Frenchman. 'Our Maginot Line is im … how do you say, im …?

'Impenetrable?'

'*Non, non* – impregnable. Did I say it correct?'

'You did.'

'And here, in our colony, rubber is a license to print money.'

They reached a fork in the path and took the left branch heading back towards the villa. Ahead of them a wooden collection wagon was pulled by a water buffalo, loaded with open barrels of freshly tapped latex. The driver flicked his whip absently, his mind elsewhere until the cart's wheel hit a rut and the wagon jolted. The last barrel of latex fell off the back and spilled into the red dirt. A plantation guard blew on his whistle and rushed over to the cart driver, who was unaware of what had happened. There were some barked words in Khmer, and then the plantation guard dragged the cart driver down to the ground and rained blows on him with a stick. The driver cowered in fear, his palms pressed above his head. Was he begging for forgiveness for his error, or trying to protect his head from the blows? Either way, it had little effect on the apoplectic guard.

Paulette looked on, shocked. She had seen beatings before, but they had only ever been on set where they were carefully choreographed and rehearsed. But this was brutal and real, and her hand went to her mouth, and she turned away from the scene. For a moment Laurent considered ignoring her reaction, but then thought better of it. He strode over to the cart, skirting the pool of sticky latex in the dirt, to where the beating was being administered. At the sight of the plantation owner, the guard dropped to the ground on his knees beside the bleeding cart driver. Levalier hauled them both up by the armpits.

'No need to be savages,' he said in French to the guard. 'Collect what can be saved and take this man to the infirmary.'

The guard looked confused.

'Well, go on then,' he added in Khmer, dropping his voice to add, 'Wait until my guest is out of sight, for God's sake!'

He smiled to the guard and steered Paulette away towards the villa.

'The trouble is, my dear, that there are millions of them, but only a handful of us. If we don't maintain control – chaos!'

'That I fully understand,' said Paulette, trying not to let her voice betray her emotion. 'It's no different to motion pictures. There can only be one person in control.'

'*Exactement*. Now, why don't you freshen up. Dinner will be served at seven. Please, if there's anything you need, just ask.'

'Nothing at all. You've been most kind to host us.'

'Think nothing of it. Expatriates thrive on variety. The monotony of the colony can leave one deflated for life, *n'est ce pas*?' His hand found the small of her back and he guided her up the steps of the villa and inside.

As soon as they had gone, however, the offending cart driver was dragged back into the trees and beaten within an inch of his life.

Back in the guest quarters, Paulette's mother waved away mosquitos as a silent Khmer servant brought citronella candles on a tray and some storm lanterns and arranged them around the room. Paulette was at the window. The beating she had witnessed made her suddenly and inexplicably sad. She left the window to a drinks cabinet and prepared another gin and tonic for herself and her mother.

'Is it the gin or the tonic that's good for malaria?' she asked, mainly to herself.

Her mother took the gin and added more to her glass. She looked worried.

'You know, sugar, we could die here, and no one would know.'

She gestured to a framed print above the drinks cabinet. Angkor Wat again.

'Maybe that's what happened. Eaten to death by mosquitos the size of damned starlings.'

Paulette smiled and returned to the window, drink in hand. Through the gloom she could just make out the rows of rubber trees beyond the lawn, and the shadowy figures of the rubber tapping army, bare-chested and wearing hitched-up sarongs. She didn't want to think about that and turned away from the window. She took from her clutch her wedding and engagement rings, put them on her fingers and admired them. The diamond glittered in the final rays of the setting sun.

'I still don't see why you couldn't have gotten married in Los Angeles like normal people,' said Alta, her gentle reproach almost protective.

'What's normal about Charlie?' replied Paulette, not really listening.

'That's true, sugar. A normal husband wouldn't abandon his wife and mother-in-law to be eaten alive—'

'We're not lost in the Congo mother! Laurent wouldn't—' and she checked herself. 'Mr Levalier will look after us here.'

But the slip wasn't lost on her mother.

Silence.

Paulette blushed at her mother's stare and looked away before popping the rings back into her clutch.

'I'm just saying … I love Charlie. Of course I do. But Selznick's offer—'

'You break one contract and the other won't be worth the paper it's printed on.'

Her mother's words lingered in the humid air long after they had been uttered. Paulette watched the moths circling the lanterns.

She knocked back her gin and tonic and poured herself another, feeling the gin take the edge off her anxiety. No, she thought. This wasn't like the movies at all. The truth was much darker than *Red Dust*. In fact, it was almost too much. But rather than consider the harsh reality of the rubber plantation, she found solace in her favourite scenes from the film. She smiled...then sighed.

'Think I'm overjoyed about it?' she said, in an excellent impersonation of Jean Harlow in *Red Dust*. 'But it's just got to be, that's all.'

But her mother didn't get the reference and stared at her in the dark.

'Jean Harlow?' Paulette added, as explanation. 'In *Red Dust*?'

'Jean Harlot,' said her mother spitefully.

'Yes, strictly speaking. She played a prostitute.'

Her mother's expression made it clear what she thought of that. She sniffed in disgust and changed the subject. 'Dinner?'

24

Charlie paced in the Elephant Bar of the Hotel Le Royal, pretending to look at the prints and artefacts, but really replaying the day's events in his mind. He was pleased with the progress of *Colonial Subjects* and the snippets of scenes that he'd worked on with Phirath. The first few days of every new idea were feverish with possibilities, all jostling for space in the unfolding narrative. His usual process was to sit in his study in Summit Drive with his notebooks, pacing, playing the violin or listening to music as he tried to organise them into some kind of story. More often than not, each idea pushed out the next and he found pinning them down on paper as difficult and frustrating as trying to hold onto smoke. But here in Phnom Penh, and with Phirath's earnest collaboration, they had neatly, almost mystically, aligned themselves into an unfolding story. His job for once was not to create or construct the story. For *Colonial Subjects*, he seemed only to transcribe it down as it unfolded in his imagination. Perhaps, he thought to himself, it was because he was developing the story in the real location, drawing inspiration from what he observed.

The arrival of the Tramp in Indochina at the port quickly repaid the audience's leap of faith into the film's unusual location.

And from that moment, emerging from the packing crate, the Tramp was sucked seamlessly into the action. He had reworked the railway scene (which had been interrupted by Phirath's voice) and decided that the Tramp would be thrown off the train for not having a ticket. Standing on the platform he would catch another glimpse of the governor's daughter leaning out of the train window as she headed off to Battambang. Her look and brief interactions would provide the Tramp with all the motivation he needed to pursue her. But before then he would wander the streets of Phnom Penh's Chinese Quarter, hungry and desperate for work. This would segue into the scene with the Cao Dai sect ending with him hiding with Phirath in the Michelin rubber truck to escape the mob of devotees. The truck would lead them right into the heart of the rubber plantations – and straight into the governor's world. The Tramp and the governor's daughter would meet up again. A romance would blossom, but more than anything, he hoped to encourage the audience to sympathise with the colonial subjects. Perhaps he could actually shoot the film on location rather than back in the studios. Relinquishing full control on a studio lot in favour of the messiness and improvisation of location shooting was something he'd never previously considered. But here in Indochina it seemed that everything was possible. He was particularly pleased with the idea that he would play both the Tramp and the governor – and imagined all the possibilities this might present with mistaken identities as the story moved towards its climax.

But just as the new story was sucking the Tramp into a new world and a new conflict, Charlie was also being reeled into a plot no less audacious, but which would prove to have very real outcomes. He was excited (and a little apprehensive) after the meeting with Phirath at Wat Botum. Even here in the calm of the Elephant Bar, the thought of it made his heart beat faster. He was involved now, not merely a spectator but a player. The adrenalin was fuel to his creative process and a tonic to the blurred months of vacation. He felt truly alive once more and itching to work. He had been wrong to say he was finished. He had been wrong to think that the technological developments in motion picture production and the advent of talkies would signify the end of his career. He had more he wanted to say.

Behind him there was a noisy argument between Victor and a handful of academics from l'École française d'Extrême-Orient. The conversation had continued circuitously for hours since dinner, and Charlie had long since disengaged. For once he was neither the centre of attention nor an expert on the subject. He spun the globe in its wooden holder finding Los Angeles before spinning it around to Indochina. With the story taking the Tramp into the world of the rubber plantations he now wished that he'd joined Paulette rather than staying in Phnom Penh and this tiresome conversation about the cultural history of the Angkorian empire.

Victor slammed his hand down on the table so hard the drinks rattled.

'And where is evidence? I tell you, water! Water, water, water!'

'Your theory is an obsession,' argued back a young woman with glasses and her hair pulled unfashionably back in a bun making her look much older than she really was.

'Fact! Not theory. Not that the EFEO seems to care for such things.'

'What other explanation has there ever been for the fall of

empires? An invading conquering army. It's no different today.'

The woman slapped a newspaper on the table beside the leather armchairs and stabbed the headline with a finger to prove her point. Charlie's interest was suddenly piqued. The headline was indeed serious. *Hitler's Third Reich army marches into the Rhineland*. It was front page news and there was even a photograph of goose-stepping Nazi soldiers, rows upon rows of them, beneath the banners, eagles and swastikas of the Third Reich.

'And you, Monsieur Chaplin? Don't you find it a tragedy what is going on in Europe?'

Charlie started at being so directly included in the conversation. All eyes were on him as he weighed up a suitable answer.

'As I've said before on other occasions, in my line of work I often find that life is a tragedy in the long shot, but a comedy in the close up.'

'Very drôle,' fired back the woman. 'And it must be easy to say, Charlot, hidden from the real world in the make-believe studios in Hollywood.'

She shoved another newspaper towards him, a regional daily. The headline was also bleak.

French Plantation Owner murdered by Khmer Workers.

'Do you also find this a comedy? Should we laugh at these events too?'

Unwilling to commit himself, Charlie muttered a few face-saving retractions and removed himself from the situation. It had in any case bored him senseless, particularly compared to the thrill of the meeting with Phirath and their plans. As he was walking back to his suite, the count rushed up behind him in the corridor to stop him. His normally animated face was a picture of concern.

'Don't listen to them, Comrade Charlie,' he offered between puffs of his black tobacco. 'Academics. They like to sit on top of the world and judge, rather than be any part of it. Come back for another drink. We will talk of other things.'

'Thank you, Victor. I won't. I'm tired and I believe it is a long drive tomorrow.'

'That is true. Seven o'clock. I come. Be ready!'

Charlie had no intention of extending the conversation with Victor and said goodnight. The truth was that the question posed by the French academic had turned his previously buoyant creativity into a depressing moral quandary. Not for the first time he found himself blaming the Tramp. He knew as well as Paulette that his silent alter-ego was what people really wanted. They wanted performance and entertainment – nothing more. Having spent the last decade wishing people would take him seriously and listen to his thoughts on economics and politics in the parlours of great men and thinkers in New York, London and Berlin, he had enough self-awareness to realise he was still being treated like the kid invited to the grown-ups' table for the first time. He was included in these conversations not for his intellectual contributions, but for the glamour his presence lent to the otherwise dull soirées. People listened politely as he put forward his views on the Gold Standard, or the situation in India, but dismissed his insights like a parent indulging a child; proud of him for taking part, but not giving his contributions any real weight. They were considered merely a groping in the dark, a naïve, childish fumbling towards a grown-up truth still out of reach because they were not yet tempered by travel and experience.

But at forty-six years old, Charlie had travelled (and conquered) the world. He'd spent time with Winston Churchill at his Chartwell residence together with politicians and economists. He'd discussed India and independence with Gandhi, and the knottiest theorems of physics and relativity with Albert Einstein. He'd met kings and rulers. He'd spent a long evening discussing political science and art with George Bernard Shaw and JM Barrie. How was it that an author who found fame through a story about a boy who never grew up could be taken more seriously than he? Hadn't *Modern Times* proved him capable of addressing the biggest issues of the day? Hadn't *City Lights* shown those who could be bothered to see beyond the pantomime, a damning satire of the pompous politicking and economic theories discussed in the abstract at dinner parties, while poverty and the Great Depression robbed millions of their humanity?

How he detested academics. How could they think so much and yet feel nothing about the subjects they discussed?

By the time he reached his suite, his anger has settled into a steely determination. With his newfound friend, he'd found a chance to combine something real, shaping material for his next picture, and sticking two fingers up to the colony that had dared to defy him by not releasing his last picture. And this next film would burst the bubble of French superiority and expose their cruelty in Indochina forever – not just under their own noses, but right across the world! He longed to see their faces when they watched *Colonial Subjects*. Would they still think him just a cheap pantomime entertainer then?

But Charlie didn't have the self-awareness to realise that his attitude was exactly the petulant defiance that kept him a child among adults, that kept him from being taking seriously as a thinker or political commentator. Perhaps this was because he had missed his own childhood. He'd leapfrogged that psychological moment and crashed into early adulthood by sheer force of his energy and drive – and had become immensely rich and successful. But it had all happened before he'd been able to work through the necessary stage of adolescent rebellion. That's why it still extended into his middle age – and why he couldn't see it. All he could think of was how he would show them. How he would bring that smug French captain down a peg or two. How he would sail above the empty posturing of the academics with his damning but comic story. How, with *Colonial Subjects*, he would make more money than the rubber plantation tyrants. He might as well have been an adolescent shouting at his parents that he'd run away and make his fortune so that he could holler, 'that showed them!'

He smoked a cigarette quickly and ferociously on the balcony, playing all this out in his head. He was about to stub the cigarette out in the ashtray but instead flicked it out into the garden – a caricature of adolescent rebellion. It was then that he noticed the car parked across from the hotel, and the dark shape of the Sûreté officer still keeping an eye on him. He returned to his desk and poured himself a large Scotch and soda. It was the drink of intellectuals. But when he took up his notebook and became engrossed in sketching the next scenes, the drink was immediately forgotten. There was a grim determination on his face as his pen flew across the paper. He was going deeper, and noticeably darker, into the story, fuelled by Phirath's long, detailed accounts of how hard life was for Cambodian people on the French rubber plantations. This would not be *just* a comedy, he fumed.

A WIDE SHOT: Dusk. The sun is setting across the rice fields.

The Michelin truck drives through the flat Cambodian countryside on a raised road. It kicks up dust behind it, smothering rice farmers on their way back from the fields, and earthenware pedlars on their ox carts. From the wood-sided back of the truck the Tramp peers out, rubbing his eyes from sleep.

The Truck turns off the highway and past a signboard for the Michelin Rubber Plantation. Abruptly the landscape changes from rice fields to rubber trees. They are planted in rows, right up to the road, and stretch back in every direction as far as the eye can see. Phirath appears behind the Tramp on the truck and they peer into the stillness of the pre-work plantation and exchange worried glances.

At the gates to the plantation, Phirath grabs the Tramp and they jump down from the rear as the truck slows. They run off into the trees towards the rubber tappers' camp. The camp itself is rows of simple wooden barracks. Behind each a small garden for vegetables. There are washing lines between them. As they skirt the edge, Phirath stops at a washing line and grabs a sarong and a tunic and a rice paddy hat and presents them to the Tramp.

CUT TO: The Tramp peers out from behind a gnarly banyan tree. He looks around sheepishly then steps out. His sarong is hitched up above his knobbly knees, but he still has on his oversized shoes. He pulls a tunic over his slight short frame and Phirath rams the rice paddy hat on his head. The transformation is complete. Only the toothbrush moustache and his shoes give him away. Phirath and the Tramp size each other up – laughing and joking. Phirath points to his shoes. The Tramp takes them off. Each one as big as his puny forearm. He doesn't want to part with them. Phirath snatches them away and tosses them behind the banyan tree. The Tramp is about to retrieve them when:

TING! TING! TING! A French plantation overseer bangs a metal wheel rim with an iron rod. The barracks in the camp spill out their labourers, shuffling into an open space at the centre of the camp in front of a flagpole flying the Tricolore. When Phirath looks around he sees the Tramp has stepped forward to join them. Work at last! But Phirath's face is a pantomime of fear. He grabs the Tramp who mouths:

INTERTITLE: Work at last!

But Phirath shakes his head furiously and nods to the treeline.

INTERTITLE: This isn't work; this is slavery! Look!

The labourers shuffle into lines. Ghoulish, gaunt, like zombies dressed the same as the Tramp and Phirath. Their eye sockets are dark, teeth and gums blackened into grimaces. It looks like hell. Some of them are women, but it's hard to tell in the gathering gloom of nightfall. Before Phirath can drag the Tramp away, the two interlopers are spotted. The French manager blows his whistle, and all eyes turn to them. They shuffle forwards, taking up a position at the back of the nearest line. A gendarme with a bayonet paces up and down the lines. Another has a rattan cane, patrolling to find any signs of defiance. A labourer staggers from exhaustion before the day has even begun. A fellow labourer steadies him. The gendarme looks to the manager for instruction.

INTERTITLE: 'Donnez la cadeuille!'

The gendarme nods and thwacks him mercilessly around the head with the cane and he crumples into the dirt. Another *whistle blows. In unison, the lines of labourers shuffle forwards like automatons towards a line of rubber tapping pails and bark knives, and separate into groups.*

CUT TO: The Tramp at the front of the line. He takes his pail and bark knife from the French assistant but doesn't move forwards. He offers the assistant his usual nonchalant grin.

INTERTITLE: What about breakfast?

For his insolence he's thwacked across his back with the rattan cane and shoved sprawling to a line of ox carts. In each of them is a vat to collect the latex from each pail.

CUT TO: The Tramp stands barefoot by a mature rubber tree deep in the plantation. An access track runs beside the line of trees and the ox cart with the collection vat waits to be filled. The Tramp empties the collection cup of latex into his pail. He looks to Phirath for further instruction, pleased with his progress. Phirath demonstrates how to cut the bark in a spiral. The Tramp drops his bark knife into the pail of latex. Holding the pail in his right hand, he dives in with his left to retrieve it, but it's sticky. He tries to remove the latex from one hand to the other, kicks over his pail by mistake and puts one bare foot into the sticky goo. His sarong slips and one sticky hand grabs the fabric to prevent it falling. Soon the tramp is a mess of sticky latex, pail, sarong and bark knife getting more and more frustrated.

CUT TO: The Tramp brings his full pail to the ox cart. He climbs up and empties it into the vat. A French gendarme watches him warily. The Tramp doffs his rice paddy hat. A woman approaches with her pail from the other side and smiles at him. An audience. The Tramp bows and his rice hat falls into the vat. She giggles when he retrieves it sticky with latex and puts it back on his head. He jumps down to make way for her.

Thwack! The Tramp receives another rattan stick beating for his troubles.

He yelps, drops his pail, and angrily turns to the gendarme, snatches the rod from him and brandishes it. The gendarme snatches it back.

Thwack!

He thrusts the pail back at the Tramp.

INTERTITLE: I've filled my pail!

INTERTITLE: Three hundred trees. Then you stop!

He's about to protest but the French gendarme's attention is taken by the young woman who has climbed up to the ox cart and is emptying her pail. The Tramp huffs and walks back into the plantation. The gendarme grabs the woman as she jumps down and gropes her, laughing. She tries to pull away, but the rattan stick soon quiets her. He takes her by the hand and leads her into the forest.

The Tramp watches it all. He's livid. He's tapping another tree when he hears her cry out as the French gendarme tries to force her. It's too much. Phirath tries to block the Tramp's path, but there's no stopping him. He switches his empty pail for Phirath's full one, and strides over to where the Frenchman has pinned the girl against the tree. Her almond eyes are screwed shut in shame and pain. The Tramp pretends to stumble and the full pail of latex flies all over the Frenchman. It has the desired effect. The gendarme stops, blinded, and wipes the latex from his eyes. It gives enough time for the woman to run off and the Tramp ducks behind a tree to hide. The Frenchman stumbles around arms out, shouting for help. Phirath grabs the Tramp and they run across the track to the other side and take up positions there.

CUT TO: The exhausted rubber tappers trudge back to camp to form a line beside the ox cart. Their eyes are downcast, avoiding contact with the French gendarmes and each other, summoning their last remaining energy to carry their pails and bark knives and put one barefoot in front of the next. In the line we find the Tramp and Phirath. A sorrowful song drifts above the line of labourers. It haunts the now empty lines of rubber trees but the latex still runs down the spiral scars and drips into collection pails.

Oh, it's easy to go to the rubber and hard to return,
Men leave their corpses, women depart as ghosts.

The Tramp looks up at the sound of a car approaching. A whistle blows. In unison the tappers move off the road and line up at the verge as headlamps sweep into view. Everyone looks down. It's not so much respect as exhaustion as the governor's open-topped automobile approaches.

The Tramp looks up. He sees the governor in the front passenger seat beside the chauffeur. And in the rear is his daughter, clutching her beloved Descartes to her chest. The Tramp's downtrodden expression brightens. Instinctively he takes a step out of the line towards her – and for the briefest of moments their eyes connect. It's all the Tramp needs. He's about to follow when Phirath yanks him back into the line. And just in time as the French gendarme who'd been covered in latex is patrolling the lines and looking for any excuse to mete out another beating.

CUT TO: The camp. The cramped barracks consist of little

more than wood floors and sheet metal roofs. Groups of workers huddle together to eat their meagre rations. The Tramp looks at the metal bowl in his lap as he slaps away mosquitos. He sniffs the food and recoils in disgust. Rice, fish bones and a fish head.

CUT TO: The Tramp is awake in his barracks. A mosquito whines around his head. He slaps at it. Misses. And lies back, his eyes wide in the darkness tracking the offending insect. Biding his time until THWACK! He slaps the shoulders of the labourer sleeping next to him. The worker starts up in surprise and looks around. The Tramp lies still beside him, pretending to snore.

Quiet returns to the camp. Until Charlie is shaken awake by Phirath, who puts a finger to his lips and beckons the Tramp to follow him.

CUT TO: With a storm lantern, Phirath and the Tramp head through the trees of the rubber plantation. Someone is following them. Phirath stops and holds his hand up for silence. A twig snaps and Saloth Sar appears. The Tramp looks at him confused as if he's surprised to see him in his story. And then they continue on their way until they hear the sound of music and laughter in the distance. Closer they peer through the plantation tree line to see the grand governor's villa at the heart of the plantation.

WIDE SHOT: the villa is lit by the moonlight and hundreds of flaming citronella torches. Its opulence is evident for all to see as a late-night party becomes more raucous in the garden. Some are dancing on the lawn. Champagne corks pop. There is food on tables. And Descartes runs between the guests who offer him choice beef morsels and tidbits from their plates. In the middle of it all the Tramp spots the governor's daughter trying to evade the unwanted attention of a French gendarme. He takes a step towards her, but Phirath pulls him back and they continue their way, with the Tramp casting longing looks back to the garden party.

CUT TO: *Jungle. Soon they've left the rubber plantation and are in the jungle proper. Here they have to clamber over huge banyan tree roots by lamp light. The forest sounds are loud and eerie. The roots claw their way over the stonework of ancient temples as they climb over blocks, and through ruined lintels until they find themselves in the middle of an ancient Angkorian temple where a meeting is underway.*

The Tramp looks doubtful, but Phirath pulls him on and they squat at the back behind a dozen or so desperate and eager congregants. The Tramp asks Phirath:

INTERTITLE: *Bandits?*

INTERTITLE: *Communists!*

At their head the communist leader raises his fist in a revolutionary salute.

INTERTITLE: *Fellow countrymen and women! Our country is ruined, we are wretched, we pay heavy taxes and duties, we are beaten and thrown into prison for the slightest offence. First they stupefy us with opium. Then they force us to work on their plantations, transporting us far away from our homes and families, to work us to our deaths.*

The Tramp looks to Phirath whose eyes are bright with revolutionary fervour. He pulls at his tunic but Phirath shrugs him off. The leader takes a knife and a gourd – a blood oath about to be taken. He cuts his thumb and squeezes drops of blood into the gourd. Phirath is up in a second, joining the band of communist brothers to do the same. The leader shouts, 'They are men, we are men too. How can we let them keep on beating us forever? Set a careful ambush, knock off one of them right away, and it will scare the wits out of the rest of them. Kill one man and ten thousand will fear you. We will live and die together!'

Finally Phirath turns to the Tramp and implores him: 'Join us, Charlie!'

But before the Tramp can respond, powerful torch beams pierce the darkness with whistles and gunshots. The Tramp dives for cover as he sees the French Sûreté break up the gathering and start their arrests. At their head is the unmistakable figure of Captain Le Favre calmly smoking his Gitanes.

* * *

Charlie snapped out of his imaginings and threw his pen down on the desk. He was becoming frustrated by the stubborn refusal of the story to move forwards without the need for speech. It was not coming together as he'd wished. He wanted to communicate the communist leader's revolutionary zeal, but the intertitles were becoming longer and longer until they nearly filled the frame. He rubbed his eyes.

He couldn't know then that his vision of the camp and the beatings and the ever-present guards foreshadowed an altogether more horrific system of forced labour camps which would become the reality for hundreds of thousands of Cambodians in only forty years' time. Nor that when he died in his bed in the comfort of his own home decades later, millions of Cambodians would be killed, and their bodies left in the rice fields. The origins of the murderous Khmer Rouge regime could be traced back to these same communist revolutionaries opposing French colonial exploitation.

25

Paulette was also awake, sitting in an armchair, glass in hand, counting the geckos on the roof and tinkling the ice in her glass. She'd had too much to drink and knew she would not sleep. Her mother had retired early, and Levalier was called away to address some urgent business affairs. So she drank alone. And too much. And now her mother was snoring under her mosquito net. The ceiling fan was turned up high and beat the air so loudly it nearly drowned out the whine of the mosquitos, which seemed utterly immune to the citronella smoke that filled the room with a cloying soporific sweetness.

It was nearly midnight and Paulette was about to climb into bed when she heard music from another part of the villa. It was a French chanson and she recognised 'Parlez-moi d'amour' and the voice of Lucienne Boyer

Paulette pulled her dressing gown tight and left the guest quarters with a lantern. She steadied herself in the doorway; was it the ceiling fan spinning or the room around it? She followed the song down the corridor, through the lounge and out to the veranda. The song was on a wind-up gramophone, but the veranda was deserted under the moonlight. There was no sign of Levalier, nor any of the servants. She poured herself a drink from the cabinet and closed her eyes, enjoying the music and swaying slightly. She didn't notice Levalier in the shadows watching her, his hand around a Dubonnet.

'You seem very much at home,' he said eventually.

Paulette spun around and had to steady herself against one of the veranda pillars. He raised his glass to her and gestured around the villa and garden as he walked over.

'How do you find my humble estate?' His voice was low; the moonlight caught the side of his face and Paulette noticed how handsome he looked, how comfortable and confident in his home estate. He seemed to know exactly what he wanted and how he was going to get it. She wasn't far wrong.

'It's not at all like *Red Dust*,' slurred Paulette back, trying to drive that thought away. But he didn't get the reference. She added, 'I'm sorry. You must think me a real bore with my constant talk of movies.'

'No more so than I fear you must be, with my talk of rubber and the colony. Tell me.'

'*Red Dust*? It was a motion picture from Metro Goldwyn Meyer,' Paulette explained. 'Directed by Victor Fleming.'

The names meant little to Levalier, but he smiled an encouragement.

'What's the matter,' said Paulette continuing as Jean Harlow. 'Afraid I'll shock the duchess? Don't you suppose she's ever seen a French postcard?' She giggled, pleased with her impression.

'A French postcard,' asked Levalier, pretending not to understand. 'You mean from Le Touquet or Nice?'

Paulette opened her mouth to explain his mistake, but then saw the teasing smile on his face and felt immediately foolish. It must have been the drink that made her feel like a naïve girl under his gaze.

'I didn't … I, er …' she stammered. Then gave up altogether. 'You see what happens when I'm allowed to speak? I get into a muddle when I do.'

'I disagree.'

Paulette was one of the most beautiful, young actresses in the world. She was dressed in a silk dressing gown, swaying slightly on his veranda evidently after too many drinks, under the magical moonlight, as all the while 'Parlez-moi d'amour' played on the gramophone. Paulette couldn't decide whether to look away or not – and if she held his gaze, how might it be interpreted – and what it might lead to. Her normally sharp mind was dulled and slow with drink. She didn't like how he made her feel. That wouldn't do.

So she doubled down, returned his look with a smile just the decent side of flirtatious.

'She was naked you know. In the barrel.'

'I've never seen the film, but now you have my interest.'

'Don't mind me, boys,' she said as a feisty Jean Harlow. 'I'm just restless.'

Levalier tucked some hair away from her face.

But Paulette didn't react. In her mind she'd gone from the memory of the picture itself – and Jean Harlow in a barrel – to the actual context of its production. She frowned, talking more to herself than to Levalier.

'Seven pictures since *Red Dust*.' Her voice faltered. 'All talkies. And in the same time that Charlie has directed one. Selznick has Victor Fleming to direct his next picture, *Gone with the Wind*. He wants me to read for the part.'

He waited for her to continue, but she didn't. Lost in her own head for a moment.

'Miss Goddard, I have to confess I honestly don't care.'

He held the ends of the dressing gowns belt playfully, neither pulling her closer, nor allowing her to move away. She swayed and pushed him away with no real force and he easily pulled her back.

'I really don't,' he said, with a more emphatic tone in his voice.

Paulette put her arms around his neck and closed her eyes and they began to move slowly to the music, alone on the veranda – about as far away as it was possible to be from Hollywood and her life and career.

> La vie est parfois trop amère,
> Si l'on ne croit pas aux chimères,
> Le chagrin est vite apaisé,
> Et se console d'un baiser,
> Du coeur on guérit la blessure,
> Par un serment qui le rassure.

The song came to a scratchy end and the vinyl jumped. They stopped dancing and stood in silence together for a moment. After what seemed an age, Levalier reached to take her hand and pulled her towards him, gently tugging at the robe straps when:

'Miss Goddard?'

It was Mr Yonamori in the doorway. They pulled apart and Paulette tightened her robe.

'Your mother is asking for you.'

Frank's interruption ruined (or perhaps rescued) the moment. Paulette put her glass down and rushed back inside the villa. She hurried back through the lounge and down the corridor, hands up to stop herself crashing into the walls or ornaments. But when she burst into the guest room, she found her mother exactly as she had left her – asleep under the mosquito net, snoring softly.

'Mother?' she said quietly. There was no response.

It was only then that she realised. Frank wasn't a fool. Of course, he always had Charlie's interests at heart. Perhaps it was just as well. There was a wry smile on her face as she sank into the armchair and pulled her knees up to her chest.

But back on the veranda, Yonamori's interruption infuriated Levalier and he was trying not to show it. He returned the needle to its cradle and poured himself another Dubonnet. He offered Yonamori one, but the Japanese manservant shook his head with a polite smile.

'Are you always so protective of Mademoiselle Goddard? He asked eventually.

'You mean, Madame Chaplin?'

Levalier stopped mid pour.

'Madame Chaplin? But I thought—'

'They were married a few weeks ago in Singapore. In secret. They plan to announce it to the world from Angkor Wat. That is why they are here.' He let that sink in for a moment, then added, 'Good night, sir.'

26

At breakfast the next morning, Charlie had lost his appetite. The croissants on his plate were untouched and the coffee cold. He was oblivious to the other guests who looked in his direction, pointing or sharing jokes in hushed tones. He was engrossed in the papers, reading about Hitler's army marching into the Rhineland in defiance of the Treaty of Versailles. The dictator's belligerence was blatant, but the world appeared reluctant to check his aggression. Charlie didn't hear Le Favre's clacking boots on the hotel tiles. The French captain stood over him for a moment, watching him devour the papers and their worrying contents.

'Maybe you would have more success with stories closer to home,' Le Favre said eventually.

Charlie folded the paper, refusing to engage, and readied himself to leave.

'I can't stop your work,' Le Favre added, so close that Charlie couldn't stand up from the table without barging the Frenchmen out of his way. 'But fraternising with, or aiding, a known subversive, a communist revolutionary, is a criminal offence. You will be arrested.'

'Captain,' said Charlie, wearied by the captain's constant haranguing. 'I don't know who you mean—'

'This is not one of your comedies, Charlot. Le Vagabond doesn't walk away with the girl into the sunset!'

Charlie stood up, forcing the Frenchman to step back a pace.

'And this, captain, is certainly not a comedy. It's tiresome, unnecessary and futile. Good day.'

For an answer, the captain tossed some black and white photographs onto the table between the croissants, orange juice and coffee. The photographs were from a plantation estate villa – one not so dissimilar to Levalier's. Lined up on the ground were the bodies of the French owner and his family, his wife and three children. They looked like they were dressed for dinner, but their throats had been cut. The blood, black as the darkest of the shadows in the photograph, seeped into the dirt. Their faces were contorted and frozen at the moment of death.

Charlie started in genuine horror.

'Your new friend, Sok Phirath,' continued the captain. 'Your solidarity with his profession may be admirable. But this "comic" actor is more than his performance on stage. These photographs, they are his father's handiwork. His father was part of an underground movement of communists who decided to strike at the heart of the French presence here – by murdering a husband, his wife and his three children. This is what happens when order breaks down in French Indochina, Monsieur Chaplin. This is also why he was immediately arrested and imprisoned. We believe that Sok Phirath is simply picking up where his father left off.'

Charlie sat back down again with a bump. He picked up the photographs and studied them properly, horrified by their obscene and graphic nature. But he'd spent many hours now with Phirath and he'd grown to respect and admire him. He couldn't imagine the young, intense, intelligent actor capable of anything so violent or criminal. Yes, Phirath passionately wanted a better life for his fellow countrymen. But not like this. He wanted to speak out. He wanted to use his theatre to entertain Cambodians, but also speak the truth. It was that combination that had brought them together.

'Are you certain, Captain?'

'Of what? That his father is a murderer of Frenchmen? Absolutely.'

'And what of his son?'

'We'll find out soon enough.'

Charlie stammered, but he couldn't find the words nor organise his thoughts. Le Favre smiled, enjoying the celebrity's distress. It was the effect he wanted. Before either could speak again, Victor blustered over, nearly crashing through a waiter clearing tables. If the count had overheard their tense exchange, he seemed utterly oblivious to the atmosphere at the breakfast table.

'Ready?' he said brightly to Charlie.

'Most definitely,' answered the filmmaker, never more grateful for the count's intrusion. 'Captain.'

He stood to leave.

'Out of the main entrance this time?'

Charlie didn't grace the comment with an answer. He strode off with Victor leaving Le Favre glaring at them. Half an hour later, Charlie packed the remaining suitcases into Victor's Peugeot 601, with the name l'École française d'Extrême-Orient printed on the doors. As he did so, he watched Le Favre speed off in a police car.

Victor was waiting impatiently.

'Is that everything?'

'My apologies. I try to travel light, but in my position I must be prepared for many eventualities.'

'Quite, of course,' said the count and almost manhandled the actor into the front seat.

'But if you don't mind, I'd like to make one stop before we leave the city.'

Victor rolled his eyes melodramatically and sat down heavily in the driver's seat. He was still in that frustrated frame of mind as the car inched through the over-crowded Chinese Quarter minutes later.

'Mr Chaplin, we don't have time if we are to pick up Miss Goddard and reach my home by nightfall.'

'Just a bit further. Now where was it? Yes, over there is fine.'

They stopped at a row of shophouses and street stalls. It was here that Charlie had first felt a spark of inspiration as he watched a young boy steal from a sack of rice as the frustrated stall owner stood on a table to fix a Chinese lantern. Charlie smiled at the memory. That's all he needed to make a scene. But how long ago it all seemed now.

Charlie climbed out and Victor pounded the steering wheel in frustration before joining him in the narrow street. They left the car and continued a few metres towards an artisan's stall. Whether by design or by accident, they saw Le Favre across the street surrounded by uniformed policemen. Charlie doffed his hat. Le Favre left his colleagues and crossed the street to join him.

Victor looked confused and displeased at yet another delay.

'You and the captain seem to like each other's company,' he complained.

'I wouldn't say that. Not from my side anyway,' said Charlie, and turned to face the Frenchman. 'What is it this time, Captain? Can't a man take a walk and do some shopping for curios in peace?'

'Oh, I'm not following you, Charlot. Not this time.' He smiled, confident in his own victory. 'We have located your friend. Wait around and you'll see the traitor arrested.'

'That's really not my business, Captain. You continually seem to misunderstand me. I just wanted to pick up a souvenir before the drive to Battambang.'

Just then there was a shout from the Sûreté officers across the street. The captain's eyes narrowed without leaving Charlie's face. Then he nodded once and retraced his steps. Charlie grinned and continued to the next stall, which was brimming with wooden handicrafts and lacquerware. Victor picked up a bowl, studied it briefly and then put it back, unimpressed.

'You came all way here for this?'

'Paulette loves wooden bowls ... lacquer things,' offered Charlie, not even convincing himself.

'There is a village near Siem Reap, gateway to Angkor. I show you real artisan's work. Real craftsmanship. We can make stop—'

'No need, Count. This will do very well.'

He looked back to see Le Favre surrounded by his policemen, perhaps a dozen in total. One of them pointed to an alleyway and Charlie followed the direction of his outstretched hand. A Khmer man had his back to them. He wore a rice paddy hat and baggy fishermen's pants. He had the same build as Phirath and was playing a game of Khmer chess. The board was on his lap between him and his opponent, and they were in a heated discussion, oblivious to the police presence. Le Favre nodded and the policemen made their way to the alleyway. Charlie changed his position to keep half an eye on the police arrest.

'How much for this one,' he asked the stall owner.

'Forty-five piastres,' said the stall owner in Khmer.

Charlie pulled out his wallet and looked to Victor to interpret. But the count looked apoplectic. He started shouting in Khmer and gesticulating with the stall owner. The haggling began in earnest, with the stall owner giving as good as he got and the conversation becoming more and more heated. But Charlie kept one eye on the impending arrest of Sok Phirath. The policeman reached the alleyway. The man turned ...

It was Phirath. He even wore the little toothbrush moustache painted on his top lip. Seeing the policeman, he jumped up scattering chess pieces and bolted. The police sprinted after, blowing their whistles loudly. Even Victor took a pause for breath to see what was going on. He quickly dismissed it. Just another French arrest in the Chinese Quarter, he thought, and returned to his haggling.

Just then Charlie noticed Phirath emerge from another alleyway entrance further down the street. As he crossed the road, Le Favre shoved forward another policeman to intercept him. But just then another man, wearing a rice paddy hat, fisherman's pants and a toothbrush moustache appeared from behind a stall. Other 'Phiraths' seemed to pour into the intersection from every direction. The policemen turned to Le Favre for instruction.

'Search them! All of them!' he barked.

The police officers rushed through the melee, twisting faces, lifting rice paddy hats, but none of them was Phirath. All of them were young Khmer men, wearing the same outfits and with the same moustache.

Charlie grinned and turned his attention back to Victor.

'I negotiate for you,' exclaimed Victor proudly. 'Forty-five piastres! He's crazy. It's not worth five. I get you for four.'

'Four?' said Charlie, in mock horror. 'Tell him I'll pay two, and that's my final offer.'

Victor looked at his new friend dumbfounded. He seemed utterly oblivious to the increasing chaos around him as scores of identically dressed men crisscrossed the streets and alleyways. Older Chinese men started laughing, hiding their teeth behind their hands, finding this the funniest spectacle they'd ever witnessed.

But Le Favre was livid.

'Two? But Charlot—'

'It's my final offer, Count,' said Charlie sternly.

Victor turned back to the stall owner and explained. And this time it was the stall owner's turn to be livid, shaking his fist, his droopy moustache shaking as he shouted insults and arguments. But Charlie didn't seem to care. He looked back to the car.

'Come on, come on—' he said to himself.

And then he saw him. Phirath and two other identically dressed young men popped out from behind an ox cart and walked quickly towards Victor's car. Ahead of them, Le Favre's men were stopping and searching everyone. Tempers were flaring, crowds had gathered to watch, further hampering their efforts. Le Favre smeared away one moustache and shoved the man away. It was not Phirath. And then he caught Charlie's eyes.

The celebrity waved the lacquerware pot in Le Favre's direction with a grin.

Phirath and his two body doubles approached Victor's car, unnoticed in the pandemonium unfolding at the crossroads ahead. As they passed, the leader opened the big boot, Phirath climbed in, and the one following at the rear closed the boot again – all without breaking their stride. It was seamless and choreographed to perfection, as only an actor could design and deliver. The two men were soon lost again in the crowd and chaos. Charlie smiled. He opened his wallet and took out a fifty piastre note and handed it to the shopkeeper.

'Fifty. *Arkuan*,' he said, timidly trying some basic Khmer. 'Thank you. Keep the change. Count, I'm sorry for keeping you. Shall we?'

And he took the bowl from the open-mouthed shopkeeper, patted an equally open-mouthed Victor on the back, and returned to the car, casually tossing the bowl up and down in the air. As if on cue, all the identically dressed men seemed to melt away, and the gathered crowd quickly dispersed. Within seconds the intersection had returned to the same daily shophouse activity as before the arrests.

Charlie climbed into the passenger seat and Victor heaved his bulk behind the steering wheel muttering to himself in Russian. As they drove past the bewildered Le Favre, Charlie reached over Victor to beep the horn, and waved the bowl out of the window. Triumphant.

Victor stared at him, ignoring the road ahead, utterly perplexed.

'You Americans,' he said finally. 'Crazy.'

Charlie was about to set him straight about his nationality but thought better of it. Instead, he settled back into the seat and closed his eyes, a smile on his face. For a long time, and to Charlie's considerable relief, Victor said nothing.

27

Charlie and Victor drove out of Phnom Penh in silence. Under normal circumstances, travelling with a grumpy companion was infinitely worse than travelling alone. Charlie was worried that his actions at the lacquerware stall had soured relations irreparably with the normally garrulous count, and that this would make the next eight hours a matter of endurance rather than enjoyment. His scowl seemed welded to his face. And Charlie's anxiety was only further increased by the knowledge that Phirath was at that very moment hidden in the boot of Victor's car. As they approached the roadblock marking the edge of the city, Charlie tried to ignore the knot in his stomach. Wooden tank traps and a chicane of barbed wire were laid across the street. There were only a score of vehicles waiting for the checks, mostly open-sided ox-drawn carts with the occasional pottery wagon from Kampong Chhnang. Sûreté officers scanned the papers of each vehicle and conducted a cursory check before waving them through. This wasn't a manhunt roadblock; it was just the regular display of control and power. They might recover a few smuggled sacks of rice or other produce, and then make an example of the perpetrators as a deterrent to others. But at the front of the checkpoint today was the battered truck transporting Phirath's Lakhoun theatre troupe to Battambang. Charlie leant out of the window to see better. The police checked the papers and then ordered the truck to the side. As soon as the engine had stopped, another officer dragged the driver from the truck's cab and marched him around to the back. The troupe were ordered down and forced to kneel on the dirt, hands on their heads. The officer walked the line, twisting faces up, searching for someone. At the end of the line was Saloth Sar. The officer twisted his head up so roughly it made the boy wince. But he was the last, and the officer hadn't found who he was looking for. Frustrated, he shoved Saloth Sar into the dirt and strode off. The boy watched him go. Every altercation, every harsh word, every slur or rough handling was being logged behind his eyes – logged in a list of grievances that was growing longer day by day, and which would eventually erupt into a pathological need for vengeance.

Victor was well known to the French officers. After a short exchange and some loud guffaws, and gestures in Charlie's direction, his car was waved through without any problem. When Charlie looked back, he saw the officers doing an impression of his walk as they moved onto the next vehicle. His shirt was sticking to his back, but it wasn't just the heat which was making him sweat. Victor crunched into gear and pulled away and Charlie settled back into his seat. In the side mirror, Charlie saw the troupe get up from the dirt and clamber back into the truck. He leaned out of the window, and for a moment Saloth Sar and Charlie caught each other's eyes. The troupe's truck farted back into life and continued its journey to Battambang. Charlie grinned. And this time it was his turn to slam the steering wheel in triumph. Victor cast a glance at him, still confused and not altogether comfortable with the strange little man, celebrity or not.

'How long will it take us to get to your home, Count Goloubew,' asked Charlie brightly, hoping to lighten the mood. He received a surly grunt in reply.

But the count couldn't stay angry (or silent) for long. Soon the open road through the sugar palms and along the Tonle Sap River had worked their magic. Victor may not have understood the American, but that didn't mean he was obliged to dislike him. He shrugged, and long after Charlie has asked the question and forgotten about it, he answered, 'Nine hours including the stop to pick up Miss Goddard and her mother. Nine hours, if we are lucky. And I feel that you, Comrade Charlie, were born to be lucky.'

Perhaps the count was referring to Charlie's rise from poverty to riches in Hollywood. The star had made no secret of his desperate upbringing, nor his subsequent wealth. When he signed a contract with the Mutual Film Corporation in 1916 for the unimaginable fee of $670,000 it had been front page news. He was the highest paid entertainer in the world. *Chaplinitis* gripped the world; shops stocked Chaplin merchandise, he featured in cartoons and comic strips, and several songs were written about him. In fact, by 1917 professional Tramp imitators were so widespread he took legal action to control his own image. The truth was that Charlie was as meticulous in controlling and guarding the narrative of his life as he was the fictional characters in his pictures. Luck may have played a part, but Charlie's tireless work ethic and fastidious control of his public persona made him both the creator and beneficiary of his own fortunes.

With the wind on his face and the roadblock far behind, he

asked the count, 'So tell me, what is there to see in Battambang?'

The count needed no encouragement. The sour mood was instantly forgotten, and he was soon chuckling and shouting and gesticulating so wildly that Charlie began to wish he'd kept quiet a bit longer.

***

Paulette on the other hand was staying in bed as long as she feasibly could, without causing offence to her host. When eventually she emerged, she found Levalier still at breakfast and reading the newspaper. There was an awkward silence as they looked at one another. Seeing her discomfort, Levalier decided to make the first move.

'Would Madame Chaplin care for some coffee?'

Paulette considered the new formality; the inclusion of her marital status changed the tone of their interaction completely. There was only one thing to do. Play along.

'She would,' she said. 'Though I dare say it's less of a "care" than a medical necessity.'

A maid poured coffee and brought it to her along with a selection of pastries, but Paulette was feeling too hungover to eat. She shook her head.

'*Arkuan*,' she managed. 'Thank you.'

The maid stifled a giggle at her attempt to speak Khmer and scurried away. On the tray was a tablet and glass of water.

'Aspirin,' said Levalier, not looking up from his paper. 'For your head.'

'Very thoughtful,' said Paulette. 'I don't suppose you have

anything … stronger?'

'This is not Hollywood,' answered Levalier coolly.

Paulette thought better of answering back with her usual sharpness and took the pill gratefully. There was another awkward pause as Paulette considered how to confront the elephant in the room. She had put off the breakfast meeting for as long as possible, but now she was sitting opposite the Frenchman she wanted to clear things up.

'About last night, I—'

'We enjoyed champagne, perhaps a bit too much. But Madame, I had no idea that you belonged to Charlot.'

'I don't "belong" to anyone, least of all Charlie!'

'I'd say your husband holds nothing dearer to his heart. If I had known of your …' he paused to find the word, 'intimacy, I would never have been so forward. So, in this case, Madame, it is I who must beg your forgiveness.'

'Perhaps when we're both done begging forgiveness in this awfully genteel exchange, perhaps we can continue to talk like human beings,' replied Paulette, eyes in her coffee but nonetheless grateful for the olive branch.

'Yes.' Levalier put down the newspaper and looks directly at Paulette. 'A scandal would be the least welcome outcome of your visit. For that we have your man to thank.'

'Frank is very loyal,' admitted Paulette, a trace of frustration there.

'So, may I speak frankly?'

Paulette nodded for him to continue. 'It has come to my attention that your husband is considering his next film in the French protectorate. I fear this would be a big mistake.'

'How did you know about that?'

'Here it pays to know everything.' He paused before continuing. 'Of course, it was rumoured he was considering the possibilities of the Little Vagabond in Indochine when he first arrived in Phnom Penh. But rumour is one thing; now it transpires that he is actively working on the subject, researching and preparing the story. I am sure he does not directly intend to create tension in the colony – but he should be aware, or made aware, that such an endeavour would threaten the equilibrium of our way of life here. Madame Chaplin, can't you dissuade him? I'd say there is no one he would listen to more.'

'Then you don't know Charlie very well at all. Once he gets an idea in his head, it will take more than a polite request to make him change his mind.'

'Then what would it take to make him stop?'

Paulette considered Levalier's question carefully before replying.

'Lift the ban on *Modern Times*, and release the picture,' she said eventually. Frank was not the only one loyal to Charlie.

28

For over an hour Charlie listened politely to Victor's theory that water shortages had caused the collapse of the great Khmer Empire, and tried not to worry about Phirath squashed into the boot of the car. The suspension had been shot by the frequent journeys to the capital and back and, as the count became more animated in his explanations, he drove faster and rougher – so much so that Charlie barely looked at the passing countryside. Instead, he had his eyes fixed on the road ahead, trying to anticipate every rut and jolt to keep his spine from shattering. Victor launched into a passionate account of King Jayavarman VII and the transition from Hinduism to Buddhism. How the Angkorian king was so obsessed with the power of his own image that he fused his own with that of Lord Buddha in the great temple of Bayon – the temple of the thousand faces. At another time, Charlie would have been interested in this subject. Image and their power were things he knew all about – albeit in a different form, time and place. But now what he longed for most was a stretch of smooth tarmacadamed road.

'And it was he who knew the importance of maintaining a constant water supply for his city. That is why he build the *borei* – the great waterworks around the temples that survive—'

But something made him stop. He held up his hand up for silence. Beneath the straining engine they heard the sound again. A bang from somewhere in the car. He shot Charlie a look and then skidded to a halt in a cloud of dust. Victor opened his door and walked round to the boot. The banging was more insistent now, coming from inside. Charlie was by his side when he opened the boot. Phirath clambered out with a respectful *sampeah* for the count and Charlie, and looked around him to get his bearings, rubbing a numb leg to restart the circulation.

'Perfect,' he said to neither of them. 'I can continue alone from here.'

And then, as if it was the most normal thing in the world for a fugitive to do, he took a leak over the paddy wall, letting out a sigh of pent-up release.

Not for the first time on the journey, the count found himself lost for words. His head jerked from Phirath to Charlie to the car and back again – a pantomime of bewilderment that would earn its place in a silent comedy.

'Ah,' said Charlie, knowing that this moment would have to come. Despite rehearsing his explanation in his head during the drive, Phirath had rather forced his hand.

'May I introduce Count Goloubew,' he said simply, and a little too casually. 'Victor this is my friend, a fellow actor, by the name of Phirath.'

Phirath shook himself off, wiped his hand on his shirt and held it out to Victor with a smile. But that was the final straw. Victor lunged for him. But the little man was too quick on his feet and they circled one another around the car as the count bellowed in Russian and Phirath barked back in Khmer. Eventually Charlie stepped between them, hands on both their chests trying to keep the peace.

'Count, please let me explain.'

But the count's blood was boiling. 'You forget where you are, Comrade Chaplin! If police find I have—'

'Do you see any police, Victor? There's just you and me and Phirath in the open countryside. Calm down, please! I need just a moment with Phirath, and then we can be back on our way. I will explain everything to you.'

Victor's eyes bulged with fury as Charlie steered Phirath off the road. But he never took his eyes off them. He cursed in Russian and lit a cigarette, pacing around the car.

'Will you be safe?' asked Charlie to Phirath out of earshot.

'They will not be looking here. And,' he added with a wry smile, 'to them, we all look the same. I can find my way. Thank you, Saklo.'

But Charlie wasn't done yet.

'What did he do? Your father?'

The mention of his father took Phirath by surprise. His smile faded; the fun of the chase, the evasion of the French authorities and Victor's comical reaction were all forgotten and replaced by a grim determination. Phirath looked hard at his idol, considering his response.

'I saw the photographs,' Charlie continued. 'The plantation owners, throats slit and tossed in the dirt. Did he do that to them?'

'I am not my father, Saklo. I have chosen my path and he chose his. He was arrested for his actions and imprisoned in Battambang. What good did that do?'

'So he did kill them?'

'No, Saklo. The photograph is a lie. Manufactured proof. The French lie to you too. This is how they always win. But not this time, Saklo. Not this time. And for that we have you to thank.'

He *sampeahed* and bowed low.

'Tomorrow night at sunset we will perform in the oldest Wat in Battambang. It will be a special performance. A performance of comedy and satire, where we will show the truth to our people. We will begin the long task of unmasking the French lies. We would be honoured if you would attend as our guest of honour.'

Charlie liked nothing more than defiance against authority, especially here in Indochina and after his altercations with the colonial police and the odious French captain. He had spent enough time in Phirath's company to respect him as a comic performer and appreciated his passion for his people. He'd gone this far to smuggle his friend out of the capital and saw no reason to stop. He nodded without a word. Phirath *sampeahed* once more, and then set off across the paddy dyke that ran between the rice fields.

When Charlie returned to the car, the count had just one word for him.

'Explain.'

Charlie nodded but gestured to the car. They climbed in and Victor turned on the ignition and the car coughed into life. He pulled away with a jolt, his anger making his driving even worse if that was possible.

'Who was that man, Charlot?'

'He's an actor like me. A very fine one, but from a traditional theatre troupe. They call it Lakhoun. Do you know of it?' The count merely glowered at the road ahead. Charlie added, 'Under his guidance, they have updated the way they perform, adding some very fine comedy. I've watched him rehearse in Phnom Penh. It's really quite something.'

Victor threw his hands to the heavens and cursed in Russian at the unsatisfactory explanation, leaving the steering wheel for so long that Charlie reached over to steer the car around a bend in the road.

'And he's not just an actor. I think he's probably my biggest fan in the whole region,' Charlie continued when the count was back in control of the vehicle. 'He knows every one of my movies, even the earlier ones.'

It was still not the explanation the count was expecting.

'He wanted a lift to Battambang where his troupe are performing a play, but he said the police wouldn't allow him to travel and I—'

'You bad liar.'

'I beg your pardon,' said Charlie, taken aback by the Count's forthright challenge.

'I'm serious, Charlot. Don't meddle in what you don't understand. These are not your people. They are not your friends.'

'I hardly think that—'

'French see everything. Know everything. Sûreté have eyes throughout the kingdom. This is not the West.'

'Then they'll be making a mountain out of a molehill!' The expression was lost on the Count. 'It's nothing! He's an actor. So am I. I'm just helping him get to his show because the French want him arrested for speaking his mind. Who would I be if I didn't help him?'

There was a silence then. Eventually he turned to Chaplin

and there was something like sadness on his face. The sadness of someone who has witnessed first-hand the full terror of sweeping political change in his home country.

'Then you are either naïve or foolish.'

Only a few miles ahead of them, a Sûreté police van sped down the same highway past a mile marker to Battambang. There was a hundred miles still to go, but as the van rounded a bend, it skidded to a halt on the dirt road. Ahead, taking up the full width of the road, was a traditional ox cart. It was laden with pottery – bowls, cups and rice-cake moulds lashed to the sides and stuffed with straw to prevent breakages. Inside the cart, ceramic stoves and larger items were stacked to the roof. The peddler and his family were from Kampong Chhnang, traversing the country and living on the road.

The Sûreté police van beeped its horn loudly but it took a while for the oxen to be cajoled to the side. The peddler was too slow, and the French driver, a Sergeant, was impatient. He grabbed his swagger stick and stepped out of the car. At the cart he waved the peddlers down with his swagger stick. They knew better than to refuse. But even so, when they moved too slowly for the Sergeant's liking, he helped them along with his stick. Soon the peddler and his family were squatting on the ground with their hands on their head.

'Don't look at me!' barked the police bully. The peddler held his gaze for a moment longer and then looked down at the dirt between his feet. In response, the policeman ransacked the cart and smashed pottery with his swagger stick. But inside there was more than ceramics. He found two sacks of rice. He beckoned over his colleagues from the police van and together they dragged out the sacks of rice and dumped them in the dirt. The sergeant then slashed both sacks with a knife and riced spilled out around his feet.

Behind them, and unaware of the incident ahead, Victor drove on. He seemed to have forgiven Charlie's earlier political insolence and softened. They had stopped a few times since Phirath's departure. Once for Charlie to marvel at the swaying emerald of the ripening rice fields. Another to watch the fishermen in the river. He'd used a few hundred feet of film in his camera. Now Charlie stared out of the window entranced by the flapping orange flags of a hilltop pagoda, only half listening to the count.

'They say colony is *mission civilisitrice* – bah! To make these rice peasants cultured Frenchmen in image of Hugo and Monet, Moliere and Degas. What they say, what they do, not same.'

'They seem to say a lot,' answered Charlie.

'Indeed. But rice farmers burn rice rather than give to French. They seem to not want to be Frenchmen.'

Just at that moment, they drove over the prow of a low hill and saw the peddler's cart and the police van ahead. Victor slowed to a stop behind them. The peasant peddlers had been put in a cangue – a wooden shackle around their necks, comprising heavy wooden poles lashed together like five-foot ladders. They squatted by the side of the road, the head of the family and his wife and children. The youngest was no more than ten years old, but he too had a cangue around his neck. The senior officer crouched by the peddler and whispered something in his ear. The man *sampeahed*, grovelling for mercy, but this only fuelled the Frenchman's sense of power and cruelty. The officer stood back, and then kicked him hard in the ribs. His wife whimpered, instinctively reaching for him and received a beating on her back. The boy cried out.

Charlie watched aghast. He'd seen the French treatment of Cambodians in the city streets, and it had appalled him there. But here in the countryside it was worse. The cangue was a brutal and humiliating means of subjection of the Khmer population. And the open display of cruelty sickened him to the very core of his being. The Tramp's defiance of authority was a staple of his comedies – and how Charlie had conquered the world in his early film. But he always played them for laughs as he outwitted and bamboozled those in power to re-set the balance for the downtrodden. Pratfalls, kicks up the backside and fist shaking saw the Tramp victorious or at least morally justified. It was a purely comic device, but there was nothing comic about what he was witnessing here. These were bullies, drunk on power and playing with the peddlers for sport. No comic choreography could help the Cambodian family. It was not the Tramp who was disgusted by their actions. It was Charlie himself. And the King of Comedy was brought face to face with the impotence of his position as a mere entertainer – in the face of a cruel and crushing reality.

He was about to get out of the car to intervene, but Victor held him back with a shake of his head and a shovel-sized hand on Charlie's forearm. Charlie settled back in his seat, trying not to watch, trying to remain removed from it. But when he saw a constable beat the peasant on his back with the truncheon for no reason whatsoever, it was too much. Charlie held back on the first whack, by the second he was out of the car and barrelling over, his face thunderous. He arrived in time to grab the policeman's baton before he could swing it a third time. The constable looked at him confused. Charlie ripped the baton from his hands and tossed it into the rice field. He shoved the bewildered policeman away without a word. But when he turned, he found the sergeant's swagger stick pressing into his chest.

For a moment the two men glared at each other. In a two-reeler this would be where the Tramp would choreograph a physical game to cut the policeman down to size. There would be no need for words. The actions would speak for themselves. But this wasn't one of his films and this wasn't taking place in the Chaplin Studios back lot.

'What you're doing is not human,' said Charlie simply, in English.

'He broke the law. Smuggling rice and owing taxes to the protectorate.' The officer knew enough English to reply. He didn't move. Neither did he lower his swagger stick.

'How much does he owe?' asked Charlie. 'I said, how much does he owe?'

'Two hundred and fifty piastres by our estimate, but that may as well be a million. He barely has twenty.'

Charlie took out his wallet, pulled out some piastre notes and tossed them to the dirt by the officer's feet. The officer looked at the money on the ground, to Charlie and back again, unsure how to deal with such an unfamiliar situation.

'American?' the Frenchman said with a sneer.

'Human,' Charlie said, his voice barely a whisper.

The pottery peddler kept his eyes on the dirt between his feet as the two men eyeballed one another. The officer leant so close that Charlie could smell cigarettes on his breath and see flecks of crusty spittle on the corner of his lips.

'You're Charlot,' he spat.

'Release him.'

'I could have you arrested.'

Not for the first time, Charlie offered his wrists to the French authorities. It was a simple gesture of defiance that pitted his fame against the offence. Once again, he triumphed. The fallout from the arrest of the world's greatest star would give the officer more trouble than it was worth. He glanced at the money in the dirt. Then shrugged and nodded to his colleague to unlock the cangue.

The family didn't move and remained squatting in the dirt, avoiding the foreigners' eyes and not understanding the change of circumstance unfolding before them.

'Now he belongs to you,' said the officer.

'You're free to go,' Charlie called over to the family. They didn't budge. 'You may go.'

The ox-cart driver finally lifted his eyes to Charlie, confused. This made no sense to him. Was it another cruel trick? Another game played by foreigners?

'Un … unlock them,' barked Charlie to the policeman. He was not even sure of the right words to use for the cangue. The policeman waited for the nod of approval from his superior and then did as he was told. Bewildered by the strange events, the peddler grabbed his wife's hand and his smallest child and they ran off the road and into the rice fields.

For a moment, no one moved. The officer was still in Charlie's face. The abandoned ox cart remained on the side of the road, with the police van and Victor's car behind it. No one spoke. There was only the sound of a light breeze rustling the rice fields, and the wooden bell around the oxen's harness.

Charlie spun on his heels, strode back to the car and sat

inside. His heart was racing. Victor looked at him sadly then put a hand on Charlie's narrow shoulders and squeezed.

'Even you can't buy them all.'

For once Charlie had no comeback. Victor pulled out and drove past the police van and ox cart and continued down the highway. It took a long while for Charlie's heart to calm and for his anger to fade as he replayed the moment again and again in his mind. Victor realised this was not the time for conversation or recrimination. It was only when the landscape began to change that Charlie felt himself relax. The calming distraction of his imagination took over as the rice fields gave way to rubber plantations. They sped past endless lines of trees on either side of the road with the occasional signboard indicating a plantation estate's ownership. Charlie found solace in his camera, and he pulled it from its case to film through the window. As he did so his imagination began to work.

29

ESTABLISHING SHOT: *A French post in the middle of a rubber plantation.*

We track along a line of Khmer plantation prisoners, each with a cangue around the neck and bare feet raised in wooden blocks. Behind them are the rows of rubber trees on the plantation estate, but they sit in the dirt in front of a police post. We continue down the line of bare feet in blocks until we find the oversized shoes of the Tramp, shackled next to Phirath. Supervising the line of prisoners is a French policeman in uniform, who flicks away flies in the heat, about to nod off. The keys to the shackles are on the desk on the veranda of the police post.

The Tramp looks along the line of feet, and up to the grim faces of his fellow captors. There's a bowl of gruel out of reach in front of them. The Tramp's stomach growls. He catches Phirath's despairing eyes, grins and tries to make light of it. Somehow his derby is still on his head. When he looks back to the desk, the officer is now asleep and snoring.

Then Descartes, the poodle belonging to the governor's daughter, bounds up with his eyes bright and his tongue lolling in the heat. He looks at the prisoners, tail wagging, but goes straight for the bowl and begins to lap up the watery gruel. The Tramp nudges Phirath. He tries to explain, silently nodding towards the dog at the gruel bowl and the keys on the officer's desk.

The Tramp whistles as loudly as he dares. Descartes' ears prick up and he looks over and slowly pads across the veranda and down the steps towards them. Phirath shakes his head earnestly, but the Tramp is on a mission. He whistles again, careful not to disturb the sleeping policeman until Descartes has come over to him. He scratches the dog under his chin and the dog barks. The Tramp puts his finger to his lips and seems to be connecting with the little animal. He points over to the keys, urging the dog on with a smile, cajoling the animal.

Slowly and with no sense of urgency, the dog trots over to the desk and looks back to the Tramp for encouragement. With an athletic bound, Descartes jumps onto the desk, grabs the keys in his mouth and jumps back down. All eyes are on the policeman. He stirs, gets comfortable again, and continues to snore. Neither the bark nor the jangling have woken him. The dog pads over to the Tramp with the keys in his mouth.

The Tramp takes the keys and pats Descartes' head. Then unlocks his feet and those of Phirath beside him. Then unlocks the cangue around his neck but fumbles with the keys and they clatter to the ground. The cangue drops off from around his neck, but the policeman wakes up. For a moment he scans the line of prisoners, thinking nothing of it. Every prisoner is still and silent, and looking down at the ground. His sleepy gaze passes over the Tramp and continues down the line until something makes his eyes widen with realisation. He whips them back to the Tramp to find his cangue missing. The Tramp grins nonchalantly as though nothing has changed -- but the policeman reaches for his whistle and gives it a shrill blast.

The Tramp grabs Phirath, still with the five-foot cangue around his neck, and pulls him away. In his other hand he picks up Descartes and the two men start running.

CUT TO: the rubber plantation proper. The police are chasing the two escaped prisoners through the trees. It's difficult to see through the rows upon rows of trees in every direction. The Tramp grabs Phirath and hides behind one. It's fine for him, but Phirath's cangue sticks out. He has to do some athletic gymnastics to position the cangue vertically behind the tree, with his neck still in it, in order to hide from view. But the plan works. The police run past, whistles blasting. They wait until quiet returns to the plantation. Then the cangue rights horizontally and we see Phirath and the Tramp peer out from the tree. The coast is clear. They're safe for now.

The walk off through the trees in the opposite direction to their police pursuers. Soon they pass a discarded rubber collection pail. The Tramp puts Descartes inside the pail and pulls the strap over his shoulder.

CUT TO: Inside the mansion, the governor's daughter sits at her window crying and calling out.

INTERTITLE: Descartes! Descartes!

The shouts carry across the lawn in front of the mansion to where the two prisoners are skirting the edge of the plantation. The Tramp turns back at the sound, but Phirath pulls him on with a shake of the head. The Tramp presents Descartes as evidence and gestures back to the mansion. Phirath sighs, then nods and they leave the safe cover of the trees and dart across towards the mansion.

30

After their awkward exchange in the morning, Paulette had left Levalier to his business and was sitting on the veranda with her mother, fanning herself with her straw hat. She was dressed simply in a light summer dress and sandals. She wanted to look her best for Charlie's arrival. Across the table, her mother stirred her drink with a finger, toying with the ice cubes. She picked one out and wiped it across her forehead. Her mother was oblivious to the incident the night before and Paulette had no intention of telling her. Nevertheless, the silence between them was awkward, and Paulette felt her mother's eyes drilling into her for an explanation. Only when they heard the distant sound of an engine backfiring and tyres on gravel did Paulette meet her mother's eyes. A maid and valet hurried down the veranda steps. Paulette fussed with her hair and adjusted the straps of her dress.

'How do I look?' she asked her mother.

'Single.' Her mother's terse reply was barely audible as she crunched an ice cube.

They watched the car pull into the driveway. Charlie and Victor were met by Levalier and ushered inside to freshen up. Moments later Charlie and Mr Yonamori were alone in a guest room. Charlie stood before a full-length mirror in more formal attire as Mr Yonamori brushed down his travel-creased slacks and folded them away. Charlie seemed lost in thought, the events of the journey weighing heavily on him.

'I bought you a wooden bowl ... lacquer ... thing,' he managed.

Mr Yonamori took the small bowl, confused.

'Very thoughtful, sir,' he replied.

'Chevalier behaved himself?' he enquired, a little too offhand.

'He's very ... French, sir,' was his manservant's diplomatic reply. And he started to buff Charlie's shoes with a cloth. There was a knock at the door and Paulette swept into the room.

'Thank you, Frank,' Charlie said, dismissing Mr Yonamori.

The couple stood apart for a moment. The short separation had weighed on them both.

'We were waiting on the veranda,' said Paulette. 'I thought I'd give you a moment to change after the journey.'

But as soon as Mr Yonamori left, Paulette leapt at Charlie smothering him in a tight embrace and kissing his cheeks and forehead.

'I missed you terribly,' she said simply.

Charlie kissed her forehead fondly. His kiss didn't have the same guilty passion as Paulette's. In fact, it was distant and he was clearly distracted. Paulette's face fell. She watched him as he unbuttoned the cuffs on a fresh shirt and rolled up the sleeves.

'Charlie?'

But instead of answering, he went over to the window and stared at the rubber plantation beyond the lawn.

'Charlie! I'm over here.'

When Charlie spoke, it was more to himself than to his wife.

'I saw a man beaten within an inch of his life for stealing a handful of rice. His own damned rice that he'd planted, grown and reaped. It was … it was inhuman! Do people in Europe know? In America? Do they know what goes on in places like this? They need to, Paulette, people need to know—'

'No. No, Charlie, not today. Please!'

His outburst left Paulette frustrated and hurt. She recognised the tone in his voice. It was the voice he used when he was obsessively fixated on a subject. Thoughts were whirling through his mind, piling up on one another. He saw himself not at the window of the Frenchman's estate, but in the corridors of power, a politician, banging his hand on the table, making impassioned speeches in the Senate or to the League of Nations, the fury of his convictions demanding and determining outcomes. But his words only occasionally caught up with his thoughts – he spluttered unconnected fragments of his anger, without context or explanation or sympathy for those who were listening. And she knew that this would not be changed by her barrage of guilty kisses, nor her desperate desire to be held close by her husband.

'You know,' Charlie continued, still avoiding her eyes, 'I feel like we were actually led to this place. We were led to Levalier's damned plantations and led to this country, here and now. I'm supposed to be here. And I'm supposed to set my next picture here.'

'We didn't come here for that, Charlie. Have you forgotten?'

'It's like the Tramp has a mission, a new injustice to expose—'

'Please, Charlie, let other people be political. Just be yourself, be funny!'

And those were the words she knew would penetrate. It may

have sounded casual, but it was as planned a line of dialogue as she'd ever heard in any movie or play.

'The world needs to laugh. Perhaps here more than anywhere,' she continued, reeling him back from the edge.

'In Indochina? No, Paulette, that's not enough.'

'*Red Dust* was funny. Can't you write me a part like Vantine?' She continued as Jean Harlow with her high-pitched devil-may-care voice, 'Gee, Denny, I don't want any ceremonies, but, but … turn around and give me the works!'

And she came up behind him and turned him around, smiling.

'The full works,' she added, and they kissed, and this time the kiss turned into something more. He slid the straps of her dress off her shoulders and carried her to the four-poster bed.

'The door,' whispered Paulette. 'What if mother comes to find out what's keeping us?'

'I'm sure she'd approve,' said Charlie. He kissed the top of her arm, then up to her collar bone.

They'd been together long enough to know exactly how to please each other, without words or reassurances. And they were both trying to push their respective and intrusive thoughts away by physical intimacy; Paulette's guilt after the dance with Levalier, and Charlie's experiences on the drive with Victor. It wasn't the anger against the inhuman treatment of the Cambodian plantation workers that festered, but the sense of powerlessness that it created. That he, Charlie Chaplin, was just a visitor, just a spectator, a member of the Indo-Chinese audience, not the director of events. So he pushed it all away for a moment and lost himself in needy breathless sex. Afterwards, Charlie washed Paulette in a copper bathtub. He poured steaming water from a pail over her back and squeezed suds from a large sponge. Paulette smiled, chin on her knees, absorbing every single touch and moment of Charlie's rare tenderness.

'Maybe I should write a scene like this,' said Charlie quietly. 'The Tramp and the governess's daughter.'

And with that their precious stolen moment together receded further, like smoke dispersing into the sky. Paulette tried not to let it upset her.

'That would get Hedda Hopper's knickers in a twist,' she replied brightly.

'Doesn't Hollywood feel like a world away?' He lifted her chin and looked into her eyes for a long silent moment. Eventually Paulette twisted away.

'You want to make a girl blush,' she said eventually, and splashed her face with water.

'Bit late for that, wouldn't you say?

'If you don't tell, I won't.'

'I love you.'

'I know, Charlie. I know.'

'You're my Gamin. The Tramp needs his Gamin. Without you – well, who'd stop me charging off, tilting at windmills, political or real? Who'd bring me back? Promise me, Paulette, promise me that whenever I get too big for my oversized boots, you'll tell me. I think you're the only woman I've ever known who has the courage to do so.'

Paulette desperately wanted to fire back, 'and you've known a few' but bit her tongue. It was not the time for sparring. So she said nothing.

In the lazy heat of the afternoon, Charlie and Paulette lay

atop the bedcovers as the ceiling fan turned above them. Paulette woke and snuggled into Charlie's chest, dressed only in a simple negligee. She carefully removed Charlie's arm and sat up on the bed. The others would be wondering where they were. No doubt Frank would have come to their rescue with an effortless believable lie – maybe about the heat, or a headache. She went to the louvre windows to light a cigarette. She was silhouetted against the afternoon sky, and when she turned back, Charlie was sitting up and staring at her, drinking her in.

'Don't move,' he whispered. He rummaged in his bag for his camera and lifted it to his eye. For a moment, only the sound of the fan and the motor of the camera could be heard. Then a *tokai*, a large grey-blue lizard, croaked from the veranda.

To-kai, it croaked. *To-kai, to-kai, to-kai*, fading out as if it was taking the last gasp of life.

Charlie walked closer until Paulette filled the viewfinder; she inhaled deeply from her cigarette, then blew a perfect smoke ring into the lens.

* * *

WIDE SHOT: *the governor's mansion.*

Against the wall we find Phirath bent double so that the Tramp can climb up the cangue still around his neck and grip the windowsill above him. He leaps athletically up and inside. Phirath hands him the pail with Descartes waiting patiently inside.

Inside her room, the governor's daughter is weeping at the window. She doesn't notice as the Tramp opens the door and approaches her shyly. He coughs and the governor's daughter spins round. He smiles and shrugs at her surprise. Then he reaches into the rubber tapping pail and lifts out Descartes, paws still stuck with latex as an explanation.

INTERTITLE: My darling!

The Tramp turns away shyly, but then realises it's not him whom she's addressing. The governor's daughter rushes over to take Descartes, covering the dog in frantic kisses.

INTERTITLE: Thank you, thank you. You must allow me to repay your kindness.

INTERTITLE: There's really nothing to repay. Just tell me your name.

The governor's daughter looks shyly back.

INTERTITLE: Angeline.

The Tramp takes off his hat with a nonchalant smile, suddenly awkward in her presence when something makes them start. The sound of shouting getting louder and louder. They rush to the window as the shouts become louder, but still a cacophony of overlapping calls.

INTERTITLE: Down with the French!

INTERTITLE: French out of Kampuchea!

INTERTITLE: Release Khmer prisoners!

From the window they look out to see Khmer farmers and rubber tappers holding flaming torches gathering in front of the governor's mansion. Phirath is amongst them. They beat bark knives against their pails as they march towards the entrance of the mansion.

The governor's daughter turns to the Tramp, fear evident in her expression. The bewildered Tramp doesn't know what to think or do. But she seems to have a plan. She takes her father's jacket

from the back of a chair and begins to dress the bemused Tramp.
She rams on her father's hat. A pleading look to the Tramp.

INTERTITLE: They'll kill us! You must speak to them.

INTERTITLE: Me? What should I say?

INTERTITLE: Anything. If you don't, they won't stop until
we're both dead. You must pretend you're my father. Pretend to
be the governor and talk to them. Tell them that in the future
things will be better.

The intertitles are growing increasing cramped as more and
more words are required.

CUT TO: the balcony of the governor's mansion.

The Tramp is shoved out onto a balcony above the lawn which
is crowded with hostile Khmer peasants. He looks completely
bewildered, dressed in the governor's jacket and hat. He tries
to go back inside, as a hush descends on the gathering, but the
governor's daughter pushes him out again. He stands before them
and holds his hand out for quiet.

A silence falls over the angry mob. The tramp surveys the
angry crowd, then speaks.

INTERTITLE: I don't want to be a governor … That's not
my business.

CLOSE UP: angry faces in the crowd. Then back to the
Tramp on the balcony. He's not sure. He takes a step forward.
Then another, looking straight ahead, directly into the camera,
and with no intertitles.

'I should like to help everyone,' he says in a clipped English
accent, adding, 'if possible. We all want to help one another.
Human beings are like that.'

There are some taunts from the crowd. Some laughter and

curses in Khmer. But Phirath, standing at their head, holds up his hand for quiet. They crane forwards to listen.

'On ... on this earth, in ... in this colony,' the Tramp stammers, 'there should be room for everyone. Our way of life can be free and beautiful, but ...' and he trails off for a moment, searching for the words. 'But we have lost our way.'

31

The sound of a car on the gravel driveway broke Charlie's imagination and brought the scene in his head to a premature end. He stood at the window of Levalier's mansion as the two-reeler slipped away. How long had he been standing there? Long enough for Paulette to have fallen asleep once more on the bed behind him. And out of the window there was no crowd of angry rubber plantation workers demanding change. Instead, he saw Levalier's car kick up dirt and skid to a stop at the main entrance. The Frenchman beeped the horn loudly and woke Paulette from her afternoon doze. She joined Charlie at the window and rubbed his shoulders and kissed his ear.

While Charlie chased the scene in his head, Paulette glanced down at the desk and saw his open notebook. Even from that distance, it was clear that he'd been writing dialogue. She smiled, moving closer to try and decipher the scrawls on the page. There was an exchange between the Tramp and the governor's daughter, the dialogue clearly marked beneath their names. But before she could make any further sense of it, Charlie snapped out of his daydream. Seeing Paulette's attention was on his notebook, he tried to snatch it away, but Paulette grabbed it first. She skipped away and ran back to the other side of the coffee table, then to the bed, with Charlie chasing her.

'Paulette, please,' he managed, fighting the urge to let his annoyance creep into his voice.

The four-poster bed was between them. Paulette was breathless, excited, not daring to believe.

'A talkie?'

Charlie just shrugged.

'And how will the Little Fellow speak?' she asked.

'I haven't decided yet,' said Charlie. Then in a cockney accent he added, 'Maybe e's a geezer, brought up by the sparra' sellers in the Spank.'

Paulette laughed, understanding none of it, but loving how Charlie's eyes lit up with the possibilities.

'Or perhaps he's a wronged country squire temporarily, rather permanently as it happens, down on his luck,' he continued with his best impersonation of a faded, fallen aristocrat.

Paulette laughed again and read aloud from his notebook.

'I don't want to be a governor. That's not my business.' She put on a posh English accent for the role, but as she read on her voice trailed off and her smile faded.

For a moment they stared at each other across the bed. Her eyes full of pain, his of resignation. She checked again, turning the pages, skimming through the handwritten dialogue.

'Paulette,' whispered Charlie. 'Please—'

For an answer, she threw the notebook at him. It fluttered and fell on top of the bedsheets.

'You don't like it?' Charlie looked genuinely upset.

'Isn't the point of motion pictures to escape reality, not confront it?'

'I told you. It's a comedy. *Colonial Subjects*.'

'A rather politically pointed one. This isn't the Tramp. This is you.'

'And what's wrong with that?' Charlie's hackles were up, as they often were when he was creating. He was very sensitive to criticism, especially from Paulette, his muse and his wife. 'Haven't I earned the right to speak my mind?'

'Oh Charlie, you've never understood, have you?' said Paulette quietly. There was a real sadness in her words. The sadness of a dawning and irreversible realisation. 'The Tramp should speak, but you should not.'

Her words lingered over the silence and settled on the bed on top of the rumpled sheets and the memory of their recent closeness.

'Then maybe,' said Charlie after a long pause, 'then maybe it's time for the Little Fellow to go.'

'You don't mean that!'

But Charlie couldn't meet her eyes. The enormity of such a decision deserved a grander moment. Would biographers look back and choose this as the moment around which his later career would pivot? Was it here after a stolen afternoon on a stranger's bed, where the sheets were still damp and the ceiling fan was turning, that he would kill his alter-ego, the character on which he'd built his fame and his fortune? The Tramp who was imitated and adored across the world from Phnom Penh to Buenos Aires, Cairo to Petrograd. The Tramp, the everyman, the plucky visualisation of hope. And if not hope, at least derision of class and feistiness against abuses of authority.

'But the Tramp is the most famous nobody the world has ever

seen,' said Paulette.

'That might be true. But who am I? They've never seen me. The real me. Not the Little Fellow. Not me the celebrity, the filmmaker, the King of Comedy. The real me.' Charlie's voice was low, almost pleading. 'I'm the most famous somebody the world has never seen.'

'Oh Charlie, that's your tragedy, isn't it? Isn't that why you're always so sad? You've hidden behind the Tramp for so long, ashamed of who you were and where you came from, and now you want to show the world the real you – but don't be surprised if no one is interested. Don't you understand? All they want is the Tramp. They just want him to speak.'

'Then that's even more reason for the little fellow to go,' Charlie said again.

'You can't really mean that, can you?' Paulette added, no longer sure.

But Charlie had already turned his attention to the window. He saw a police car arrive and park behind Levalier's limousine. Le Favre stepped out and greeted Levalier like they were old friends.

'Charlie, answer me. You don't … you can't mean that.'

'What does he want now?' Charlie ignored her, and the troubling direction of her questioning. He didn't want this to be that moment, so he deflected his attention elsewhere.

There was a knock at their door and that pivotal but fleeting moment was lost in the business of being a house guest. They never spoke of it again, but the image of the ruffled sheets and Charlie's notebook cast atop them would stay with Charlie for a long time.

They dressed in silence. Moments later, Paulette and Charlie waited at the top of the steps with Victor. Levalier and Le Favre were deep in conversation. Le Favre tossed over a set of big keys to a uniformed plantation supervisor. The police van reversed away and Le Favre finally spotted the couple on the steps.

'Monsieur Chaplin!' he called out, smiling.

'Odious little man,' whispered Charlie to Paulette, but waved and smiled. Paulette dug him in the ribs but waved too.

'Mademoiselle,' Le Favre said.

The little bow was so damned French that Paulette nearly laughed out loud.

'The governor has made a special request for me to personally escort you to Battambang. I had hoped to catch you before your arrival, but the count drives too fast.'

'That's very kind of you, above and beyond,' said Charlie back.

The captain didn't understand the expression. But he pushed on as he climbed the steps towards them. 'The countryside can be dangerous for Frenchmen these days.'

'I'm not French.'

By this point Le Favre was right up in Charlie's face.

'You are to them,' he said.

And pointed to where the supervisor and some Sûreté policemen pushed a line of eight Khmer prisoners forwards. They had cangues around their necks. Their sarongs were hitched up, and it was evident that they'd been both beaten and broken under the French supervisor. They were loaded into the back of the police van.

'Deterrence is the only way to maintain control of French

assets,' Le Favre said, as lightly as if he was considering a mixer for his afternoon Dubonnet. 'Wouldn't you agree, Laurent?'

Levalier shrugged indifferently.

Before the prisoners could reach the van, one tried to break free. He was still in the cangue and ran for the cover of the trees, but he didn't get far before the Sûreté police caught him again. He was hauled back and beaten on his back and legs until he crumpled onto the lawn. Wood against flesh makes a dull sound but the man's cries echoed off the walls of Levalier's villa. Paulette turned away in horror. Eventually two officers brought the staggering prisoner back to the police van and slung him inside.

Paulette buried her face in Charlie's shoulder.

Victor saw Charlie's expression and leant in to whisper to him. 'Now perhaps you know why I care only for ancient temples.'

'Where will they be taken?' asked Charlie.

'In my country, we have gulag. Here it is Battambang prison that creates the same fear. Officially, there are four hundred political prisoners there. But I hear it is three times that.'

Le Favre calmly tapped out a cigarette on its box and put it to his lips. He relished the display of his power and control – not just over the Khmer prisoners, but the effect it had on the problematic guests of the French protectorate.

'Actions speak louder than words,' he offered casually. 'A sentiment I believe you share.'

Charlie thought twice about wiping the grin off the Frenchman's face with his fist, and instead turned away. Le Favre lit his cigarette and waved off the police van.

'I will see you in Battambang,' he said and disappeared inside Levalier's villa.

A hand slipped into Charlie's. Paulette gave him a reassuring squeeze and pulled him away to the shade of the veranda. Chaplin paced, itching to go back inside to give the captain a piece of his mind, but Paulette held him back.

'What's the use of trying,' she said, as the Gamin from the final scene of *Modern Times*. She hoped for the response from the Tramp that followed, but instead she received only a steely stare. She nudged him further. 'Buck up! Never say die.'

'Easy for us to say.' It was all Charlie could manage at that moment. 'Let's go.'

'Finally, something you've said that makes sense, dear. We've stayed here too long.'

32

Half an hour later the guests were nearly ready to leave. Charlie waited by the car, impatient to leave the plantation and its insufferable cruelty. Levalier swaggered over and offered Charlie a cigarette, but the filmmaker declined. He wanted it to be absolutely clear how he detested his host and the way he and the other Frenchmen conducted their business in the colony.

'As you wish,' Levalier said and lit his own, leaning on the car. 'I don't understand you. You are wealthy beyond measure, a global star. The world loves you. So why do you need to continue making films?'

'Because I'm a filmmaker,' said Charlie tartly.

'Didn't I read that you're retired?'

'So the French press would have you believe.'

'Perhaps you should, Charlot. The twenties are over, and the cruel reality of the world is once more upon us. Haven't you earned the right to sit back and enjoy it?' He paused and then added, 'With your wife.'

Charlie didn't respond. The truth was that just a few days ago, this was exactly his thinking. Those closest to him knew he was prone to protesting he was finished with motion pictures after each and every film. But this time, Charlie really thought he had.

Talkies had eclipsed his silent Tramp. New stars and new stories were needed for new times. He didn't need to make another picture ever again – not for financial reasons in any case. His legacy was as secure as his wealth. But then, he was also only in his forties. What else would he do?

'I should find out what's keeping them,' he said finally, not liking the direction of his thoughts.

'She'll leave you, Charlot,' said Levalier as he was about to go inside.

Charlie stopped.

'In her heart, I think she already has.'

Charlie retraced his steps until he was right up in Levalier's face. He was slight compared to the Frenchman, but there was no doubting his passion, and Levalier took an involuntary step back. Charlie leant closer still.

'Perhaps she will,' he said with a smile. 'But never for the likes of you.'

Just then Paulette, her mother and Mr Yonamori came out of the villa, ready to leave. While Frank added the last items of their luggage to Victor's car, Charlie held open the door for his mother-in-law and his wife. He climbed in after them and they drove away without a backwards glance. Once out of the gates, Charlie finally relaxed and took Paulette's hand in his and squeezed it.

'To Battambang then,' he said.

'To Battambang,' shouted the count and pounded the steering wheel.

* * *

As Charlie and his party drove towards Battambang, a sampan arrived before them and pulled up at the river's edge. A Khmer man staggered off, holding a bottle of rice wine and singing drunkenly. Ahead of him was a French checkpoint. He stumbled over and two French officers blocked his path. It looked like the man had pissed himself, and the smell was overpowering. The officers were half stern and half laughing as he tripped and tumbled into the arms of the nearest who shoved him away in disgust. The drunk went sprawling but managed to save his precious rice wine at the expense of cracking his head on the brick wall. He lay there for a while and started to sing. The French officers exchanged glances. Then they walked over and heaved him up by his armpits. He offered them a swig from his bottle, but they recoiled from his breath and shoved him on. He staggered away from the checkpoint, zigzagging, barely able to stand.

It took him a while to weave his way past the colonial townhouses, through the market building and on towards the pagoda. Inside the compound, the theatre troupe had already erected the bamboo stage in front of the vihara steps. They were busy unloading instruments, costumes and trunks of props from their truck while Saloth Sar stayed at the entrance to keep guard. In Phirath's absence it was the prince who took charge, barking instructions and preparing for the performance.

The drunk swayed past Saloth Sar and staggered straight over to the prince and offered him the nearly empty bottle of rice wine. The prince shoved him away, busy with the preparations and cursing Phirath's absence. But the drunk was insistent. He tripped again, and this time collapsed into the prince. But as he did so he pulled him back behind the vihara wall. In an instant, the drunk's manner changed. It was Phirath of course. Sober. Serious. Determined. He took off the simple disguise and stripped off his stinking clothes.

'Everything is ready?' he asked in Khmer. The prince nodded. 'The weapons?'

'Everything is as you planned.'

'Good.'

'Phirath, the Sûreté are looking for you.'

'And they'll find me soon enough,' Phirath replied.

33

If Levalier's villa was designed to show off French culture and colonial superiority, Count Victor Goloubew's estate was far less ostentatious. Perhaps once it might have been considered the height of colonial style. There were still peacocks roaming in the grounds. The landscaped garden had banyan trees and tamarinds, but the bougainvillea had taken over. It crawled through one wing of the crumbling mansion, eating further and further into it. Many of the roof tiles were missing and sheets of tarpaulin covered swathes of the roof. It looked abandoned.

The guests exchanged nervous glances and Paulette's mother looked aghast. The last visit had been a disaster, and this was looking even worse. Why could they not just get on with their business, get out of the country and back to civilization?

But Victor was clearly delighted to be home again. The car lurched to a halt. He parped the horn triumphantly and flung open the car door. He breathed deeply, grinned, and then gallantly opened the door for Paulette's mother and offered her his hand. She took it hesitantly and climbed out, scanning the crumbling villa. Mortified.

'Are these the ruins of Angkor?' she whispered icily in Paulette's ear.

'On academic salary, this is not to Levalier's standard. But welcome is no less – how do you say? – hearty?'

'Yes, hearty,' said Charlie. 'Thank you.' Then he whispered to Paulette, 'Hearty or Hearsty?' He took her hand and followed the count. 'It's like a poor man's version of Hearst Castle.'

'Without the champagne fountains,' smiled Paulette. 'Or zebras.'

She was referring to Sir William Randolph's Hearst's extravagant San Simeon castle in California. She and Charlie had been to quite a few parties there. But they belonged to another world and another time, even if the Count was, in his own way, no less eccentric than the infamous newspaper baron. In fact, Victor's grounds had such a sense of faded grandeur and charm that Charlie immediately fell for the place. He felt his spirits return as they crunched up the gravel towards the entrance. Levalier's villa might have been immaculate, manicured and with all the modern facilities, but it was built on the blood and toil of the plantation workers who lived on the estate. This felt altogether less tainted.

Victor strode up to the house, kicked away a chicken on the veranda and threw open the double doors. The guests followed him in.

Inside was as eccentric and unkempt as the outside. The entrance hall was a time capsule to the early 1920s and he ushered his guests into a kind of parlour room which had the feel of a Victorian collector's study. It was cluttered with books, lithograph prints, sculptures, maps, stuffed animals, sketches, even a scale model of the Bayon temple. He cleared away some space on a chaise longue and offered it to Paulette's mother. She sat down so gingerly it looked to Charlie that she was actually hovering above it.

'Neang!' shouted Victor opening the shutters. He flicked the switch for the ceiling fan. Nothing. On and off in rapid succession, and then gave up with a shrug. 'Please, please, sit. Anywhere you can. Nothing is important. Move anything. Neang! Damn the girl.'

And then a side door opened and a flustered middle-aged Khmer woman, the housekeeper, appeared. She saw the guests and froze in an almost comic pantomime of sheer terror. She would have been even more terrified if she knew who they were.

'We have *fourth* guests,' bellowed Victor in broken Khmer.

The housekeeper didn't move. Was it shock? Or was his Khmer so bad she didn't understand? Paulette hid her giggles behind a sudden fascination for a series of maps on an open bureau, beside a stuffed mongoose.

'Make the guest rooms,' he said in Khmer. Then gave up. 'See to it!'

And he followed her out, shooing. She batted him away playfully but scurried off down a corridor. They heard a light squeal and Charlie and Paulette smiled. At the bureau Charlie put his arm through hers. He peered at a series of prints of apsaras from the temple walls, dancers with serene faces, fingers twisted into the classical gestures – and bare-breasted.

'Like what you see?' asked Paulette.

'Are they even anatomically possible?'

'How's a poor wife to compete?' And she elbowed him in the ribs and returned to her mother. The housekeeper marched back in and beckoned the ladies to follow her. Charlie nodded to Yonamori to attend to them.

A moment later Victor returned to find Charlie alone in the entrance hall admiring the various ornaments and clutter.

'Are you an adventurous man, Mr Chaplin?' he said. 'Or would you like to freshen up with the ladies?'

It was more of an invitation than a question. Charlie shrugged with a smile and that was all the encouragement Victor needed. He gestured for his guest to follow.

'You may wish to bring your camera,' he added.

At the back of the house was an outbuilding of sorts. Victor pulled open the creaking wooden door. Chickens clucked and scrammed, and there in the straw and dust was an open-topped Ford Model T.

Charlie was over to it in a second, running his hands across the bonnet and admiring it. 'I used to have one of these you know.' He peered inside. A rueful shake of his head and he put the memory away. 'But later,' he added, 'well, it was Ford's production line factories that I was so against in *Modern Times*.'

'Yes,' said Victor, not having a clue what Charlie was talking about.

'Ford Model T. Somehow I would have expected something more ... *grandiozhny*.'

'Big car belongs to *lycée*. For myself, car is car. And this is ... sufficient.'

'And this is the adventure?' asked Charlie doubtfully.

'*Nyet!*' Victor laughed at the very idea. 'Would you?'

He held out the starting crank. Chaplin took off his jacket and flung it on a table which erupted in a cloud of dust. He rolled up his sleeves and put the crank in place as Victor dropped into the driver's seat. The car's rudimentary suspension creaked in protest.

'Ready?'

Chaplin turned the handle. There was a loud backfire and it coughed into life.

Maybe it was the childish thrill of an unexpected adventure, or maybe it was the distance from Phnom Penh's pomp and protocol, or maybe he just wanted to forget the awkward moment at Levalier's villa – and the even more difficult decision he knew he must soon make – but despite himself, Charlie grinned and leapt athletically into the car.

'Drive on, Count Goloubew!' He gestured forwards. 'Adventure beckons!'

Chickens squawked in all directions and the Model T roared out of the barn, just missing a peacock whose proud display went limp in alarm. They were soon a cloud of dust racing through the gates and out onto the open dirt road.

Victor's driving on the way up from Phnom Penh had clearly been toned down out of respect for the Peugeot 601's owners at the *lycée*. With the Model T he had no such qualms. He drove it hard down the dusty track, veering into thickets and riding up ditches. They turned off onto a paddy dyke which led away from the centre of town. It was barely wider than the car but Victor drove as erratically as if driving along the Champs-Élysées itself.

'If thing works, I use. If not, I replace. Model T never fail.'

Charlie considered setting him straight about the conditions in the Ford assembly lines, where human beings had been turned into automaton slaves for profit and progress. It was the inspiration for the factory set up of *Modern Times* of course, but he knew that Victor was unlikely to care about his political treatise. And to be honest, his mind was more focussed on the track ahead. He hung onto the car door, trying to anticipate every jolt and roll, but Victor continued as if he was talking over a cup of tea in the hotel lobby.

'Progress always comes. Bolshevik, fascist, industrialist, peasant. All same to me.'

It was not the time for Charlie to discuss his own political leanings, nor the part he'd been asked to play in Phirath's performance. Fortunately for Charlie, the count seemed to have forgotten the smuggling of the comic actor across the French checkpoints out of Phnom Penh. Out of the capital the count's mind was focussed instead on his real passion, the magnificent, ruined temples of Angkor.

'Where are you taking me?' asked Charlie beginning to worry about leaving Paulette and her mother behind for so long.

'When you see from air, you will know. Everything else? Nothing!'

And with that they burst through a knot of sugar palms and arrived at a wide river. Next to a wooden jetty bobbed a seaplane. Victor skidded to a halt and the dust billowed around the car. He killed the engine and suddenly everything was still and quiet.

Victor jumped down and Charlie rubbed the small of his back taking a moment to recover after the drive. The sight of Victor striding towards the seaplane made him nervous. Was this the adventure? The CAMS37 biplane had a single propeller behind the wings and looked like a relic of a major air battle. Bullet holes had strafed one side. The holes were rusty. It must have been a long-forgotten battle. Charlie was doubtful whether there had been any maintenance since.

Victor walked down the jetty and climbed into the cockpit,

and there was nothing else to do but follow. It took Charlie a while to find his footing up and into the cramped seat beside the count. When he had settled in, Victor switched on the engine without any explanation or briefing. The huge propellers turned 180 degrees but sputtered out. Victor shifted the throttle. This time the engine took and held, and the propellors spun until they were a blur with just the yellow tips creating a circle. Black smoke billowed from the engine casing.

'Are you sure she'll fly?' shouted Charlie.

He received a thumbs up for his troubles. Victor put on some goggles and gestured for Charlie to do the same.

'I do most of my work from the sky!' he shouted over the din. 'Only from sky can you see all. Are you ready for real adventure?'

He didn't wait for Charlie to reply, and soon they were thundering down the river before lifting off gently into the sky. They cleared the treeline as the river snaked round to the west, and then climbed steeply. Charlie looked down as they flew over the dense jungle. He could see the shadow of the seaplane rippling over the tree canopy below. He leaned out and filmed with his camera, gripping the strap tightly. Seeing this, Victor banked in the direction the camera was pointing and Charlie felt his stomach lurch. They flew in low, coming out of a big dive and straightening up. Through the viewfinder, Charlie focused on a clearing and a small village pagoda. A few Khmer farmers looked up at the noise and waved. They had evidently witnessed the seaplane flying overhead many times. Charlie smiled and filmed more. He wished he'd brought more film stock. He tracked the farmers as they passed behind them until he felt Victor's hand tapping his shoulder and pointing forwards.

Charlie looked ahead. The smile faded; he lowered his camera. There, behind the setting sun, the five towers of Angkor Wat rose majestically from the tree canopy. Silhouetted, they became both massive and delicate as they pointed up towards the sky. They emerged from the unbroken expanse of the jungle like an offering from the natural world to the gods. For someone who prided himself on exploring, celebrating – even championing – the minutiae of the human condition and human behaviour, Charlie was utterly unprepared for the feeling on seeing the temple for the first time. He'd seen big. He'd witnessed engineering scale and grandeur. He'd mesmerized the world with machines and industry, satirically juxtaposing scale with his own rather slight frame in *Modern Times*. Yet here, erupting from the jungle was a sight he could never unsee. Without any people or any other structures to measure or compare, the scale of Angkor Wat was difficult to assess. It could have been a mile wide or an inch, a black crown on a velvet cushion, or what it was – the largest religious complex ever built on Earth.

They flew closer, skimming as low as Victor dared, and then Charlie realised that the jungle wasn't a constant dark unbroken shadow in the failing light. There were gaps and glimpses of other ruins overtaken by huge trees. Buddhist flags flapped at the hilltop pagodas. This wasn't just an ancient ruin but a living temple. The sounds of the seaplane's engines faded. Charlie felt himself like a bird gliding on the evening breeze. Were birds the luckiest creatures on earth to be able to see this wonder whenever they chose? They flew over the Elephant Walk towards the Bayon temple and Charlie's mouth opened even wider at the sight of a thousand massive rock-hewn faces looking in every direction, each identical, each serene but intense, each one seeming to follow their flight.

Charlie leant out to see the *boreis* – the vast irrigation channels that ran between the ruins. They banked again and headed west towards the setting sun. Ahead, the widest of the *boreis* reflected the five towers of Angkor Wat itself in an almost perfect symmetry. The height of human creation reflected on a timeless natural mirror.

It didn't disappoint. It was incomparable.

For a while Charlie didn't realise that he had been holding his breath. It was only when the temple grounds gave way again to the jungle and Charlie could see the shadow of the plane dance on the treetop canopy below that he finally exhaled.

Victor looked behind and saw in Charlie's face the same dumbstruck wonder as he himself had felt when he first saw Angkor Wat. Victor still felt the echo of that feeling with every new visit or flyover – but it would never be as intense as the first time. His smile was tinged with jealousy. He'd spent his adult life chasing that first hit, like an opium addict trying to recover their first high.

They circled round and flew by one more time – but it was the first time that made the greatest impression. Afterwards, they headed back to the river with the sun behind them. Victor saw Charlie's whimsical faraway face, but he knew better than to interrupt his new friend's thoughts with words. In fact, they would never speak of it again. Some things, as Charlie knew only too well, were better without language.

During the flight back, Charlie began to finally understand where Phirath drew all his passion, dedication, and determination.

Angkor Wat was more than a religious temple. It was a reminder of where the Khmer people had come from; or rather, by 1936, how far they had fallen into slavery. And finally, he realised the enormity of what he'd promised his friend. This wasn't about sticking two fingers up at the French, cocking a snook in the style of the Tramp. There was something far greater at stake, and something far more complex that needed to be said. But that battle was still to come. He didn't want to think about that now. He wanted to cling to that sense of wonder for a while longer.

34

It wasn't long after Charlie and Victor had left for their adventure that Paulette found herself in a rather less agreeable adventure of her own. She was freshening up with a jug of water by the chipped enamel basin when she heard a scream from the bedroom. She rushed in to find her mother standing on a rickety chair. Alta screamed again, holding up her skirts. Beneath her a snake slithered between the chair legs, which rocked with every scream, nearly ready to topple. Paulette stopped in her tracks. The chair legs steadied. It was quiet enough to hear the snake hiss. The snake and her mother eyed her, and Paulette couldn't tell which look was more venomous.

Footsteps echoed from the corridor. Frank Yonamori entered and assessed the threat without breaking his stride. Over at the dresser, he took Paulette's hatbox, calmly removed a broad straw hat, grabbed a broom and took on the snake. A few prods and pokes later he had successfully pushed and cajoled it into the hat box and replaced the lid.

'Anything else, Ma'am,' he asked without any hint of insolence.

The two women realised they'd both been holding their breath – and let out a sigh.

'Very good. Then I'll dispose of our unwelcome guest.'

As soon as he'd gone, Paulette's mother collapsed onto a threadbare chaise longue and fanned herself with a magazine.

'The faucet don't work. Bathing is an endurance test,' she muttered, her accent slipping slightly back towards Utah. 'There are damned serpents in my room!'

Paulette laughed. Now the threat had been dealt with, she felt rather carefree.

'Oh, buck up mother. Have some fruit.'

There was a plate of dragon fruit in a bowl on the coffee table. She brought it over to her mother, who looked at the pink scaley skin doubtfully.

'Do I eat it or attack it?'

'Don't be silly, Mother!' But she regretted her sharp tone immediately. She added more softly, 'It's only for two nights.'

'I won't sleep a wink. Not a decent night since we left that mediocre hotel.'

'We have been slumming it rather,' retorted Paulette. She sliced the dragon fruit down the middle and scooped out the white flesh spotted with tiny seeds. But when she offered it to her mother, Alta merely shuddered and shook her head.

'Where's your sense of adventure?' chided her daughter.

'In my hat box!'

Alta's breathing steadied and with it her determination. She sat beside Paulette and took her hands in hers. 'Let's get to this damned temple, announce your damn marriage, and then get back to an unruined civilisation!'

Paulette set the plate of fruit down with a bang.

'What do you think we're doing?' And she stormed out.

Moments later she was rushing through the house calling Charlie's name. But he was nowhere to be found. Neang, the housekeeper, came running to see what the fuss was about and tried to explain to Paulette that the two men had gone up in a plane, but the gestures made as little sense to Paulette as her Khmer mixed with Russian. She started to share her mother's frustration and walked out into the overgrown garden instead. She wanted to be alone.

The truth was she was beginning to doubt the announcement herself. The marriage in Singapore had been a quiet, almost stolen affair. As usual Frank had made the arrangements and surpassed himself by misdirecting the press to Raffles Hotel, while they had sneaked off to a rather drab administrative office to make their vows. It had all felt rather underwhelming. She wasn't one of those girls who grew up dreaming of white dresses and thousands of guests and a wedding day fit for a princess. But she had married one of the world's greatest and richest celebrities with as much fanfare as signing a cheque in a banking hall. She had no doubt that Charlie loved her. And she loved Charlie equally in return, but after only a few short weeks she sensed that something had changed. She'd been excited by Charlie's newfound passion for his work and thrilled that after all the usual announcements about quitting motion pictures forever, he was back to creating. But there was something different about this. If they'd been back in Summit Drive and the studio lot, she would have been more relaxed about it. He could be disagreeable while he was working on a new project – curt, dismissive, wrapped up in himself. She knew that this was his process. She'd seen it with *Modern Times* from start to finish. Here in Indochina, he was no longer surrounded by the people who could keep him on the right track. His studio manager, friends, investors and partners all played their part. Here he was adrift and wandering – and was spending too much time by himself. After their argument in Levalier's villa, and her own guilt about how close she'd come to kissing the Frenchman, she was feeling anxious and uncertain about their future. They were husband and wife, but since the marriage, they seemed to have drifted apart. The more she thought about it, the less she liked where her thoughts took her. Did she love Charlie because of what he could do for her and her career? Or was the truth that she loved him for who he had been, rather than who he now wanted to become? Perhaps this that was behind her outburst about the politics of his script *Colonial Subjects*?

She flicked the mosquitos away and made up her mind to talk to Charlie when he returned. But when he returned, he was distant and circumspect, and refused to talk about where he'd been other than a vague reference to a long talk with the count about the politics of the colony.

The count was as energetic as ever, but surprisingly avoided any talk of where they'd been. He'd decided on a whim that he would host a party for his guests, despite their protests. He disappeared into his study with Neang and busied himself with preparations, bellowing orders, ordering drinks and food, and calling his friends and acquaintances.

It was already past seven and dark when Charlie seemed to suddenly snap out of his deep introspection and suggest to Paulette that they take a stroll along the Sangkae river. Despite Alta's protests and Paulette's clear reluctance, he wouldn't take no for an answer. He whispered some instructions to Frank and told a bewildered Victor that they would be back in time for the party. In fact, Victor was grateful that his guests would be out of his way while he prepared for the party.

They walked from his villa into town. But news of their arrival had soon spread and by the time they'd reached the market, the group had swelled with curious Frenchmen and other expatriates eager to see and be seen with the celebrity party. Someone had also alerted the press, but they hung back respectfully. And skulking in the shadows lurked the ubiquitous Sûreté police.

Mr Yonamori held a parasol for Paulette's mother while ahead Paulette and Charlie strolled along the riverbank, watching the sampans. But as much as Paulette was desperate to steer the conversation towards their relationship and future, Charlie was still wrapped up in his own head. The seaplane adventure had lifted his spirits, but at the expense of questioning his film project. After the majesty of Angkor Wat, his project felt rather small and inconsequential. He spoke aloud to Paulette, but really he was talking to himself.

'I create a labyrinth,' he said, arguing with himself. 'I put the Little Fellow into an impossible situation and challenge myself to find a way out of it. But this time I can't do it. Not without words. I can't do it. Maybe I don't want to do it.'

He broke off when he realised that Paulette had stopped and was staring at him. She smiled when he finally realised and focussed his attention back on her.

'Mrs Paulette Chaplin. Your wife?'

And she held out her hand as a mock greeting. Point taken, but Charlie was not amused. In fact, he almost seemed to be sulking. Paulette softened.

'Perhaps we've been away too long,' she offered. 'I feel a little homesick if I'm honest. Maybe we should cut short our trip and head home.'

'But there's something about this place. Don't you feel it?'

'I feel the heat. I feel the bite of the mosquitos, but Charlie I don't feel like we belong here.'

'I don't recall suggesting we should pack up Summit Drive and move here?' replied Charlie, irritated now. And he walked on. Paulette joined him. She put her arm through his.

'Darling, you've only just released *Modern Times*! And you've been telling everyone you've retired. Relax and enjoy yourself.'

'I don't get you sometimes, Paulette,' hissed Charlie. 'You want me to work on a new film, but you also want me to retire? You threaten to leave me and star for Selznick. You're thrilled I'm working on a new script, but you tell me I shouldn't speak? What do you want? '

'Honestly, I want you to forget *Colonial Subjects*. It's … it's affecting you in a way I don't much care for. You asked me what I want. The truth is, I think I want to go home. When we're back you can work on something there.'

But what she hoped would calm him, had the opposite effect.

'I can't! What's the point of all this, what's the point of being who I am if I can't do a damn thing about anything? He's got to talk. It's the only way.'

And he pivoted away from talking about himself to talking about the Tramp. The two were increasingly fusing together. Paulette thought better of challenging that line of thought.

'So let him talk. But something else.'

'Another comedy?' This time it was Charlie who spat out the

word like a mouthful of sour milk.

'You're the King of Comedy.'

'I was.'

Seeing him so despairing was more than Paulette could bear. But she already knew the backlash he'd received for *Modern Times* and the picture's supposed communist tendencies. A political film might be the end of him – in more ways than one.

'Darling, I promise you. I won't even consider any other offers if you do. Not from Selznick, or from any of them. But stay away from politics, I beg you. Don't try to change the world with your motion pictures. It'll change with or without you.'

Chaplin chewed over her words, considering his reply. But before he could respond, a flashbulb exploded only feet away from him. He hadn't even noticed the photographer walking alongside them. He was momentarily blinded but shoved the photographer away irritably. Frank rushed up to intervene and head off any further confrontation. When Charlie looked around and saw there was a group of reporters and photographers following them, he seemed to have a sudden change of heart. He checked his watch and smiled. The pointless discussion with Paulette was forgotten. She watched him suspiciously.

Charlie smiled for the cameras and offered them a few steps of his iconic walk. The press surged forwards, encouraged by the celebrity's engagement.

'Charlie, over here Charlie!' called out one. Charlie looked in the opposite direction.

'Charlot,' called another, and Charlie looked up as if being addressed from the heavens.

'Mrs Chaplin!' tried another.

Paulette turned to the camera and the flashbulbs exploded and fizzed.

'Do you think Mrs Chaplin suits me, boys,' purred Paulette, neither answering nor refuting their claim. If it hadn't been thirty degrees in the shade, she'd have worn her furs for the moment. But up ahead Charlie caught sight of the uniformed Sûreté and his smile faded. He made an about turn and addressed the press.

'Tonight we are privileged to be the guests of a traditional Khmer theatre performance right here in Battambang. You are all invited.'

The announcement was a surprise to the reporters. There was a hubbub of raised voices until one rang out clearly and in English over them.

'Are you aware, Mr Chaplin, that the governor wants this particular show banned?'

It was the reaction Charlie wanted.

'I am. And he does. And maybe he will ban it. Like he's banned *Modern Times*. Is that what we have become? Are we to burn books like Herr Hitler in Germany too? My god, the show is just a comedy, nothing more. Has anyone ever died from laughter?'

He had their full attention now. He could feel Paulette's eyes boring into his back, but he wasn't done yet. This is what he wanted. It was what he'd planned with Phirath just a few days earlier in the gathering twilight at Wat Phnom. The press were silent.

'Are you telling me that comedy is now a threat to colonial security in Indochina? My friend in the Lakhoun theatre only does what I also strive to do in my motion pictures – combine comedy, entertainment and a bit of satirical finger-pointing. Or would you have laughter banned in your protectorate?'

No one challenged him.

He held out his arm for Paulette to take. She gripped it hard, pinching him under his bicep. Charlie didn't react and guided her past the Sûreté towards the archway which led to Wat Sangkae.

The reporters followed, sniffing now a story more interesting than Charlie's romantic relationship with his co-star. What was he up to?

35

Charlie's entourage had swelled to two score or more as they passed under the pagoda archway and up the tree-lined approach to Wat Sangkae. An elderly abbot was waiting for the group when they arrived. Behind him, the stage was set with a painted backdrop of a palace scene. It was circled by lanterns, and coconut husks were burning on either side, bathing the stage in a warm glow and lending the whole occasion a kind of magical – almost mystical – aura.

The guests exchanged glances. None of them had any idea why they were there, nor how Charlie had made the arrangements. But at the same time, the place hummed with an expectation that was impossible to ignore. The abbot was an old man with gold-rimmed glasses, wrapped in dark red robes and an expression on his face like he'd just woken from a particularly vivid but heart-warming dream.

Charlie stepped forward and respectfully *sampeahed* the abbot, palms pressed together in front of his face with a little bow. The group, colonial dignitaries and the press were ushered to some benches at the front and Paulette and her mother took their seats, unsure what to expect – and what Charlie had planned. The formality was a little awkward. The abbot handed Charlie a bundle of incense sticks and gestured for him to follow. Inside the dimly lit vihara flashbulbs momentarily illuminated the bright colours and tableaux of the life of Buddha, against which the image of Charlie in his tropical whites seemed somewhat incongruous. In front of the Buddha, Charlie lit the incense sticks, shook them out and placed them with a bow. He was grateful for the moment inside Wat Phnom with Phirath, where he'd learned the correct and respectful way to behave in the pagoda. But Charlie was not there for a religious reason. He had something far more political in mind.

By the time Charlie had joined Paulette and her mother on the benches, Le Favre and members of the Sûreté had arrived and loitered at the back in the shadows. Monks and novices took their places behind the Western guests, and the enclosure soon filled with men, women and children from the surrounding streets. There was a hum of expectation, hushed whispers from the press, muted laughter from the Cambodian audience – but Charlie and his wife said nothing. Even Alta kept silent. She was uncomfortable in the heat and swatted away the persistent mosquitos but muttered only to herself. Paulette gripped Charlie's hand tightly, all smiles for the camera, but when she got the chance she whispered fiercely in Charlie's ear, 'What's going on, Charlie?'

Charlie feigned surprise at her question. 'We're just taking in a show, darling. Pretend it's Broadway.'

Paulette didn't look convinced. 'Off Broadway. Very far off.'

When everything was ready, a gong sounded deep and sonorous. It lingered long into the silence as a hush descended on the gathering. The Lakhoun theatre troupe musicians took their places. A drum beat for quiet. But there was no need. Everyone, including Le Favre, was silent with anticipation.

The painted backdrop behind the stage was of an elaborate palace scene. A boy brought a throne onto the stage. It was Saloth Sar. He nodded to Charlie and then disappeared behind the stage. There he found Phirath finishing his thick make up and making final changes to the giant's black and white mask. If Phirath was nervous, he didn't show it.

'He's here. And he's brought all the press with him,' said Saloth Sar.

Phirath grinned. 'Didn't I tell you he would?'

'The Sûreté are also here,' the boy added.

'Then I hope they enjoy the performance,' retorted Phirath, but there was a tension in his voice. There was no turning back now. Phirath took a deep breath, stealing himself for what he was about to do.

The drums beat to a crescendo and then suddenly stopped. The moment of silence seemed to last for an age. The actors took their positions behind the stage and then the performance was underway. It was exquisite, almost mesmerising, but there was little explanation. The costumes were elaborate, the face paint equally so. These were kings and queens, giants and princesses. The delicate, coloured glass beads in the headdresses caught the light and glinted. A royal tragedy was unfolding as the princess was abducted from the court and the prince vowed to get her back.

But after the first few minutes of fascination with the spectacle of the movements, costumes and music, Paulette's mother began to fidget, unable to interpret the carefully choreographed dance nor understand the story. Paulette was as hypnotised as Charlie, letting the mysterious, impenetrable performance wash over her. The music built to a fever pitch as the giant and the prince fought, their sticks clattering together, the feet stamping over the stage.

A final beat of the drum and the stage fell silent.

'Is it over now,' whispered Paulette's mother, not as quietly as she intended.

'Wait,' murmured Charlie in anticipation.

Two comic actors ran onto the stage as if they were being chased. One was Phirath but beneath all his make-up it was hard to tell. He wore a small toothbrush moustache and Paulette caught Charlie's eye with a smile – and a question. He gestured her back to the performance.

The two comedians pushed and shoved one another, a pantomime of slapstick comedy owing everything to the celebrity guest in the audience. That continued until they heard the heavy footfalls of someone approaching. They hid themselves behind a bamboo thicket, as an actor playing the colonial governor stomped onto stage, with a fat belly and a red face.

'Ho-hi-ho-hi-ho!' he bellowed in nonsensical French.

The Khmer audience laughed nervously, surprised by this comic and contemporary addition to the Lakhoun tradition. But the French guests in the audience were less amused. Paulette covered a laugh with her hand, trying to remain neutral. Phirath swaggered up behind the governor with a Chaplinesque walk, kicked him up the backside and whipped back behind the bamboo. The governor spun round enraged.

'Ho-hi-ho-hi-ho!' he exclaimed again.

This time the Khmer crowd didn't hold back and roared with laughter. Even the monks' impassive faces creased a little in amusement. There was another kick from another direction as the governor's back was turned. More laughter. Then the comic actors took up their sticks and drove the apoplectic colonial governor from the stage.

At the back of the pagoda, the Sûreté officers looked to Le Favre for a signal to intervene. Whistles in their mouths, one unclipped the holster of his pistol. Le Favre shook his head. Not yet.

As soon as the colonial governor had gone, Phirath strode to the centre of the stage. He took off his rice paddy hat and scanned the audience. He had their full attention now. He paced up and down before finally addressing them directly.

'Ladies and gentlemen, *mesdames et messieurs*, members of the press,' he started, slipping seamlessly between French and English.

Le Favre nearly spat out his sugarcane juice. He whispered into the ear of his sergeant who nodded and snapped his fingers for two officers to follow him. They made their way through the crowd as Phirath continued.

'Is this how things must be forever?' Phirath challenged the audience. 'Foreign invaders exploiting our homeland. Raping this country of kings, stealing the resources of its lands and its people?' He switched to Khmer. 'Our citizens rot in jail. Four hundred and more as political prisoners, held without charge, for over a year, for daring to challenge our occupiers.' And then in French, 'Is this the reality of the *mission civilisatrice*?'

In the front, Charlie's smile faded and his face paled. This is not what they had agreed. This was no longer comedy. He froze, his grip on Paulette's hand tightened. What was happening? One thing was clear. It was too much for the sergeant. He leapt up onto the stage and the musicians stopped playing. A flashbulb exploded, capturing the moment when the sergeant gripped Phirath's arm and tried to drag him away. But Phirath was surprisingly strong and held his ground. He continued regardless.

'Our honoured guest today is the King of Comedy himself. He has travelled from America to witness first-hand the way our people and our artists are treated. Come! You have something to say. This is your chance. Mr Charles Chaplin. Speak.'

Phirath wriggled free from the Sergeant and ushered Charlie up on to the stage. His hand was out, beckoning him up.

Charlie didn't move.

Nothing. Not even his eyelids.

The sergeant looked to Le Favre for instruction. The captain gestured for him to wait but pushed through the seated guests and up to the stage himself.

'Come up to the stage and speak, Charlot,' implored Phirath. 'Give the press the news they are waiting for. Show your support for our struggle against colonial oppression. Show your support for the international communist movements. It is your time! Come, comrade Chaplin. Come!'

Still nothing from Charlie. He sat motionless as around him the world seemed to slow on its axis. He felt all eyes zooming in on him as he himself seemed to retreat away. He was outside himself, looking back at his face with a director's eye – seeing the perspective warp as the camera lens shifted. Phirath's mouth moved in slow motion, imploring Charlie to join his Communist anti-colonial protest. Charlie could feel the world zooming out as all the eyes in the pagoda tracked in on his face. It was a visual effect that would not be used for another twenty years but how well it represented what he was feeling. How well the effect suggested that growing feeling of alienation and dislocation when even the light seemed to bend in the dawning realization that Phirath had tricked him. That this was not a pantomime of comic solidarity across language and culture but a political trick – and that he, the King of Comedy, had fallen into this trap. He pinned Phirath with a stare, like a bug on a board. The betrayal was too hard to bear.

'Monsieur Chaplin? Saklo? Don't let us down, take a stand! It is what you have come here for. You too are a communist, are you not? You are one with us!'

Another officer climbed up on stage. He took out his revolver, ready to shoot it into the air but Le Favre pulled down his arm. The press all turned to Charlie – the centrepiece of Phirath's spectacle, more powerful than the slapstick French governor and the cheap laughs he'd drawn moments before.

'Monsieur Chaplin,' said Le Favre. 'Do you have anything you wish to add to this pathetic spectacle of insurrection?'

'Tell people what you've seen, Saklo,' urged Phirath, a hint of desperation creeping into his voice. 'Tell people what you think of Indochina and the colonial subjects. Tell the press. Tell them how you will expose it all in your next motion picture. Tell them how we have worked together to create a film that will end the cruel exploitation between the colonists and the people. Shout it out, Charlot. Let it be heard from here to Paris and all the way to Los Angeles.'

More silence. Nobody moved.

The crowd, the press, Paulette and her mother all looked at

Charlie, but he stared straight ahead, unwavering. For Charlie, there were only two people in the scene – him and Phirath. His Khmer doppelgänger on stage; his number one fan; the disciple and his idol. But Charlie had been duped. The betrayal was clear in Phirath's eyes as the officers grabbed him by the arms. His last desperate plea to Charlie was barely more than a croak. And his last look was one of crushing disappointment. Phirath had met his idol and found him wanting.

All movement slowed and stopped, like a dancer in a music box, unwound and on its final revolution.

'Arrest him and clear the stage!' barked Le Favre.

More policemen jumped up to the stage. Another actor was arrested. The actor playing the governor returned to the stage and presented his wrists for arrest. Then a voice rang out, clear and proud.

'For the Free Khmer!' It was Saloth Sar, and it was a pre-arranged signal.

All at the once the movement flooded back. Musicians scattered into the darkness leaving their instruments. Other members of the troupe fled, stagehands dropped everything and vaulted the pagoda walls or hid behind the vihara.

In the mayhem a gunshot rang out.

The crowd panicked. Whistles blew, the police tried to maintain calm. Paulette's mother screamed and clutched Paulette.

But all the while, Charlie remained frozen in his seat as if he couldn't see or hear the chaos unfolding around him.

The sergeant managed to drag a kicking and thrashing Phirath off the stage, but it took two other officers to hold the little man as he was hauled through the audience. Le Favre made sure they brought him right past Charlie. As they did, Phirath stopped struggling for a moment and glared at his hero.

'What is the point of your power, Saklo, if you refuse to speak?'

Charlie boiled inside, but his face was a mask. He couldn't even acknowledge the stinging rebuke. As Phirath was removed from the pagoda, he stared straight ahead towards the lingering empty space of that final challenge. Paulette snapped her hand away from his. On the stage he saw Le Favre standing tall and triumphant.

'I warned you, Charlot,' said the captain. There was an ugly victorious sneer in his voice.

Charlie snapped out of his trance. 'So, are you going to arrest me too?'

'And give the people a hero, and the press their moment? I don't think so, Monsieur Chaplin. You said nothing. You did nothing. You changed nothing. You are nothing. Even here.'

As the captain was walking away, Charlie shouted after him, 'We'll see what the papers print tomorrow!'

'You're free to go,' the captain called back. 'Enjoy your evening.'

And it was that freedom which bound Charlie more tightly than any handcuff or cangue or rope. It was not only the freedom of colour, privilege and wealth; it was the crushing freedom of inconsequence. He didn't matter. Charlie was shaking with impotent rage as Le Favre walked through the emptied pagoda, laughing with his policemen, as casually as if he'd just left a bar. Once outside, the captain snapped his fingers, and his officers immediately circled the press demanding the camera films. The press knew better than to argue. They handed over cameras and the rough hands of the officers ripped reels and exposed the film. There were to be no pictures of what had happened. There was to be no story, save the one the French agreed upon.

Inside the pagoda, Paulette's expression said it all. She turned away from her husband, feeling numb and distant.

'Paulette, wait—' Charlie managed, but she was already standing. She turned her back on her husband and left with her mother.

Charlie Chaplin found himself completely alone and in the dark, an audience of one, beneath an empty stage.

36

Charlie remained on the bench beneath the stage for a long while. The pagoda was empty, the coconut husks had burnt away to glowing embers and the lanterns had been extinguished. He didn't register the movement of the monks, stepping up to the vihara or skirting around the stage. The abbot watched him for a while, serenely but sadly, until he too walked away.

Eventually, Charlie left the compound, and walked in a daze along the tree-lined approach back to the archway onto the main road. For a long time he wandered the dark streets of Battambang. He walked along the river, past the market, past the shopfronts and food stalls, smoking continuously. And then he stopped. It wasn't that he was lost. He could find his way back to the count's house with ease, but first there was something he had decided he must do. He flicked his cigarette away, although he'd barely smoked half, and approached a line of rickshaws outside a Chinese shophouse. He stepped into the nearest with the ease and familiarity of someone who had grown up in the French colonies.

'Police station,' he said to the puller. Off his blank look, he added, 'Gendarmerie.'

The police station was a colonial building of shuttered windows, high arches and pillars. Under the lamplight, it managed to appear both elegant and foreboding. But its colonial elegance didn't extend past the façade. Once inside, the paint was smeared and worn, and the tiles cracked. Even the faded portraits of French President Lebrun, Governor Robin and King Sisowath were faded and withdrawn, haunting the hallway like spectres. This was a place for the French to see from the outside to reassure them of their control, rather than to experience the dim and desperate interiors. The only European eyes to see the gendarmerie under electric light were the officers on duty, no strangers to the building's cruel secrets. It smelled of sweat and dirt.

When Charlie crossed to the desk, the dour duty officer started in surprise. He was even more surprised when Charlie gave his name and demanded, in faltering French, to be taken to the cells. He was told to wait. The officer disappeared into a back room. An indistinct voice relayed his request; another questioned it, and so it proceeded up the chain of command. A phone eventually rang. Somebody somewhere, perhaps Le Favre himself, granted permission. Charlie imagined the triumphant sneer on Le Favre's face. But this time it didn't anger him. A subdued and compliant Charlie was led down a dingy corridor towards the cells. The officer in charge stopped at one cell and gestured for Charlie to approach. Then he disappeared.

The cell was a tiny brick hovel with a barred door. Inside Phirath squatted in the dirt, with his back to the rear wall. He was naked except for his *krama* – a red chequered scarf - around his waist. He had evidently been beaten; his left eye was nearly closed. Looking out of the gloom, his right eye just managed to pick out Charlie at the cell door, but he scoffed and turned away.

For a long while Charlie stared at this shadowy sinewy

creature in the dark. He didn't know what to say, and the purpose of his visit seemed to have faded away. After a while he sank to the filthy floor, the rusty bars smearing a line down the back of his once crisp white linen jacket. He and his fan and admirer were separated by more than the bars.

'Why did you do it?' Charlie asked finally. His voice was as cracked and thin as it had been when he first arrived in Cambodia only days earlier. There was no reply. His voice trembled as he continued. 'What will happen to your troupe, Phirath? They're your family. They look to you, and you've given all that up for a few stupid words.'

'I haven't given anything up, Mr Chaplin,' replied Phirath from the darkness. He was as calm as Charlie was agitated. 'I'm exactly where I need to be.'

'What about our project? What about *Colonial Subjects*?'

At that, Phirath shuffled over to the cell door and crouched beside Charlie.

'There never was a project. That was all you, not me.'

'He could talk,' offered Charlie. 'I could talk. That would help, wouldn't it? Maybe then—'

'It won't make any difference.'

'But I have to do something.'

'You had your opportunity, Saklo. I gave you that chance. But you see, this isn't the Tramp's battle. It's mine. It's ours. The people of the Free Khmer. You are merely another white visitor, arrogantly thinking you can change our world, when it is a world you neither know nor understand.'

Charlie turned to find Phirath staring intensely at him, with his other puffy, bruised eye mocking Charlie's inaction. The actor was crouched, calm and determined as if he'd planned this whole affair. It only infuriated Charlie further.

'You lied to me. Back in Phnom Penh you begged me to help you escape. You told me it was simply to put on a comic performance at the pagoda. But you lied to me. You used me,' said Charlie quietly. On his aimless walk through Battambang he'd thought of everything he'd say to Phirath, but now faced with the reality of his broken body in the cells, none of his words expressed what he really wanted to say. 'That wasn't comedy. It wasn't entertainment. It was politics. Propaganda.' The words sounded like they were coming from someone or somewhere else.

'Of course. What did you expect?'

A knot of police officers approached then, their bootsteps echoing off the scuffed walls. Charlie's face hardened. He was running out of time.

'So, Le Favre was right then? About your father and what he did?'

'Don't believe what you read in the French newspapers, Saklo,' said Phirath, quoting Charlie back to himself.

'Stand aside,' barked the nearest police officer in French and Charlie hauled himself to his feet. His brief meeting with Phirath was over. They opened the cell doors and dragged the beaten comedian from the cell but as he passed Charlie, he ripped himself free from their grasp and lurched right up into Charlie's terrified face.

He said nothing. A final lingering exchange of looks – betrayal in Charlie's eyes, and disappointment staring back at him. A thwack on his back and Phirath crumpled. But he was smiling as he was dragged out of view. A policeman locked up the cell.

'Where will he be taken,' asked Charlie.

'Battambang Prison,' the policeman replied.

'Without a trial? Without any judicial process?'

The policeman laughed. 'A trial? For what? We all saw what happened.'

The visit to the police station left Charlie depressed and confused. He left then, convinced that he could hear the group of French officers sniggering and mocking him. He lit up a cigarette, not wanting to return to Victor's home and certainly not wanting to face Paulette and the inevitable, perhaps irreversible, showdown that this would entail. He strolled aimlessly once more through the dark streets. He retraced his steps past the market and on past the French lycée, and there he stumbled across a new Art Deco theatre hall. The marquee advertised the latest French releases, but the building was shuttered and dark. The coming attractions board had posters for movies – Hollywood movies with Clark Gable, Shirley Temple, Errol Flynn. *Mutiny on the Bounty, Captain Blood, Top Hat*.

Charlie stared at these motion picture icons. They mocked him even here. Thousands of miles away from Hollywood, the stars of talkies and the studio machine laughed at his stubborn resistance to speech. Yes, he thought. He was done. Hadn't he known that the moment he'd released *Modern Times*? Hadn't he told the world he was retired from motion pictures? But he'd at least gone out on a high. Like the Tramp himself, he'd disappeared into the sunset, only not down a dusty track with his Gamin, but with Paulette on the SS *Coolidge* on a long trip to Asia. Maybe he would never return.

As he walked off with these maudlin thoughts swirling around his head, he heard a metal door banging and looked down the narrow alley beside the picture house. Steps led up to an exit, and the open door was banging in the breeze coming off the river. He wandered over, up the steps and peered inside.

The side entrance opened into the balcony stalls. The wall lights were shaded by misted glass, in block shapes. He stepped silently down the banked rows of seats, and down the steps. The picture house had two floors, with the projection room beneath the balcony stalls. There were signboards there, screwed into the walls, segregating the auditorium into Khmer and French sections. Like everything else in the colony, it represented a world of haves and have-nots; one for the Khmer people, the other for their occupiers. The French section was the balcony above, away from the mosquitos, above and superior to their subjects below. But Charlie was too tired to think about that now. He climbed back up to the balcony and took a seat there looking down onto the raised stage below. The quiet and solitude was a tonic, and for a while he sat in the empty theatre staring at the blank screen below until the emotions of the day overcame him and he began to weep silently into the dark.

37

It was nearly midnight by the time he returned to Victor's home to find the party well underway. Not for the first time in the Kingdom of Cambodia he'd avoided a party held in his honour. But he'd missed the governor's garden party days before because he was caught up in the fervour and buzz of a new creation. This time, it was a very different feeling. Peering over Victor's walls, Cambodian faces gazed at the opulent excess in a mixture of fascination and bewilderment. Charlie passed through the gates, but the music and the laughter and eccentric strangers irritated him. Guests had gathered on the lawn. Flaming citronella torches lined the approach to the house and some lanterns hung beneath the banyan trees. Victor Goloubew's booming voice carried clearly across the overgrown lawns interspersed with the guttural call of the confused peacocks. He felt like a stranger, not the guest of honour, and honestly, he wanted it to stay that way. Once again he wished he could separate himself from himself, not as he'd done so many times before, into his alter-ego, the Tramp, but to pass through the party as someone else. Someone ordinary. Someone who wouldn't turn heads, who wouldn't be the focus of questions and curiosity. Someone who didn't matter.

He caught sight of Paulette by a trestle table bar, dazzling in the centre of the party, like the pole star in a winter sky. She was dressed in a shimmering satin evening gown, dangling anecdotes to star-struck guests, who hung on her every word, punch-drunk on the lightness of her laugh. The sadness he'd felt in the police station and the empty cinema swelled inside him again, threatening to overwhelm him. If that unremarkable moment in Levalier's villa with Paulette had signified the death of the Tramp, then this moment had no less significance. He instinctively recognised it for what it was; this was the moment that foreshadowed the end of his marriage. It was destined to be stillborn before it was even announced to the world. He could pay Paulette all the money in Hollywood to stay – and he would – but it would never be enough to buy what she really wanted. He couldn't take his eyes off her. How she loved to talk. How effortlessly she dazzled, but somehow still managed to put people at ease. She was born to it, as she was born to shimmer on the silver screen, a mesmerizing light in the darkness of a movie theatre. And with a pang of loss, he realised that his darling wife would no longer be content to stand in his shadow and wait for her time. She was young, her star was rising, and it was only Charlie's stubbornness, like straining guy ropes on a hot-air balloon, which held her back from soaring. He knew then, in his heart, that he would have to let her go. He found himself wishing he'd stayed in the projection booth in the dark of the cinema. The projectors, the smell, the celluloid running through the projector gates and the flickering images on a screen – yes, that was enough. That's what he could do to make up for his earlier cowardice. He was finished in the United States anyway, but perhaps he could bring happiness and laughter to the French colony. Perhaps here he could disappear into the cinema never to be seen again. For a moment he imagined how the press might cover his disappearance. How the police would be called in to search for him but would do so half-heartedly. They wouldn't care about a silent movie star, and would casually, and erroneously, dismiss him as an American. A forgotten movie star only dimly remembered. A comedian who was no longer funny, but who once had kicked the Kaiser up the backside in a vaguely recalled silent two-reeler. And how years, maybe decades later, when his name would take a few moments to register in audience's minds, they might re-discover him and his work, perhaps after he was already dead. By then people would remember him as the elderly eccentric hermit in an Indochinese cinema, a projectionist sustained by the flickering images of others, who had once travelled the world but whose world was now the walls of the picture house, a prison of his own making ...

He shook his head vigorously as if to scatter these thoughts. He could feel the licks of depression and the tortuous spiral of self-despair. Better to be angry than that. Anything but that. And then, like a moment in a lesser movie, Paulette scanned the party and her eyes settled on Charlie in the shadows by the gate. There was no doubt she'd seen him. Her gaze rested on him for the briefest moment – just long enough for him to know. Then she turned back to the guest beside her. He was ignored. She knew how Charlie hated to be ignored, to be invisible. Her anger at Charlie's pointless political dabbling at the pagoda had not dulled with the champagne and company. He knew that look all too well. This wasn't over.

The thought of their star-crossed trajectories reaching their inevitable point of departure soured in his mind and began to set.

It wouldn't take long in the mood he was in for them to harden into ugly malice. He skirted the party in the shadows, unseen by everyone except Paulette, and entered the villa from the back entrance, disturbing the flustered housekeeper.

In the guest room, Charlie quickly washed and gave Neang his filthy stained suit and picked out an evening suit. As he was checking himself in the mirror, Paulette entered. She lit a cigarette, studying her husband.

'Where were you?' she asked eventually. 'I'm getting sick of asking that question.'

Charlie didn't answer. Instead, he inspected an ornately carved bone opium pipe on a holder, trying to hold back the simmering rage building beneath his calm expression.

'Suit yourself. I hope you're happy with your latest crusade. Next time, you might wish to consider if those around you, those you're married to, might not actually want to take part in it.'

'What's that supposed to mean?' thundered Charlie.

'Charlie, I'm real! There's a me behind the screen.'

'A desperate Utah farm girl who slept her way into Hollywood?'

She slapped him. Hard.

'I swear to God, I'll take Selznick's offer as soon as my feet touch the ground in Los Angeles.'

'Not while you're under contract! You're *my* star. *My* wife. You belong to me!'

'For better, for worse.'

'You're nothing without me!'

'For richer, for poorer.'

Charlie flung her atomiser from the dresser across the room.

It smashed against the floor. Shards of the bottle scattered like stardust across the tiles.

Silence.

Charlie was mesmerised by her perfume sliding slowly down the wall and staining it. He stared at that, rather than face Paulette, whose eyes still seemed to taunt his political and creative impotence. Her eyes could be as cruel as they could be adoring.

'I own you,' said Charlie quietly, already aware that he was losing her.

Paulette's lips turned into rueful but mocking smile.

'Oh darling, don't look so glum. God knows, you've wanted to own everything you ever could since you earned your first dime on the vaudeville stage. You own your studios so you can own your films. You own your stars, your crew, dear old Frank, your servants. Christ, you own every room you ever walk into. But Charlie, don't for one second think you've ever owned me.'

That spirit which first attracted him, now taunted him.

'Our guests are waiting. They want their moment with a star. Shall we?'

She offered her husband her arm, but the tenderness they shared at Levalier's villa had vanished and was replaced by the cold emotional distance of a performance. But she could still put on a show. 'We owe that to the count, don't you think? He's been nothing but generous to us.'

The large doors opened to the back garden and Paulette and Chaplin stepped out as the celebrity couple. The press had been invited, as had other guests of Victor's – academics and businessmen, government officials and artists had all gathered. The events at the pagoda seem to have made little impression on their desire to enjoy the attention of the world's most famous couple. There was even a ripple of applause as they entered the garden.

'Charlot, Paulette!' It was the count and he rushed over with a breathless Alta just managing to hang on to his arm and her hat. He pumped Charlie's hand, gallantly kissing Paulette's with an over-the-top bow.

'Where the devil have you been?' snarled Paulette's mother.

For once, neither Charlie nor Paulette replied. Her mother's face fell, her anger replaced by concern.

'What's happened? Darling—'

'You were there, mother,' said Paulette. 'Don't you remember? You'd think it would leave an impression. Charlie championed a communist and then backed down when it really mattered. But it was just a piece of theatre, *n'est ce pas*? All in the past?'

But she was looking at Charlie when she said so. The moment hung ugly and barbed. Before he could respond, groups of well-wishers and rubberneckers pressed around them. And this time Charlie was happy to lose himself in their banalities. For Count Goloubew the evening was a tremendous success. He was happy to host such famous people as his guests. Battambang had its own identity and community. It was fiercely proud of its small expatriate enclave so far from Phnom Penh, but so close to Siem Reap and the Angkorian temples. By the end of the evening the gramophone was playing polkas and there was dancing between the peacocks on the lawn. The events of the day faded with the alcohol and the heat and the laughter, and Charlie and Paulette put on a wonderful performance of enjoying themselves.

But less than an hour later, after many guests had left, Charlie found a way to excuse himself from the group. He walked behind the main house towards the outbuilding, holding a paraffin lamp in the darkness. There he creaked open the doors to the makeshift garage and climbed into the old Ford Model T. He sat with his hands on the steering wheel, imagining himself driving away from all the anxieties that he could no longer keep at bay. When he was like this, minutes could easily turn to hours. He replayed the arguments with the precision of a movie projector on the screen in his head – from every angle, with every intonation, like he was making edits and cuts in a strip of celluloid. There was no doubt here that this was a talkie.

'You said nothing. You did nothing. You changed nothing. You are nothing. Even here.' Le Favre sneered his victory.

'You are just a visitor, thinking you can change a world you don't know or understand.' Phirath crouched in the cells like an animal and snarled his rebuke.

'Charlie championed a communist and then backed down when it mattered.' Paulette's laughter was mocking and cruel.

Paulette had changed in the space of a few hours. Or maybe she hadn't changed at all. Perhaps she was the same as always, and it was he who had changed. He was mulling over all these things, as he chain-smoked cigarettes, finding himself tortured by the same opposing desires. He longed for anonymity as much as he longed for popularity. More than popularity he wanted to matter, to be heard, to be relevant and taken seriously for once. And perhaps most of all he longed to be a million miles away from Indochina and its rubber plantations, from Count Goloubew and his Angkorian obsession, and from Le Favre with his irritating moustache and smug manner. Most of all he wished for some space from Paulette, time to be himself without needing to perform to the world, not as the Tramp, but as Charlie Chaplin.

The remaining guests danced and drank into the small hours. They noticed, of course, Charlie's absence but put that down to the price of fame. He'd graced them with his presence, lightened their night for an hour. Could they expect any more? Only Paulette knew the real reason and knew intimately how he would be feeling and how the black dog would be snapping at his heels. She'd already said what she had to say to her husband. The music and laughter and conversation masked the sound of a crankshaft turning. Beneath a joyful polka, they didn't hear the cough of an engine. And they didn't notice Charlie driving out of the outbuilding in the Ford Model T, without headlights, towards the gates and into the street beyond.

38

Charlie spun the steering wheel and turned left out of the gates, flicking on the headlights. As he did so, he noticed a shadow running beside the car. It jumped onto the running board, out of sight from the old gateman and from any casual observers in the house.

It was Saloth Sar.

'What do you want?' shouted Charlie above the engine.

'Keep driving,' was the only response.

Before long they were roaring through the empty night streets of Battambang. The shophouses were closed, the stalls packed away. A lone drunk staggered across the intersection beside the river and Charlie swerved around him, past Sangkae Wat, over the bridge and out of the city proper. Saloth Sar issued directions at every junction.

'Where are we going?'

'Left.'

'Get in,' said Charlie, 'before you kill yourself.'

But the boy shook his head. His eyes were fixed on the road ahead and he clung to the passenger door. Before long they had left the city and its few streetlights. Even the glow from the braziers and rubbish fires were behind them. The Ford's headlamps made a tunnel of light in the darkness, just enough to see the rough track ahead. As they swung round a bend between two sugar palms, the beams picked up a rocky outcrop in the distance, silhouetted against the moonlit sky. Saloth Sar pointed to it.

'There.'

Moments later, the Model T stopped outside a sheer rock face and Charlie cut the engine. In the sudden silence, Charlie heard crickets and the night insects all around him. The boy reached into the passenger seat and took one of Charlie's cigarettes and lit it as casually as if they were lifelong friends.

'Where are we?'

'Battambang Caves,' said Saloth Sar in Khmer.

'In English? I heard Battambang, but –'

'You in Free Kampuchea now. Now you must speak Khmer.'

'Free Cambodia?'

'It will be. No thanks to you.'

'No offence taken.' The boy blinked, not understanding. Charlie continued, 'Wait for the newspapers tomorrow. They will report your cause, and the arrest of Sok Phirath. Isn't that what you wanted?'

'You have not been here very long. You don't understand.'

'What else did you expect me to do? I'm not a communist. I couldn't very well agree with Phirath, accuse the French publicly, take his side. I brought the press as agreed. Phirath lied to me. He never said he was going to ask me to join the Communist Party in full view of the press. Do you have any idea what that would have done to me? To my reputation.'

His outburst made no impression on Saloth Sar. Probably he didn't understand.

'No, you are *barang*. White foreigner. You don't care.'

'You're very perceptive,' Charlie said sarcastically, adding more to himself than to the boy, 'And, as it happens, I do care.'

Charlie snatched the cigarette from the boy's mouth, glowering at him. Then took a puff and exhaled with a sigh.

'What will happen to him?'

'You'll see.'

'He's in prison.'

'Exactly. Where he's supposed to be. Tomorrow night, Saklo, tomorrow night.'

The boy punched the air with his fist. With a cheeky grin he left the bewildered Charlie, jumped down from the car and ran off into the darkness towards the mouth of a cave.

Inside a fire was lit.

'Wait. Wait! Why did you bring me here?' But the boy had gone, and Charlie was left wondering exactly how he'd ended up in such a situation. He sighed, defeated, grabbed the crank handle and stepped out of the car. As he passed the bullhorn he parped it loudly, once, twice, three times.

He slotted the crank handle in place, but something made him straighten and he looked again towards the mouth of the cave. Saloth Sar was silhouetted in the entrance. He pulled his *krama* up to cover his face and suddenly he wasn't a boy anymore. He was a fighter. He was joined by the actor who played the prince. He too lifted his *krama* to cover his face. Before long other members of the theatre troupe who had escaped the arrests at the pagoda joined them, standing in a line at the mouth of the cave, *kramas* covering their faces and the fists raised in the salute of the Free Khmer.

Charlie barely had time to take that in before a stream of bats few out from the caves. Not just a few, but thousands upon thousands, a cloud of them screeching and beating the air with their wings, so dense that they blocked out the moon.

39

The next morning Charlie took breakfast on the veranda alone. He was up early and had sent the housekeeper to bring the newspapers, eager to see how they would report the previous evening's incident in the pagoda. He was flicking through them when the doors opened, and Paulette joined him.

'Nothing,' spat Charlie in disgust. 'Not a single word.'

Paulette sat down, newspaper in hand.

'Good morning,' she said ignoring his filthy mood. She handed over her newspaper. 'Not quite nothing.'

As she poured coffee, Charlie scanned the headlines from *The Straits Times*. There was nothing there. He looked up confused.

'Page four. Below the fold.' There was a triumphant tone in her voice.

Charlie flicked through and found a tiny article at the bottom. Barely two inches.

'"CHAPLIN DEAD" is the unconfirmed rumour in Asia,' it read.

'A Reuter's dispatch from London early this morning,' read Charlie aloud, 'says: "It is strongly rumoured here that Charles Chaplin died in Indochina. No information is presently obtainable." He glared at Paulette above the paper. 'That's it?'

'You're dead apparently. Maybe I should confirm it.'

Charlie slapped the paper down on the table, livid.

'That's the captain's work, I bet. Do I look dead?'

Paulette didn't know whether to laugh or console her husband. They were no strangers to rumours in the press. From exaggerated claims to entire fabrications, Charlie had, like every celebrity, faced his share of press inventions. And he understood more than most that the rumour was out now, and alive and thriving. There would be disbelief in London and Los Angeles. Charlie's studio manager in Hollywood would scramble to confirm the terrible news regarding the death of his boss. But this was 1936. It may take only a moment to start a rumour in the press, but it would still take an age to track down and refute the source to get to the truth. Was this the real reason behind the newspaper headline? Was it nothing more than spite from the captain of the French Sûreté, who used his control of the press to metaphorically kill, at least on paper, the star who was making waves in the French colonial pond?

'What did you think would happen, Charlie? You sided with a Communist revolutionary. Surely you must know how damaging that would be. Not just for you, but also for me –'

'I'll tell you something,' fumed Charlie, cutting her off. His blood was boiling. 'That French bastard has killed someone. I'm not talking about his political prisoners and damn rubber plantation workers. And I'm not talking about me! Do you know who he's killed?'

Paulette glanced up from another broadsheet. Her eyebrows furrowed and there again was the wrinkle in her nose that Charlie used to adore so much.

'He's killed The Little Fellow. The Tramp. Le Vagabond!'

'Charlie—'

But Charlie wouldn't be stopped. Not this time.

'The Tramp is dead. I've made up my mind. Done. Finished. Never again. But I won't give that small-minded, smug captain the satisfaction. He won't … he can't kill me! And neither will he silence me. I'll speak now. I'll shout. I'll tell the whole damn world. Frank,' he shouted. 'Frank!'

A flustered Mr Yonamori rushed over.

'Get me a damned telephone. And find Captain Le Favre.'

'Ah, sir. You see …' his manservant stammered.

'What?'

'He's already here, sir. He's been here since dawn. He wants a—'

Charlie leapt up and stormed inside. Paulette and Mr Yonamori exchanged glances, and then Paulette followed her husband inside. They scurried to catch up as Charlie strode through Victor's cluttered house and down the corridor on a mission. Le Favre approached from the opposite direction. Seeing Charlie black with rage, he smiled.

'Bonjour, Charlot,' he said brightly.

Charlie shoved the newspaper into the captain's chest, barely able to hold himself together. Le Favre made a show of reading the offending article.

'Dead? *Mon Dieu!*'

'Fuck you.'

The insult hung in the air. Le Favre smiled once again.

'No decorum. No protocol. No manners. You Americans.'

'I'm fucking British! And if you think you can silence me with a cheap press—'

'I warned you not to—'

'Don't threaten me, Captain!'

Charlie squared up to the captain. He might have been smaller but there was no doubt that he would have taken on the captain and the entire Sûreté in that moment. 'Do you really think a policeman can stop me? I've been outsmarting the police since I was a boy!'

'Not, I believe, in the real world,' countered Le Favre, but his smile had gone.

Charlie was already thinking of his next move. This encounter was done. He shoulder-barged past the bemused captain without looking back. Le Favre leered at Paulette, a faint bow and he turned to watch the retreating Chaplin walk away down the corridor.

'I lied before, Charlot! I've never seen a single one of your motion pictures. They are stupid.' Charlie didn't respond. 'Childish. Facile—'

'Not unlike you then, Captain.' Le Favre was surprised to hear Paulette defending Charlie. 'Well done,' she continued sarcastically. 'I hope you're ready for him.'

She rushed off after Charlie, leaving the captain perplexed at her reaction, and concerned about what the couple might do next.

If the French and English newspapers had failed to report the arrest of Sok Phirath and Chaplin's refusal to admit his communist ties, the Khmer newspaper printed little else. Around the Battambang market, groups of Khmer men huddled around the cheap newsprint. Those who could, read aloud for those who could not. By a sugar cane stall, as the owner shoved the stalks through the mangle, the patrons huddled around a student who read aloud in Khmer.

'Who then will speak for us?' he read, his voice low so that the men had to crowd closer to hear. 'Who will tell us, "Enough!" Who will wake us from our thousand-year sleep to break the cangues that we ourselves have made? Who? Not Mr Chaplin for sure.'

The student looked up to see some French Sûreté cross the street and head towards them. He hid the paper, and they drank their sugar cane nonchalantly. The policemen passed, casting them suspicious looks, but as soon as they'd walked on, the student continued.

'Monsieur Chaplin, who claims to be the champion of the poor and the dispossessed, who claims sympathy with our communist cause, is revealed in Kampuchea to be interested only in one thing – money. He has made his fortune from his silence. That continued yesterday at Wat Sangkae in Battambang. We know he is a man of no words. But yesterday we learned that he is also a man of no action.'

Behind them the Sûreté officers continued to a café where Le Favre sat with his morning coffee. He pretended to read the paper, but he was scoping the group of men by the sugar cane stall. They were not the only huddle he could see. Something was building. He could sense it. His officers saluted, but he paid them no attention.

'Do not look to the West for heroes,' the student continued, voice even lower, but no less triumphant. 'The French are our oppressors, supported by the British and Americans. Do not look to the East. They are our oppressor's servants. The Free Khmer needs Khmer heroes. Who will heed this call for action? Who will seize this moment?'

That call had already been answered, and preparations were already underway.

40

While Le Favre considered the potential impact of Charlot's visit to Indochina, Charlie himself was on the phone in Victor's office. A peacock chattered unnervingly in one corner as if it was lost and looking for a way out. On the other end of the line, Governor Robin's office was a picture of bureaucratic organisation – the opposite of Victor's cluttered passion. Behind him, the Tricolore flag hung perfectly in its holder, along with framed pictures of himself, French President Lebrun and King Sisowath Monivong. The Frenchman leant back in his chair, the phone to his ear. He spoke with the full authority of the protectorate. He had initially looked forward to the distraction of receiving a bona fide Hollywood star in Indochina, but in the end it had given him nothing but headaches. And they were headaches which piled on top of the already febrile mood in the country. He had in front of him the newspaper proclaiming the rumour that Charlie Chaplin had died in Indochina. Finally, something about the irritating comedian had made him smile.

'I read this morning that you had died,' he said, relishing the moment.

But Charlie wasn't in the mood for frivolous sparring.

'Over the years, I've had many impersonators, Governor,' he

replied. 'But this is me.'

'Then give me one reason why I shouldn't instruct Captain Le Favre to arrest you,' he continued. His smile had already gone.

'For what? Attending a show?'

'For aiding and supporting a known dissident. A firebrand, leading the Free Khmer independence movement. That, Monsieur Chaplin, would be grounds enough for treason.'

'Governor, I think you have been misinformed,' said Charlie. There was no trace of emotion now in his voice. He was calm and controlled. 'I kept my silence. In fact, it is my belief that I was tricked by the man in question. He abused our common interest, then assumed a political alliance. In that he was gravely mistaken.'

The governor thought about that for a moment. It was possible that Charlie was telling the truth. It wouldn't have been the first time that a foreigner had fallen foul of a friendship and been duped into something more serious. But it was more commonly financial – or at least transactional – rather than political.

'Go on,' he said.

'I give you my word, Governor Robin, that I'll leave the protectorate tomorrow. I'm sure your captain has told you of my intention to set my next motion picture here. But let me promise you this: no Indochina film project, no press, no meddling.'

'Your presence here has caused us great concern—'

'On one condition, sir.'

Now he had the governor's full attention. He leant forward in his chair, phone close to his ear waiting for Charlie to continue.

'Release *Modern Times* before I depart for China. Allow me one public screening in Battambang. There is a movie theatre right here—'

'You don't get to dictate—'

'One screening, that's all I ask.' Charlie cut him off and paused to let that sink in before he continued. 'Otherwise, I promise I'll give the press what they want. You may have ordered your secret police to muzzle the press here, but beyond your shores I'll speak to anyone who will listen. And believe me, there are a lot who still will. I'll give dozens of interviews about my experiences in Indochina. I'll tell the truth about the harshness of French rule and the contempt with which you hold your subjects. And make no mistake, Governor, I will continue with my film and produce such a damning indictment on the colonial ... endeavour, that your superiors in France will demand your removal from office. Is that what you want?'

Charlie held his breath. For once, he spoke more confidently than he felt. The peacock strutted out of the door, head high like it disapproved of the down and dirty negotiations being conducted.

'I'll need to discuss this with—'

'Who?' Charlie cut him off again. 'With whom? Are you not the Governor? Your word is all it takes. It must be tonight, and I give you my word I'll be on my way out of your dominion in the morning.' He lingered on the word dominion, hoping it added to his argument. 'And tell your captain that I don't need a damned escort!'

With that he slammed down the phone.

When he turned, he saw Paulette standing in the doorway. Perhaps it was the adrenaline, but the image of the haughty peacock somehow transforming into Paulette lodged in his mind.

'Don't do this Charlie,' she begged. 'Don't spoil it.'

'It's done,' he said simply.

'Then I believe it truly is,' she replied.

He knew exactly what she was implying as he pushed past her and into the corridor. Paulette watched him walk away. There was no swagger to his walk, nor the carefree gait of the Tramp heading into the sunset. He was not performing. Charlie was a small man, but his back was straight, and he walked fast and with a purpose so intense that she knew immediately that it was futile to try to stop him. When he was like this, he had neither friends nor lovers, only servants to his will – or opponents to it. But she also realised then that there was no coming back from what Charlie was about to do.

An hour later, Charlie and Victor entered the entrance foyer of the Battambang picture house.

'A screening?' asked the count. 'But the authorities have made it quite clear that the film has not been approved for release.'

'Not anymore. The governor agreed to one public screening. Right here in Battambang.'

'You, *monsieur*, like to seek out trouble. It will be your end.'

'Not this time, Count Goloubew.'

The Art Deco façade was new and in the daylight it felt bright and airy. There were two doors to the auditorium, one marked 'Khmer' leading to the ground floor seats, and the other marked 'French', which led up two flights of stairs on either side of the box-office to the balcony stalls. Charlie peered through the doors to the Khmer section. There were rows of empty seats and curtains covering the screen on its raised stage. At another time, it might have felt sad – a picture house without an audience. But now it felt pregnant.

A little door led into the projection room. He checked inside.

The huge film projectors sat idle. There were film cannisters on a trestle table, a daybed in one corner for the projectionist. One wall was covered with movie posters from the US and Europe. Victor looked doubtfully over his shoulder, but Charlie just grinned.

'Are you an adventurous man?'

And with that the count burst into a loud guffaw and clapped Charlie on the back.

'Sir?' Mr Yonamori called out from the entrance foyer. He carried a stack of film cans labelled Modern Times and a roll of posters and publicity material. Charlie had been so sure that the governor would accept his ultimatum that he'd instructed Frank to arrange for the prints and posters to come up from Phnom Penh the night before. They'd found a driver willing to risk a pre-dawn departure. Everything was falling into place. It was, Charlie now firmly believed, fate rather than planning which was guiding him towards this auspicious occasion. This screening had nothing to do with box office takings. No, it was destiny, a final act of defiance against the overwhelming control of the French protectorate. A minor victory perhaps, but a moral one.

'An adventure!' shouted the count. 'Ha! Very well, Mr Chaplin. How may I be of assistance?'

Charlie's triumphant mood was infectious and even Mr Yonamori managed the smallest of smiles on his thin lips. For the next few hours they worked tirelessly on the preparations and publicity for the screening. On Victor's suggestion (and with the help of the count's energetic translation), Mr Yonamori dispatched a rickshaw with a loudspeaker to criss-cross the city. This was guerrilla marketing, partisan publicity. There was excitement and energy about their sanctioned rebellion.

Charlie stood back from the Coming Attractions board outside the picture house. He could barely hide his smug satisfaction as the posters for *Mutiny on the Bounty* were covered by those for *Modern Times*. 'Les Temps Modernes' they read in French. A caricature of the Tramp straddled the cogs of a machine, derby and cane in one hand, an oil dispenser in the other, oiling the cogs. Another had a photograph of the actor as the Tramp. And a third split the central figure: the left half was the Tramp as a simplified cartoon in roller-skates, while the other half was a mechanical representation of a human form, with bolts and a key like a Meccano figure. In the Tramp's arms were miniatures of the Tramp and the Gamin holding a pole with a bag tied to the end.

From lunchtime onwards, the news of the screening spread throughout the town and soon there was talk of little else. European shoppers in the main store forgot their groceries and gossiped about the film and its ban. Rumours about Charlie's death were countered by wide-eyed accounts of his presence in Battambang and how he mysteriously vanished from the party given by the eccentric count. Others confirmed actual sightings around town declaring that he'd been putting up posters himself, and that the news of his death was nothing more than a publicity stunt. Of course, some were dismissive of the Tramp and his comedy. But even those most sneering of Chaplin's comic genius were already making plans to attend the screening. It may not have been their glass of Dubonnet, but there had not been such a buzz of anticipation in this sleepy town for as long as the small expatriate community could remember. No, the news had been too dour, too dark for too long. From home there were only reports of

Herr Hitler's annexations and expansions. From the colony, only febrile fear of insurrections and killings on the rubber plantations. The opportunity to escape into a motion picture bubble for two hours was almost as tantalising as the rumours about the filmmaker's untimely death.

As the day wound down and government offices and private stores prepared to close, older people fondly recalled his earlier films as they slammed shut leather ledgers, snapped closed padlocks and rammed home the bolts in shophouse gates.

But the buzz was not confined to the European Quarter. In the market, hand-painted signs in Khmer were stuck to the pillars and walls. Even the protests in the Khmer newspaper of Chaplin's earlier cowardice, couldn't dim the excitement expressed in the curly Khmer script of a one-night – and one-night only – screening in Battambang of the King of Comedy's latest and communist motion picture. From high-minded servants to down-trodden rickshaw pullers, they hid their smiles behind their palms, or attempted an imitation of Saklo's famous walk. Whatever they might have thought about Chaplin the filmmaker, Saklo the character was as loved as he had ever been. Before the sun set, Khmer and Chinese groups were beginning to congregate close to the picture house doors, waiting for the moment to purchase tickets.

Back at the movie theatre, everything was set up. With Victor's sometimes unhelpful translations, they conveyed every last detail to the bewildered elderly projectionist. Charlie was finally satisfied that everything was ready. Everything except for one final task. Mr Yonamori found Charlie in the projectionist's booth and presented him with a screwdriver. The final task.

Charlie entered the lobby and unscrewed the signs segregating French and Khmer patrons.

'There should be no divisions in comedy,' he told Frank, in a voice more solemn than he intended. He handed the signs to the projectionist, whose eyes widened in fear. Charlie's actions were tantamount to open rebellion – and the punishment for that was all too familiar.

'You can blame me,' he added, seeing the fear in the old man's eyes. 'Victor, tell him that I take full responsibility.'

Victor's polyglot translation somehow conveyed the meaning, but the old man did not seem convinced.

While Charlie planned his evening of entertainment, not five hundred yards from the picture house doors was Battambang Prison. Here, Phirath faced an altogether darker situation. The prison reeked of death and squalor. He and the other new prisoners had their manacles removed and were shoved out of a low door and into the bright morning sun in the prison courtyard. The high walls and watchtowers loomed over the crowded yard. Sullen and broken faces barely acknowledged their arrival. Guards looked down from the watchtowers on heightened alert, fingers on their carbine triggers. Others patrolled the yard in pairs looking for any sign of trouble.

Phirath scanned the courtyard looking for someone. This was the final but vital part of his plan. It took him a while but eventually he found who he was looking for. An old man sat by himself against the wall with his back to the yard. Phirath made a beeline for him and stood above the crouched figure for a moment before he spoke.

'Father?' he said.

When the old man turned, he looked much older than his fifty years. He was tired but his spirit had not yet been broken, and the presence of his son, even in the confines of the notorious prison, lifted the clouds from his eyes. Despite one swollen eye and bruising on his face and arms, there was no denying the defiance in Phirath's stance and manner. It was a defiance they both shared. Phirath dropped to his knees and *sampeahed*, respecting his father in a tradition that went back centuries. His father lifted him up and, with their backs turned to the suspicious guards, they punched the air in a salute for the *Khmer Isssarak*, the Free Khmer.

'We're ready,' he said simply. And his father nodded.

By nightfall the prison loomed dark and foreboding against the sky. There was barely any sound from within, save the cicadas and the faintest of rustles through the banyan trees. Then footsteps approached through the grass of the banks beneath the walls. Saloth Sar and a number of the theatre troupe revolutionaries skirted the walls in the shadows – keeping an eye on the watchtowers and picking their moments. The boy watched as the prince, now in the dark clothes of the *Khmer Issarak* placed a stick of dynamite against the prison outer wall. The gift from the communists in Saigon had arrived in its final destination. He nodded to the others who followed suit, taking up positions and laying more dynamite. When they'd set the charges and were in position, they squatted on their haunches in the shadows to wait. Whether they succeeded or not was no longer up to them. They'd laid their plans, and now they muttered prayers for the moment to come.

41

By seven o'clock that evening, the cinema had filled beyond
capacity and there was a hubbub of chatter throughout the
auditorium over the sound of a gramophone playing from the
stage. French and Khmer patrons sat uneasily together. There was
no segregation inside, but the mutual distrust and suspicion was
all too evident in the looks and comments from both, muted only
by the anticipation of what was to come. Outside on the street,
European, Khmer and Chinese groups tried to push into the box
office to buy any remaining tickets. The ushers tried to squeeze
more patrons in, filling every seat, and into the aisles and stairs
until there was hardly room to move. Outside, the darkness had
taken the edge off the heat, but inside there was no respite. It
was stifling. The whine of mosquitos couldn't be heard above the
hum of conversation, but the slap of hands against flesh made it
clear that they were present in swarms. Ladies fanned themselves
with whatever they had to hand. Sweat beaded on foreheads and
forearms. Those who'd dressed up for the occasion, now wished
they'd chosen lighter, cooler clothes, but it wouldn't have made
much difference. Cotton stuck to skin, regardless of its colour.
The cinema had never been so full.

Charlie looked through the projection booth window, pleased

to see every seat taken, and every step and aisle filled. He saw Paulette and Mrs Goddard towards the back, dressed up for the occasion and suffering in the humidity and heat. On a table beside the rolls of film he had placed a derby hat and cane. His hands hovered over them for a moment before he checked his watch.

It was time.

Charlie fed the film into the projector himself. The elderly projectionist watched mesmerised. When he grinned at the filmmaker, his teeth flashed gold. Charlie flicked the switch – the beam pushed through cigarette smoke and dust and hit the curtains over the screen. Charlie nodded to the projectionist and left the booth.

The wall lights dimmed, the gramophone scratched and stopped, and a silence settled on the gathered crowd. The curtains were pulled to the side and the screen came to life. Charlie leant on the back wall beside the projection booth watching the audience as the first image played.

A clock.

As *Modern Times* screened only for the second time in Cambodia, the crowd laughed as one. There was no French and no Khmer anymore, just an audience. Their evident enjoyment of his film moved Charlie more than he cared to admit. He stopped biting his nails and his eyes were moist with emotion.

On screen, the Tramp was force-fed by a faulty feeding machine, shovelling food and spinning corn into his overwhelmed mouth.

But in the police station, Captain Le Favre was taking no chances. His years of experience putting down insurrections, policing the protectorate and serving the French authorities had given him more than a sixth sense for trouble. He held the phone to his ear, cigarette in one hand, another lit and abandoned in the ashtray on his desk.

'It's a mistake, sir,' he insisted in French.

'How so, Captain? Sok Phirath is in prison. Our dear little friend, Le Vagabond, has assured me he will leave in the morning, and I believe him. Captain, I'd say he has done us a favour.' Governor Robin was tired of the whole affair. He agreed with Levalier. *C'est beaucoup de bruit pour rien.* The whole thing had been blown out of all proportion. If they'd agreed to screen the film in the first place, none of this would have happened. There were other pressing issues to attend to and Chaplin's visit had given him more than enough headaches and paperwork for something so inconsequential.

'He's up to something,' was all that Le Favre could manage. The tone in the governor's voice was final.

'He's an American with an ego the size of Texas. Indulge him for one more day, Patrice, and we can put this whole affair behind us.'

It was not a request.

The governor hung up and Le Favre slammed the phone back on the cradle. He glared at it, like the phone was the cause of all his troubles. But he was not one to linger on the stand-down from the governor. He grabbed his hat and left the police station, making a beeline for the picture house.

In the cinema, the Tramp entertained customers in a restaurant with a song sung in fluent gibberish. The crowd erupted into laughter. There was no French laughter or Khmer laughter – just universal laughter, like a steam valve releasing the pressure. At the back of the hall, even the score of Sûreté officers on duty were laughing despite themselves and the task at hand.

At the prison gates, two guards heard the sound of laughter and music. The cinema was no more than five hundred yards from the prison, and a crowd had gathered outside. They'd heard about the screening, of course. Who in the town had not? The rest of the city of Battambang was unusually quiet and all the sound came from the picture house. Ushers held back the crowd, but there was a kind of Chinese whispers in play as those in the entrance foyer, who could actually catch glimpses of the film through the auditorium doors, relayed their account of the film to those behind. The laughter rippled in waves from inside to the crowd on the street, delayed by a few moments until it became almost continuous. One of the prison guards did an imitation of the Tramp's walk. The other followed suit, overtaking him and stepping closer to the theatre, for a moment leaving their post.

Watching them from the shadows on the opposite side of the street was Saloth Sar. He was dressed almost entirely in black, with his red *krama* tied loosely around his neck. Although it made the 11-year-old boy look much older, he had been disappointed when the older revolutionaries had sidelined him in their planning. He was to play only a small role in the events to come. As soon as the prison guards were more than thirty yards away from the gates, slowly drifting towards the picture house, the actor who played the prince gestured for his fellow revolutionaries to follow him. They ran in a crouch across the street towards the prison gate. Perhaps after all, Chaplin was helping their cause. The timing of the screening had increased their odds of success.

On screen the final moments of *Modern Times* played out.

The intertitle read: 'What's the use of trying.' There was no French version, but the intention was clear in the scene and there was no need even for these words.

'Buck up – never say die. We'll get along,' read the next intertitle as the Tramp consoled his Gamin and lifted her from despair. The Tramp and the Gamin walked towards the camera, an endless road stretching behind them. The reverse angle showed them walking off in silhouette towards some distant mountains.

By this time the prison guards were halfway to the picture house on the edge of the crowds. Inside the theatre, the projector flickered to white. For the briefest of moments there was a hush in the hall so intense that even the celluloid flickering through the end reel could be heard from the projection booth.

And then thunderous applause. The audience in unison rose to their feet in a standing ovation for the movie, clapping and shouting.

'Saklo, Saklo!' shouted the Khmer audience.

'Charlot, Charlot!' shouted the French.

Charlie pushed his way with difficulty through the crowd to the front of the auditorium and climbed the stage. He bowed to the applause and cheers.

'Ladies and gentlemen,' he started, but he was drowned out by the applause and no one could see him in the darkness. So he pulled up a chair to the stage and stood on it. He was right in the projector beam, lit like a spotlight. He put on his derby hat and clutched his cane. The projector beam threw the silhouette onto the screen behind him, larger than life, known and adored across the world. And the audience roared their appreciation.

'Ladies and gentlemen,' he called out again, hands raised for quiet, but enjoying the moment of adulation after the difficulty and tension of the previous days. Eventually a silence fell, and all eyes turned to him. He unfolded a piece of paper, a speech he'd rehearsed a hundred times. But Charlie was not a confident speaker at the best of times.

'Thank you, thank you,' he started. 'I ... I ... thank you. I used to ... I ...' he stammered. He checked the paper in his hand before continuing. 'I used to think it was enough to be an entertainer,' he managed, shielding his eyes from the projector beam. But then he saw Paulette watching him in the audience. There was pride there, a recognition of his determination and genius. But more than that, there was a sadness in her eyes in anticipation of where this was going. She shook her head – a tiny movement across the large auditorium. But it was enough for Charlie to know that she knew exactly what he wanted to say – but was imploring him to stay silent.

Charlie pressed on regardless. He couldn't be stopped now. This was his moment. He needed it. He had to speak now, if nothing else to make up for his cowardly silence at the pagoda the night before. There was something he had to say and here, with a captive entranced audience, there would be a power in his words – if only he could get them out. Speaking wasn't as easy as he'd hoped, and his words barely carried beyond the first few rows.

'I used to think it was enough to be an entertainer,' he repeated gaining confidence, trying to project his voice. 'To make the world laugh. But when I see suffering from any corner of the globe, it feels more inadequate than ever.'

He was speaking in English and the Khmer audience didn't understand. They kept silent at first, out of respect. Saklo was speaking, and he was there in the flesh, not just on the screen. Much of the French audience didn't understand either. The hall was hot, and the mosquitos whining and biting. And Charlie's speech seemed to stick in his throat, and the words he uttered seemed brittle and slight. In every pause, the coughs and mutterings of the crowd grew louder. What was he saying? Translations and mistranslations fed back to those standing by the door, then out into the lobby, and then finally rippled outwards to the crowd on the street. With each retelling, his words and intentions were mangled.

Charlie shielded his eyes again, peering around the projector beam to see Le Favre pushing his way forcefully past a group of Khmer men, clearing a space against the back wall. His face was impassive, but beneath the calm, Charlie recognised that cold calculating malice and it made his heart beat faster.

'Greed has poisoned men's souls,' Charlie added, back to the task at hand. He'd thought about every word and phrase. Rehearsed it, imagined the great speech for the people in the auditorium. On screen he knew exactly how he would direct this scene, but this was not a sound stage in the Chaplin Studios in Hollywood. When he played it out in his mind, he saw himself as a great orator, but in the front of an increasingly distracted crowd, he began to doubt himself.

But he couldn't back down now. He stumbled on.

'Greed for rubber for our factories, gained at the cost of the dignity of those who work for it.'

More restlessness at his words. Confusion as the phrases were translated and passed back.

'More than industry we need … er, we need humanity. We

think too much but we feel too little.' He knew the power of his words on the page, but once uttered they floundered and faded like waves on sand and seeped away into silence.

He cleared his throat. Steadied himself, checking the paper, ready to speak again—

BOOM!

An explosion, so loud and so close that dust fell from the ceiling into the projector beam. French and Khmer and Chinese faces in the dark turned away from Charlie.

'Ladies and gentlemen—'

BOOM! BOOM!

There was no doubt now. The first exchanges of confusion gave way to real fear and a scramble to leave the hall. The desperation further fuelled by the sound of gunshots in the distance and shouts of alarm.

Le Favre pinned Charlie with a glare of pure venom.

For a moment it was like there were only two of them in the room. White, Khmer and Chinese faces blurred into a boiling sea of fear beneath his piercing gaze. Charlie's world seemed to slow and stop. He felt himself falling … or perhaps shrinking. The thirty-foot silhouette behind him was getting somehow smaller, he was shrinking on his chair, fading out as if the reels were slowing and the frames were flickering into stillness.

Le Favre gave a loud blast on his whistle – and the enormity of what was happening flooded back. He rounded up his officers with a shout. More gunshots, the staccato rat-a-tat of a carbine and the ear-splitting crack of a rifle.

The audience stampeded to the exits.

'Please, ladies and gentlemen,' Charlie continued. He wanted to say his piece, he had prepared it all. He was finally ready to speak.

'Listen,' he implored the audience.

But there were no expectant faces turned to him now. They had their backs to him, cramming through the doors and into the street outside. Shouts of panic drowned out his well-chosen and well-meaning words. He held out his hands for calm, but no one could hear him, and in that moment they didn't care a jot for what he had to say.

Paulette was one of the last to leave. She gave Charlie a sad look, then helped her mother into the foyer. Charlie watched them until they were lost in the crowd.

For a moment Charlie stood stock still, the iconic silhouette projected behind him. And then the projectionist switched off the projector. The auditorium was empty. Charlie stood in darkness on a chair in front of the screen.

Powerless, eclipsed and utterly ignored by the real events taking place outside the movie theatre, and beyond his control.

42

The attack on the prison was brief but precisely coordinated. Dynamite blasted openings in the prison walls, and the Free Khmer revolutionaries poured in. Saloth Sar was furious that he'd been told to wait outside. He felt he'd earned the right to fight alongside his comrades in the real battle within the prison itself. From his position he could see that the prison had been breached and was in flames. A pillar of smoke poured from inside its notorious walls. The guards shouted and scrambled to maintain order, holding their positions at the main gates as best they could. From the watchtowers they shot to kill anyone who was not in uniform. But the Free Khmer had launched an attack on three positions simultaneously – a coordinated and planned assault to free the political prisoners held inside. Carbines emptied from the watchtowers. Pistol shots echoed off the walls.

Inside the prison, Phirath held onto his father's hand and ran down a corridor. A final explosion blasted through another section of the perimeter wall. A French guard was shot and tumbled into the courtyard below. Soon their sheer numbers had overwhelmed the guards at the gates. Sirens wailed and reinforcements arrived. Sûreté offices and regular police poured out of a dozen police vans, guns out, firing indiscriminately.

Phirath looked again to the breached perimeter wall and the battle taking place around the main gates. He checked the coast was clear then nodded to his father.

'Not the gates. This way.'

He dragged him crouch-running in the shadows along the back wall of the courtyard. They ran towards a missing section at the base, of the perimeter wall. It had been dynamited and the hole was big enough to crawl through. Other prisoners made their escape, and out to the freedom of the river on the other side. Phirath pushed his father through and followed. Finally on the outside, they embraced, but there was no time to lose. Saloth Sar was waiting for them, still frustrated by the small part he'd been given in the attack. He held out a bag to Phirath and the actor pulled out a communist cap, a radio, and some food.

'They're waiting for you. This way,' Saloth Sar whispered to Phirath. He pulled out a pistol and held it by the muzzle to hand it over. 'We're to meet by the river—'

But his voice was cut off by a single pistol shot. Amongst all the carbine automatic fire, this one single crack seemed strangely loud and distinct. A bullet cracked through Phirath's father's skull and sent the old man flying to the ground.

Phirath dropped to his knees beside the body. His hands were covered in his father's blood. He looked at them confused for a moment, barely noticing that a prison guard was firing in his direction through the hole in the wall.

Bang! Bang!

Two shots fired so close together they sounded like a ricochet. The prison guard spun away, bullets to the chest and head, and collapsed back into the hole in the wall. Saloth Sar held a smoking pistol.

'Quickly!' He dragged Phirath away as other guards struggled to remove the body from the hole to chase down the fleeing prisoners.

Scrambling down the steep muddy bank, Phirath and Saloth Sar reached the river. There was no time for shock or despair or grief. They crept beneath the wooden stilts of the Khmer houses that lined the bank, moving from cover to cover. The gun shots behind them were more sporadic now and seemed further away than they really were. Saloth Sar stopped, small chest heaving, but Phirath pressed on, wading westwards. The boy grabbed his bloodied shirt and held him back. He gestured to a sampan moored to a floating jetty. There were people half-submerged in the water beside it. In the moonlight, Phirath saw the familiar faces of his theatre troupe and his comrades-in-arms. They beckoned him over. Saloth Sar followed the actor-turned-revolutionary into the water towards the waiting sampan. But Phirath had not gone far when he turned back to the boy and shook his head.

'You can't follow me where I'm going.'

'I'm coming with you,' Saloth Sar pleaded.

Phirath shook his head once more. And suddenly the grim face of a battle-hardened revolutionary crumpled into that of a disappointed young boy once more. He lowered his *krama*.

'Where will you go?' he asked quietly.

'Hanoi. Then the forests. I'm a fugitive now. But I'm free – thanks to you, thanks to our comrades. We are few now, the real Free Khmer. But when we come back it will be to liberate our people from the French.'

'Then let me come with you. I'm Free Khmer too. I've been

with you from the beginning. Haven't I've earned the right to follow you, and fight with you?'

'You have, and much more. But your destiny is to stay in Phnom Penh. Forget about us for now, leave our struggle and finish your studies. Use the pagoda at Wat Botum, use your connection to the palace, use whatever means you have to learn the French ways. When your time comes, you'll know what to do.'

Saloth Sar knew better than to argue with Phirath. There was a command in the actor's voice that was both gentle and firm – a paternal kindness absent in his relationship with his real father. He may have only been eleven years old, but he had already experienced more than most children of his age. He had known privilege as the son of a wealthy farmer; he had known the Buddhist discipline and teachings of the pagoda; he had witnessed the sycophancy in the palace where his aunt was a member of the king's royal ballet; and he'd seen first-hand the cruel superiority of the French colonialising mission. But it was with Phirath's revolutionaries that his young heart had found its place and destiny. He had stormed the prison and he had killed for the revolution. This would stay with him forever.

Saloth Sar handed over the pistol and Phirath shoved it in the bag with the other items. But seeing the boy's face, he took the communist cap off and put it on Saloth Sar's head. He tightened the *krama* around his neck and lifted it again to cover his mouth and nose. He looked like a real revolutionary now. A glimpse of the real revolutionary he would later become.

His impatience was understandable for his age.

'But Phirath—' he started, hoping for one last chance to change his hero's mind.

'My name is no longer Phirath.' He was no longer an actor. He knew he must now leave that old identity behind forever. 'I've left that name behind and so must you, or it will lead you into trouble. Little brother, from now on I will be known only as Original Khmer, my nom-de-guerre for the fight that is to come.'

'Then I want one too. I want to fight.'

Phirath laughed and held the boy's shoulders.

'Little brother, if my comrades had a quarter of your courage, the fight would already be won. But now you must study, and watch and listen until you're ready, until you've reached your full revolutionary political potential.'

'My political potential?' Saloth Sar sounded crestfallen.

'Yes, little brother. Return to Phnom. Start now before it is light. Tomorrow, be back at the pagoda, and start praying for victory and prepare yourself for your time. It will come, of that I have no doubt.'

And with that he waded out. The others had pulled the sampan into the shallows. He climbed in and the comrades pushed out from the river and joined the current. As if on a signal others did the same. A flotilla of sampans headed into the middle of the river under the moonlight, away from French control and into an uncertain future beyond the law.

For Saloth Sar, there was no time to mourn his hero's departure, nor react to the killing of the French guard. He'd taken a life, a Frenchman's life – and he was not yet twelve years old. He pushed his emotions somewhere deep and distant inside himself. Phirath's words floated down the river with the sampans, but they were to leave an indelible mark on the impressionable boy. His own future as a revolutionary would eventually become synonymous not with freedom, communism, or anti-colonial action. Instead, he would forever be associated with the worst excesses of a genocidal regime that would bring death and suffering to millions of his own people. But Saloth Sar's evolution into the notorious Pol Pot, the leader of the Khmer Rouge, was still a long way off. How he became what he did is an altogether different story. For now, the boy scampered away into the darkness, flinging away his *krama* and stuffing the communist cap into his pocket. He melted away back to Phnom Penh, back to the pagoda and the palace, waiting for his time to come.

43

The prison break was not fully over until the early hours of the morning. Many prisoners had escaped, but many more had been killed trying, or had been recaptured. Most of them were political prisoners, but not all. The police had set roadblocks within an hour of the first shot being fired, but they were more for show. Those who had escaped would seep into the land itself and disappear. The roadblocks were designed for one thing – retribution for the killing of the French prison guards, and for daring to carry out such an audacious attack. It was not just at roadblocks either. Police patrols in Battambang and other cities were hastily arranged. Everyone would be stopped. Any sign of insolence would be met with force; random arrests would be made, livestock killed and produce smashed or confiscated. Unsurprisingly, Khmer and Chinese alike stayed at home.

By the time dawn broke, the prison was back under French control and the prisoners back in their cells. Those who hadn't escaped, or who had not even tried, knew that the next weeks would be a different kind of hell. Extra police had been brought in to insure it. Le Favre was in a filthy mood as he looked at the hole in the breached wall and gestured for the guards to lay rolls of barbed wire as a temporary measure until it could be repaired.

He strode back across the courtyard past line upon line of dead prisoners, scores of them laid out on the stones, uncovered, with their faces frozen in the moment of death. Flies buzzed everywhere. But Le Favre paid them no attention, until he passed Phirath's father. For a moment he stood over the body. Beyond the bodies of the prisoners, lay five dead prison guards and two police officers. A tatty Tricolore lay across three of them, a bloodied sheet over the face of the fourth. The others were uncovered.

'Two more are in critical condition. Seven with severe injuries,' said the prison warden. The captain saluted the dead.

'Heroes of France, all of them. To the end. And the prisoners?'

'Over three hundred escaped, scattered into the jungle. Thirty are dead. We've secured the rest.'

Le Favre picked up a rusty machete from the cache of weapons seized or captured from the prisoners and the Free Khmer. He felt the weight in his hand as if considering a personal and brutal mission to chase them.

'The governor is aware?' he asked.

'Acutely.'

Le Favre slammed the machete into the wooden door frame and left the courtyard. A Sûreté officer scurried to keep up.

'Where is Le Vagabond?' he asked, but the officer simply shrugged, confused. Why would he care about an American actor after the events of the night?

Charlie had not slept. He sat at the window in Victor's house as the dawn came up. His desk was scattered with discarded notes and torn pages from his notebook. The rage and the frenzy had abated and all that was left was resignation and a brutal realisation. With all his status, with all his fame, with all his money, he had failed.

Behind him, Mr Yonamori took Charlie's clothes from the cupboard and packed them up into suitcases. The derby hat and his cane lay on the turned down sheets.

'Le Favre agreed?' he asked his manservant without looking at him.

'He did. He offered to personally escort you back to Phnom Penh and out of Cambodia by river steamer. But yes, he agreed that on the way, he will allow you one stop to see Angkor Wat. He suggested an early start.'

Charlie nodded and lit a cigarette. Then asked, 'And Phirath?'

'From what I have been able to ascertain, sir, he was not among the dead at the prison.'

Charlie nodded again. The door opened and Paulette entered, dismissing Frank with a gesture. For a long moment she looked at her husband, but he stared stubbornly out of the window. He didn't want to see her face; he could feel the reproach in her gaze.

'Tell me you didn't know,' she asked eventually.

'How can you ask me that?' replied Charlie, but his voice was a resigned and tired whisper.

'So it was a coincidence? The timing? The pagoda, the screening. Tell me you didn't plan this all with that … that man.'

Charlie shook his head and stubbed out the cigarette. To be honest he was not thinking about the prison break, or the speech he never made, or about Phirath and how the actor had used him as a diversion for his own political purposes. He understood finally why Phirath was so determined and driven to fight the French. But in his mind all he could see, all that he could bear to see, were the faces of all those men and women and children in the cinema watching *Modern Times*.

'French, Khmer, Chinese, Annamese, Montagnard – it didn't matter,' he muttered, continuing the train of thought out loud. 'They forgot all their differences, all the politics, all the resentment and fear and laughed together. That's all I wanted. I can't do anything more.'

Paulette wanted to scream at him. Who the hell did he think he was? Where the hell did he think he was? But seeing him sat in the window seat even smaller against the large window frame, she didn't have the heart.

'Not here,' said Paulette. 'And certainly not for a very long time.'

'But I can't stop, now I've started. I can't go back to how things were. My old life seems so ... so trivial in comparison. You do understand, don't you? You're the only one who might.'

'I do,' she said. Aware of the irony, she took off her rings and put them on top of the derby hat beside the cases. Finally, Charlie was looking at her. He acknowledged her actions, accepted them even. She was right, but it still hurt.

'I can't work without you. I can't write without you.'

'You've never had me, Charlie. We just shared the road for a while. But I'm twenty-eight. I'm at the beginning of my journey. My future lies ahead of me. Yours will take you in a different direction.'

'I'll release you to Selznick. I'll help you with auditions.'

Paulette nodded. But there was a sadness in her smile.

'I'll write you a talkie. Not here, but somewhere closer to home.'

'It's a deal,' she said.

'I don't want a deal.'

'That's all I can offer. You see, Charlie, under all this--,' and she span around in her elegant outfit, 'I'm still just that desperate girl from Utah.'

The quiet rebuke stung more intensely than any argument or raised voices. She meant it to. A few days ago, they would have argued and fought with passion. But here in Victor's house and after the events of the past twenty-four hours, there was nothing more to be said. They both knew it.

Before she left the room, she turned back and offered Charlie a brighter smile. They could still be friends. She wanted that.

'Don't look so glum darling. It's been a wonderful ride. Like I told you once, "We'll get along."'

But as soon as she'd left, and was walking down the corridor, her mask of confidence and defiance melted away. She collapsed into a chair and fought back her tears.

44

Paulette and Charlie were dressed in whites. They sat drinking strong black coffee on the veranda surrounded by their cases and jungle hats. The departure of Charlie and his guests from Victor's home was a muted affair. The count, despite his eccentricity and obsession, knew full well how Charlie's actions had caused the group, and himself, significant trouble with the French police. As his guests, he was also truly saddened to realise that this was not just a political crisis but a personal one between Paulette and Charlie. He put on a brave face as the guests waited for the police cars to arrive. Even Mrs Goddard was less huffy than normal.

'You won't be disappointed,' was all Victor could manage, trying to lighten the mood. 'Once you see Angkor, none of this,' – and he waved generally to incorporate the situation and the policemen packing up the cars – 'none of this matters!'

They drove in silence from Battambang to Siem Reap, skirting the vast inland lake of the Tonle Sap. Le Favre led the convoy in one police car, with another trailing behind. He was taking no chances. He had agreed to escort the celebrities to Angkor Wat, then back to Phnom Penh and see them off – personally – onto the river steamer for Saigon. Only then would he turn his full attention to the aftermath of the prison break and insurrection and put in place his plans for swift and punitive action that would stamp out any further expression of anti-colonial action.

For once, Le Favre was sure that the troublesome tourists would not try anything again, given the severity of the events of the previous days. So convinced was he that he had even given in to Charlie's demand for the press to be informed of their itinerary. And Mrs Goddard was only too pleased to see a few photographers at Victor's gates, snapping pictures of their departure from the count's ramshackle home. The trip had been a disaster, but perhaps Charlie and her daughter could recover something from their experiences when they made the announcement the world was waiting for from Angkor Wat. She knew her daughter had argued with Charlie but was unaware of how deep the rift had grown.

They left the tiny, quaint town of Siem Reap and drove down a narrow road through the jungle. Then, for no apparent reason, the convoy stopped, and everyone climbed out. The tourists left the police cars and waited in silence in the shade. There were no other tourists. The sounds of the jungle were loud. There was no sign even of the temples themselves, save a few ruined blocks of carved stone that served as the only place to sit. Le Favre was happy to wait. He had scheduled a three-hour stop before the drive on to Phnom Penh and the longer they waited alone in the jungle, the less opportunity for trouble.

The sun was already high in the sky, and Mrs Goddard fanned herself. What now? Where were the press? Where were the damned temples? But no one knew and no one wanted to check with the huddle of uniformed police and Le Favre. They didn't want to give him the satisfaction. Alta kept her opinions to herself for once, but there was no hiding her sharp intake of breath when two elephants arrived. They'd heard the call from the mahout around the bend, before the lumbering giants kicked up the dirt and came to a stop beside the blocks of stone. Their ears flicked and their trunks reached and explored up to the howdahs strapped to their vast backs. Alta stared, her mouth open in surprise and trepidation.

'This way, Madame,' said Victor as calmly as if he took an elephant every day on his daily commute. Before Mrs Goddard could protest, she was taken by the hand, climbed the stone blocks and sat down with a bump on the cushions of the howdah.

'If the good Lord had intended humans to travel on elephants—' Mrs Goddard began but broke off with a squeal when the elephant's trunk reached back over its head towards them. Even Mr Yonamori's normal mask of impassivity broke and he actually smiled – not the modest smile that was his usual display of appreciation – but a broad grin.

Charlie filmed the others on their elephant for a while. It was impossible to stay discouraged and disillusioned in the presence of such incredible and improbable creatures. When Le Favre tapped his watch, bored with their excitement, Charlie helped up Paulette, and joined her on the leading animal. The group entered the Angkor Wat complex through the South Gate – a towering stone wall topped with a vast carved head above a wide opening below. Even so, the elephants had to pass in single file. Charlie filmed through his 16mm camera, but these weren't the visual sketches of his imaginings. He was no longer making visual notes to inspire a film for the Tramp set in the East. This was merely a rather prosaic record of their travels, and a futile attempt to record the majesty of the scale and craftsmanship of the temples built a thousand years before. Charlie and his entourage had only been in Cambodia for a few days, but it felt much, much longer. As the sun rose in the sky, it was hard to remain obsessed with the political events of the previous days; they faded into insignificance in the context of the passage of centuries, and the collapse of a once mighty empire. The ruins inspired such wonder that it hushed them all into a stunned silence.

In the howdah behind, lurching with each elephant stride, were Victor, Mr Yonamori and Mrs Goddard. Despite the count's protests, Charlie had managed to keep the garrulous count away from Paulette and himself. Paulette was not in the mood for his overwrought phrasing and linguistic contortions. Mrs Goddard looked distressed but was putting on a brave face. She clutched her hat with each rolling step, barely noticing the temples beyond her, or the long elephant walk – the parade ground of the Angkorian kings that led from the South Gate.

'There! Look!' shouted Victor, standing up in the howdah and nearly overbalancing. 'Angkor Wat. Largest religious structure in the whole world. Consecrated to Vishnu in twelfth century.'

But details of dates and provenance and construction were irrelevant. They saw the five majestic towers reaching up into the sky.

'Vishnu,' Victor said, his voice reverently lowered to a whisper. 'Protector. Preserver. It is written, 'Whenever righteousness wanes and unrighteousness increases, I send myself forth …'

But the sound of his tour patter faded away. It felt again to Charlie that the world had stopped turning. That the globe in its holder (an image to which he would soon return) had been steadied and stopped by an unseen hand. Time was no longer relevant. He lowered his camera. Some things were not to be recorded and fixed on celluloid. Instead, he listened to the sound of the elephants' feet, their breathing, the rustle of the leaves in the forest canopy and the call of birds.

They dismounted at the bridge. Paulette and Charlie led the way across the wide stone walkway and into the main complex, leaving Mrs Goddard to walk with Victor who held a parasol to shade her from the sun. The scorching morning heat rebounded off stone, reflected off water and punished the tourists. Victor was only too keen to show off his knowledge. But if his language was normally a muddled affair, it lay in verbal ruins in his excitement for explaining every known fact and theory of the Angkorian wonder.

Charlie didn't want the temples explained. He was not interested in the facts of their construction and dimensions, the king who built them and why and how. He and Paulette dawdled through the main temple, following the cloistered bas-reliefs anti-clockwise around the lower part of the temple.

Behind them Victor pointed out the stone depictions of the Churning of the Sea of Milk and explained the battle scenes and the *apsaras*, but even he trailed off after a while. The chanting of monks carried over the stone walls and came from deep within the temple itself. They arrived in an inner chamber dominated by a vast seated Buddha. Incense curled up in the shafts of light, and a monk made offerings. This was not just a relic to the past but a living religious space. Charlie and Paulette hung back respectfully, until Paulette pulled him away leaving the monk to his prayers.

They climbed the steps into the main temple. As they reached the highest point, the sun beat down and they were witness to an almost mystical moment. The ice-crystals in the high-altitude cirrus clouds refracted and reflected the sun's rays, creating a halo of light above the highest point of the temple. It was like a sign from God – or the Gods – that despite the fall of men, the fall of empire, the inevitable passing of time, wonder would still remain. The bitterness of the previous days, the harsh words and recriminations, the rebukes and insults, passions and frustrations no longer seemed significant.

But if Charlie was struck silent by Angkor Wat, it was the temple of Ta Prohm which really put his life's work into perspective. Charlie and Paulette climbed under a stone lintel and across moss-strewn slabs. Ahead was a vast banyan tree. Its roots snaked across the stonework, clawing it back into the jungle. Charlie ran his hands over the roots almost reverently. A city of one million people, reduced now to ruins and reclaimed by the jungle. Nothing, he realised sombrely, was built to last. From this perspective his fears about being eclipsed by technology or fading from fame seemed petulant and childish. Would his films last? Would his studios? Would his legacy? Where were the stories from Angkorian times now? A kingdom of wonder, a city of god-kings overflowing with stories and legends and myths. And what remained of them? A handful of anthropologists trying to decipher the stories contained within the bas-reliefs of the remaining stones not reclaimed by the jungle. What chance was there of his own work surviving against the long march of time?

'Stay with me,' he said quietly to Paulette.

For a moment it was tempting. Surrounded by the majesty and meaning of the temples, all of the Hollywood business, motion pictures, marriages and careers seemed utterly insignificant. But Paulette knew that this wasn't real or lasting. Yes, they could lose themselves in the temples, and leave that world behind them. But only if they never left. The real world beckoned them back and all her imaginings and daydreams vanished in the moment of thinking them.

'Charlie, don't,' she whispered. 'Not now.'

'One more picture,' he pleaded. 'Together.'

'I know you, Charlie. One, and then you'll ask for another—'

'Not this time.'

Paulette looked at him fondly. Her husband, who had conquered the world and was known in every continent, but in this place was just an insignificant little man in white flannels and jungle helmet, running his hands over roots thicker than his own torso which were slowly, like a constrictor, squeezing and breaking the biggest achievements of men.

'What kind of film?' she offered as an olive branch.

'A talkie. But something political. Something that matters.'

'So the Tramp will talk?'

'Not the Tramp. A comedy without the Tramp.'

When he had threatened this before, Paulette was sure that it had been the petulant outburst of a man-child used to getting his own way. But there was a sincerity and honesty in his voice now. A calm after the tempestuous events of the previous days. In fact, Paulette was one of the few people in the world who knew what this really meant – and what he was really saying to her. He was offering to let go of his alter-ego for her and for her career and future. And that was a huge moment for Charlie. The Tramp had walked with him his whole career. A Chaplin movie without the

Tramp was almost inconceivable.

As Paulette considered her reply, a barefoot girl, probably less than ten years old, ran across the temple stones towards them carrying a tray of purple orchids and offered them to the tourists with a shy smile. She didn't know who they were. To her they were just two more strangely dressed red-faced foreigners. Paulette smiled at her and took one, and Charlie left a piastre coin on her tray. When she'd scurried away, Charlie gently took the orchid from Paulette's hand and placed it behind her ear.

'One more,' she said to Charlie.

'Just one more.'

'We can manage that, can't we?'

And she wandered off to examine some carvings around a doorway. In Angkor Wat everything seemed possible – so long as the spell wasn't broken by leaving. There was no paperwork, no lawyers, no studios, but in that action he and Paulette wordlessly agreed a new contract of sorts. The only witnesses for it were the stones and the temple itself, but the contract had as much power and weight as any he had ever signed. For a long while Charlie couldn't take his eyes off Paulette. Standing there and in that moment, thought Charlie, she was more beautiful and dear to him than at any point in their relationship together. Ta Prom was forgotten, and the world and all its temples and treasures existed only for his Gamin, his muse, his beloved Paulette.

A tug on his arm snapped him out of his introspection. The little Khmer girl had returned and was looking up at him. She had big eyes and shiny black hair and gestured for him to follow. When he protested, she simply raised her fist in the now familiar Free Khmer salute. For a moment she held his gaze, and then as suddenly as she arrived, she skipped away. Paulette was admiring the bas-reliefs on the temple walls. When she looked up, she saw Charlie disappear out of view, beyond a collapsed temple lintel.

'Charlie?' called Paulette. 'Charlie! Where are you going? Wait for me.'

45

The girl led Charlie across Ta Prohm's courtyards and open spaces and then skirted along the ruined temple walls. Huge blocks of carved stone were scattered between the trees – like the discarded remnants of a giant's game. Charlie struggled to keep up, nearly losing his footing many times. But the little girl was light on her feet and was frustrated at his slow progress. She beckoned him again from the doorway into the temple itself and Charlie found himself a little out of breath and sweating by the time he stepped into the cool interior. The temple's inner chambers and halls were cold to the touch, mossy and shaded. Still the girl stayed just out of view as Charlie scrambled across fallen stones, collapsed lintels, and damaged *lingas* and bas-reliefs. From somewhere increasingly far away he could still just hear Paulette's voice, but it bounced off the stone walls and seemed to come from everywhere and nowhere all at once. He pressed on regardless and soon found himself crouching to squeeze through a narrow low entrance to a dark inner chamber. The stone walls smeared black-green against his white linens, and for a moment he could barely make anything out as his eyes adjusted to the dark.

It was not what he saw that first made an impression, but what he heard. There was a thump like a heartbeat, and it echoed around the stones like the double beat of heart ventricles. It thumped again and, as his pupils dilated to capture the scant light, he noticed Phirath approaching through the darkness.

'Listen,' said Phirath, as casually as if they'd just met in the street.

Charlie stood still. Even Paulette's voice didn't reach him here and only the silence filled the chamber, thick and solid. Phirath let out a low-pitched hum and thumped his chest. The space was an echo chamber, by design or by chance. Phirath altered the pitch of his hum and started murmuring words like a Buddhist monk's chant. He thumped his chest again, and again.

'Monks use this place to pray for peace and enlightenment.' He held out his hand for Charlie and they shook. 'I come here to pray for victory.'

Their friendship had only spanned a few days, but it seemed to Charlie, standing in the echo chamber of a thousand-year-old temple, that they had known each other, been bonded to each other, since time began. He stared at the intense little man, dressed now all in black and he recalled that first meeting, outside the palace gates when he'd not been recognised at all. And then later in the theatre troupe's house and their impromptu performance together. He remembered the thrill of frustrating Le Favre in the Chinese Quarter when Phirath had hidden in the boot to be smuggled across the checkpoint. The memories of their journey from creative partners, imagining a new project for the Tramp in the East, to the betrayal at the Lakhoun performance in Battambang, was carved into his memory as indelibly as the ancient carvings of the temple itself. But so too was Charlie's cowardly silence, Phirath's subsequent arrest, the prison break and the abandoned screening of *Modern Times*. All these memories jostled for prominence in a split second. Charlie felt the same thrill again, but with it a familiar anger and frustration of being used as a pawn in the Cambodian's political plans. He knew that the entire French administration was hell-bent on finding Phirath – and that if they found him, he would be executed for treason. He had so much he wanted to say and ask, but once again, he couldn't find the words. The humming continued, the double beat of the thumped chest and echoed response.

Eventually he whispered, 'Phirath, if they find you here, if they find you with me—'

'I needed to see you again before you leave Indochina.'

'To apologise?'

'Would that make a difference?'

Charlie considered that for a moment. He shook his head in the darkness.

'We must take risks, Saklo. How else will we ever make a difference?'

He thumped his chest again.

'Try.'

Charlie did as he was told. He hummed first, then thumped his chest. The sound echoed around the chamber. He smiled at the result and tried a double thump. Phirath grinned back at him.

'One day people will know of our struggle.'

'I would like to help.'

'Like you did at the pagoda?' The rebuke stung and Phirath immediately softened. He'd already made that point. It didn't need underlining again. 'You see, Saklo, what you have to understand is that this is not your struggle. The whites in our country don't understand. You haven't yet realised that this is our story, not yours. And even you can't change the world with a movie.'

'Perhaps.'

'We need our own heroes, Saklo. And very soon, you will need yours, back in your own countries, closer to home. That is where you should focus your energy.'

He raised a Free Khmer fist. Charlie did the same.

'I'm glad I got to meet you, Saklo.'

'And I you, Phirath.'

But there was little trace of the comic actor who Charlie had first seen flying over the handlebars on the drive from the docks. The man who stood with him in the echo chamber was now a single-minded revolutionary. He had abandoned more than his name – his whole former identity had been packed away, belonging to a former life. And with that, the connection the two men once shared also disappeared. He ducked back out of the chamber entrance. Charlie looked around one last time, beat his chest, and listened for the echo. When the beat had faded, and the silence engulfed him once more, he followed Phirath out. But when he stood in the antechamber, under the ruined roof, Phirath had vanished.

'Phirath?' he called out.

After a few further attempts, he realised that this had been Phirath's final goodbye. There was nothing left to be said. They would never meet again. Their shared passion, which had drawn them together like gravitational attraction in Indochina just days earlier, had gone. The momentary ties that had bound them were undone, forever. He stepped across the sea of broken stones and the collapsed outer walls and into the cool of the shade of the nearest tree and lit a cigarette. That was where Paulette found him moments later. Her initial annoyance of him leaving her alone in the temples vanished when she saw his face.

'Where were you,' she asked quietly.

'Just thinking. It's the kind of place that rewards solitude.'

'If you say so.' She walked off but realised that Charlie wasn't following. 'You can't stay here, Charlie. The press are waiting. We called a press conference, remember? We have an announcement to make.'

46

By the time they made their way back through the temples to the entrance of Angkor Wat, a sizeable knot of journalists had gathered in the shade, waiting and grumbling. Some of them had been following the couple since their appearance at the Hotel Le Royal in Phnom Penh. The heat and the difficulty of reaching the location had put them in a particularly critical mood towards the whims of Hollywood celebrities. Mrs Goddard, Mr Yonamori and Victor waited for the couple at the cars. Le Favre leant against the nearest, smoking and muttering about the time. But the press brightened when they saw Charlie and Paulette holding hands and approaching down the walkway from the main entrance. Charlie waved with a smile.

'Good afternoon.'

Cameras clicked and wound. Mrs Goddard shoved through the press to the front and positioned herself near the couple. She had been waiting for weeks for this news, and she beamed with pride as she inched closer. Finally, they would be announcing their marriage to the world. Perhaps afterwards they could go home. Paulette smiled, waiting for Charlie to speak. But he seemed lost for words and she leant close to his ear.

'This is your moment, not mine, darling.'

He nodded. She wasn't going to save him again. But he didn't know how to begin.

'Say what you need to say. Just make sure you really mean it,' she whispered.

Charlie cleared his throat.

'Paulette and I,' he started, 'have had a wonderful vacation exploring Indochina these past days.'

Mrs Goddard's face fell. Paulette let go of Charlie's hand and pulled her mother closer.

And then Charlie recounted the highlights of his travels over the past few days. He talked softly about the treatment of Khmer rubber plantation workers, but also of the hospitality he and his group had enjoyed from the French expatriates. He thanked Levalier and the count for opening their homes to them, and for Victor's knowledge and passion for the Angkorian temples. He told them of his flight above the temples in Victor's seaplane. He spoke of his joy at seeing traditional Lakhoun theatre. But when it came to the Angkorian temples themselves, he was unable to put his feelings into words. He trailed off.

'Some things are best left as an experience rather than recounted in words,' he offered.

The press exchanged glances. Was that it? They had been promised some kind of scoop. Le Favre watched it all. Was the irritating little man planning something once more?

'Did you know there was going to be an attack on the prison last night?' asked one journalist in the silence after Charlie's account.

'Of course I didn't.'

'But you knew the leader Sok Phirath. A wanted terrorist.'

'I didn't know of his intentions. I met him as an actor, and we shared some thoughts about theatre and comedy. That was all.'

'And what about the incident at the pagoda the day before?' pressed another.

'I didn't read about it in the papers,' says Charlie. But he was looking at Le Favre when he said so. Touché.

'Your friend was arrested for insurrection.'

'A deeply regrettable moment. I had merely made the acquaintance of a fellow comic actor in Phnom Penh. When he met me by chance in Battambang he invited me to his show and I showed him the professional courtesy, one actor to another.'

'So, you don't share his political views?'

'I must confess we never discussed his political views. In fact we discussed only that which could be communicated by physical comedy. His political views are part of his story, not mine.'

'So, you deny that you'll be setting your next motion picture in Indochina?'

'Categorically. Although I will admit the possibilities of doing so have intrigued me. No, my next motion picture, should I direct another, will be set closer to home.'

'So, where do you stand on the Cambodian independence movement?'

The questions were pushing Charlie to speak out one way or the other, to take a stand for the French or the people, but he wouldn't be goaded into taking sides. What was supposed to have been a marriage announcement, was rapidly turned into a political interrogation.

'I think France, or any country for that matter, which involves itself in the affairs of another should do so with kindness and respect. I admit, I have witnessed some behaviour here which falls short.'

Le Favre signalled to his officers. They approach from the line of cars, ready to intervene if necessary.

'Do you condone violent uprisings?' asked a French journalist.

'Perhaps the power they took from the people will one day return to the people,' he offered as an enigmatic reply. He seemed to be talking more to himself than the press, but they scribbled down his words in their notepads.

'As for this Kingdom of Cambodia, let me say this. The country and the people I have met in our short stay have left a lasting impression in my mind which I will cherish. I ... we are all sad to be leaving and I fear that Hollywood on our return will seem quite dull in comparison. Thank you.'

He waved again and found Paulette's hand again. He led her through the press towards the waiting police cars.

The press watched them go, furious.

'Traipsing through the jungle and the heat for a damn goodbye and cheerio?' fumed an American journalist.

'Damned celebrities,' agreed his French counterpart.

The Sûreté officers escorted them to their cars as the disgruntled press shuffled away. Before he climbed in, Victor battered him on the back and pulled him in for a bearlike hug, squeezing the air from his lungs.

'It's been ... quite the adventure,' said Charlie.

'Adventure, yes! But some, adventures best stay in here.' He rammed a forefinger against his temple. 'I believe that you, Monsieur Chaplin are most adventurous American I ever met!'

'Ah, but you see, I am not an American.' Charlie finally put him straight.

The count's mouth dropped open. It was such a perfect pantomime expression that Charlie wished he could cast him in a movie. He was like a more eccentric Henry Bergman, the big comic foil for the Tramp. He must find a part based on him he thought, as Victor kissed Paulette's hand and opened the door for Mrs Goddard.

'One hour only to see all temples!' he muttered. 'Very well. Au revoir. *Do Svidaniya*. Goodbye and *choum reap lear.'*

The two cars pulled away and the police cars slipped in before and after. They drove in silence, each member of the group staring out of the window at the blur of the forest, content with their own thoughts, replaying the events of the past days, the arguments and expectations, the sights they'd seen and the people they'd met.

'Damn climate has really gotten to my adenoids,' complained Mrs Goddard eventually.

'Lozenge, Madame?' offered Frank Yonamori.

47

The drive back to Phnom Penh took the remainder of the day and was uncomfortable but largely uneventful. After the first stop, Charlie asked to sit with Frank to go through their itinerary and arrangements. Paulette didn't argue. There was both too much to say, and nothing left to be said. They drove fast and the rice paddies and sugar palms and villages, which had so entranced Charlie on the drive up to Battambang, no longer held any fascination or curiosity. In fact, Charlie longed to leave the country. This was perhaps the only view he now shared with Paulette and her mother. The convoy kicked up dust from the roads, but it soon settled back down until there was no trace of their presence at all. Life in the colony would continue with or without them, mulled Charlie, suddenly and acutely aware of the pointlessness of his visit. He had achieved nothing there. His project, which had swept him into a creative fever days earlier, lay abandoned in his notebooks, never to be revived. His attempt to influence the political context had been snuffed out by a combination of his own cowardice, the effectiveness of the French police, and in any case completely eclipsed by the passionate actions of a Cambodian actor. And his marriage had come to an end before it had even been announced.

By the time they arrived in Phnom Penh and checked into

the Hotel Le Royal it was already late at night. Paulette and Alta weren't hungry and didn't feel like drinking in the Elephant Bar. Charlie had no desire to speak with the press who would no doubt be there. Looking in the mirror of the bathroom, Charlie recalled how he'd stared at his reflection in the very same mirror days earlier and dabbed white shaving foam on his eyebrows and moustache. He was not feeling playful now. You never look into the same mirror twice, he thought, just as you never step into the same river. Paulette busied herself in the bedroom. When Frank knocked and entered with a message, Charlie was inclined to decline the request for a final meeting before their departure from the kingdom. But Frank told him how insistent the royal visitor was. And Charlie couldn't bear the silence in their suite.

'How do you refuse a prince,' shrugged Charlie and went down to the bar.

The young Prince Sihanouk, who had been so star-struck by Charlie's presence at the royal screening, was waiting for him in an upright chair. His high-pitched voice could barely contain his excitement at the opportunity to snatch a conversation in private with his idol. Despite his initial reluctance, Charlie found the boy's questions and curiosity a much-needed tonic and distraction. There was no talk of politics in the kingdom, or of the situation back in Europe. Instead, Charlie enthralled the 14-year-old boy-prince with anecdotes from his filmmaking journey and life. He talked to him of his technique, about how he would develop the ideas for his first two-reelers, all the way to the obsessive precision and care of his later films at his own studios. The boy let him speak, absorbing the filmmaker's joy and love for cinema, only occasionally interrupting for more detail or clarification.

It was gone midnight by the time Charlie checked the clock on the wall above the globe in its wooden holder. As they said their goodbyes, Charlie presented the prince with his beloved Keystone A-7 16mm film camera. He didn't know then of course that the boy who would become the king of the independent Cambodian nation two decades later, would also emerge as an avid filmmaker and film champion, directing a number of films himself. Under his patronage, there would be a cultural expansion across all the arts, and a golden age of cinema in the late 1950s and 1960s. Was his love of cinema born from these meetings with Charlie?

They boarded the steamer the next morning, heading down the Mekong Delta back to Saigon. Charlie held Paulette's hand and waved his hat at the well-wishers on the dock and the bustle behind them. Le Favre was there of course, making sure they actually left. But as the steamer steered away and swung out into the river and the docks were lost to view, Paulette pulled her hand away. Charlie was lost in thought staring at the turgid brown of the Mekong and she left him there, let him go, and clip-clopped back into the lounge bar of the steamer from where piano music played and laughter carried across the water.

Charlie stared into the muddy expanse where the four rivers intersected. As he was carried downstream, he found himself considering the personal intersections he had encountered in the past days. He had no camera to film the departure, but perhaps somewhere in the palace the young prince was already experimenting with Charlie's gift, beginning his lifelong love of cinema. In the cool of Wat Botum's pagoda, Saloth Sar was perhaps studying with the orange-robed monks, unable to concentrate on the Sanskrit texts, because his young mind was brimful of memories of his first act of political defiance and violence. Charlie would be nearly at the end of his life by the time Saloth Sar and the Khmer Rouge took over the country in 1975. Known then as Pol Pot, would Charlie recognise him in the papers or remember his encounter? Would he have behaved differently to the boy knowing what he was to become in the decades that followed? Could he have altered the course of history if he'd behaved differently? Could he have influenced the boy-revolutionary against a course of action that would in time almost entirely destroy the fabric of Cambodian society? Or was Charlie pondering Victor's obsession with the Angkorian temples and the count's absolute refusal to accommodate any political interference with his work? Perhaps Victor was airborne again, mapping the temples, happily soaring above the problematic relationship between the country and its political future? And what of Le Favre? He'd waved them off from the port, happy to watch them leave his sphere of influence into another jurisdiction's problem. He'd soon be back in his offices, puffing on a Gitanes and using his network of informers and spies to track down the escaped prisoners of the Free Khmer.

But most of all, Charlie's mind turned to Phirath. Where was he now? Hiding in some distant jungles, plotting the revolution that would be delayed until decades after his death? Would he ever perform again with the Lakhoun theatre troupe? Would he live to see a Free Cambodia?

Of course, Charlie couldn't know how the lives of those he had met would influence this quiet backwater of colonial exploitation or how he may have influenced them on their journeys. Instead, he found himself looking down at his patent shiny shoes on the railing of the snub-nosed prow of the steamer and the water passing beneath him. In just a few days he had been inspired by the kingdom, fallen in and out of love with it. He had met kings and princes, been humbled by Phirath's actions, enraged by the captain's control – but in the end it all flowed away, and this realisation left him feeling hollow and lost. Was it time to hang up his derby for good as he'd been considering when they arrived?

Inside his cabin, Charlie finally acknowledged how utterly exhausted he was. He sat at a desk with a glass of iced water. Mr Yonamori entered with a tray of newspapers. Charlie grabbed the first and skimmed the headlines.

'Will that be all, sir?' his manservant asked.

'For now, thank you, Frank.'

Charlie selected another paper, this time *The Straits Times*. There was a portrait of Hitler on the front page under the headline 'The Dictator of Germany'. There was that damned moustache. Charlie stared hard at the picture ignoring the words. Then he took his pen and sketched a derby hat on top of the photograph. The likeness to the Tramp was uncanny. And he inserted a word in the headline so that it read, 'The Great Dictator of Germany.'

Perhaps that was the moment when he realised what he would do next. Or perhaps it was later when he listened to Phirath's advice and turned his creative intentions to a danger closer to home. All he knew then was that despite the widening rift between them, Paulette would help him, one last time. It was a promise he knew she would keep, and he loved her for it.

Epilogue

Charlie and Paulette never announced their marriage, fuelling speculation that it had never taken place at all during their tour of the Far East. But as he had promised, when they returned to Hollywood, Charlie worked with Paulette on her audition for Selznick's picture, *Gone with the Wind*. Her screen tests for the audition survive, although that role would be given to Vivien Leigh. And true to her word, she and Charlie worked together on one final picture four years later. It was Charlie's first talkie. The vestiges of the Tramp remained in the character of the Jewish barber and the Tomainian dictator, Adenoid Hynkel. But perhaps these doppelgängers owed as much to the pairing of the governor and the Tramp. They existed only as abandoned sketches in his notebook, provisionally titled, *Colonial Subjects*.

The Great Dictator would be Charlie's most commercially successful film and the last time he and Paulette worked together. Unlike his previous marriages, which had ended in bitter divorces, paternity suits and settlements, Charlie and Paulette divorced as quietly as they had married, an amicable agreement reached in Mexico just weeks after *The Great Dictator* was released in 1940.

Anti-colonial pressure in Indochina was interrupted by World War Two. The Free Khmer movement was officially formed in

1940 but it was the young film-obsessed King Sihanouk who oversaw the bloodless transition to Independence in 1953. As for Saloth Sar, he returned to Wat Botum and later the lycée in Phnom Penh. He completed his studies in France and returned to lead the Khmer Rouge under the name Pol Pot. During the late 1970s, the dream of a Maoist agrarian utopia fused with a national pride of the ancient Khmer Empire. But the dream turned into one of the 20th century's most brutal genocidal nightmares.

Charlie found his voice somewhere between the production of *Modern Times* and *The Great Dictator*. In the latter, he played the Jewish barber, mistakenly pushed onto the stage to speak to the various armies of Tomainia, after impersonating his doppelganger, Adenoid Hynkel. He made an impassioned speech. But really this speech was Charlie himself, direct to camera. His plea for peace and humanism was one of his lasting and most pertinent legacies.

'To those who can hear me,' he said, looking uncomfortable at first but growing in confidence, 'I say – do not despair. The misery that is now upon us is but the passing of greed – the bitterness of men who fear the way of human progress. The hate of men will pass, and dictators die, and the power they took from the people will return to the people.'

How much of this really happened? Many newspapers mention the visit of Charlie Chaplin to Phnom Penh with Paulette and Mrs Goddard, and their arrival on 18th of April 1936. In the archives you can find his answers to questions from the press conference held at Hotel Le Royal. He was asked if he might consider setting his next motion picture in the East. Another asked if he intended hunting – for elephants, the newspaper records. And another enquired whether Paulette and he were married, a question he carefully evaded. He and his travelling companions had an audience at the Royal Palace with King Sisowath Monivong, before continuing their journey to the ruined temples of Angkor by car. By the 22nd of April 1936, they had left Indochina and were continuing their grand tour of the East, up the coast of China and towards Japan, before returning to the United States on the 11th of June of that year.

What else happened in those few days remains a mystery. There are only sketchy details and an enigmatic and unconfirmed rumour that he had died on the trip. Had Charlie's experiences unfolded as imagined in the pages above? And does it even matter? Or is it enough to enjoy a story that, somewhere in the multiverse of infinite possibilities, could perhaps be true?

Acknowledgements

Many friends and colleagues helped in the research and writing of this book. In particular, I would like to acknowledge the support of Jon Smith, my screenwriting partner and friend, who indulged my fascination with this story and offered his advice and guidance throughout. Also to Justin Deimen, Mary Hare, Claire Fryer, Stephen Angel, Clive and Gina Seaton, and to Shaun Whitehouse and the staff of Lanes Hotel.

LEFT TO RIGHT Victor Goloubew,
Paulette Goddard and Charlie
Chaplin, Angkor Wat, 1936.
[Charlie Chaplin Image Bank]